Title:	It Ends at Midnight
Author:	Harriet Tyce
Agent:	Grainne Fox
	Fletcher & Co
Publication date:	February 21, 2023
Category:	Fiction
Format:	Hardcover
ISBN:	978-1-7282-6384-7
Price:	$27.99 U.S.
Pages:	320 pages

This book represents the final manuscript being distributed for prepublication review. Typographical and layout errors are not intended to be present in the final book at release. It is not intended for sale and should not be purchased from any site or vendor. If this book did reach you through a vendor or through a purchase, please notify the publisher.

Please send all reviews or mentions of this book to the Sourcebooks marketing department:

marketing@sourcebooks.com

For sales inquiries, please contact:

sales@sourcebooks.com

For librarian and educator resources, visit:

sourcebooks.com/library

IT
ENDS
AT
MIDNIGHT

a novel

HARRIET
TYCE

sourcebooks landmark

Published by Sourcebooks Landmark, an imprint of Sourcebooks
P.O. Box 4410, Naperville, Illinois 60567-4410
(630) 961-3900
sourcebooks.com

Originally published as *It Ends at Midnight* in 2022 in the United Kingdom by Wildfire, an
imprint of Headline Publishing Group. This edition issued based on the hardcover edition
published in 2022 in the United Kingdom by Wildfire, an imprint of Headline Publishing Group.

Cataloging-in-Publication Data is on file with the Library of Congress.

Printed and bound in [Country of Origin—confirm when printer is selected].
XX 10 9 8 7 6 5 4 3 2 1

To My Friends

PART 1

THE FOX

The fox hates fireworks. While they're going off, she'd rather keep herself hidden, curled up in a bush somewhere quiet. Hogmanay is the worst, Edinburgh one big explosion. Normally she'd wait till they were finished, but tonight she's too hungry. Slim pickings lately; it's time to scavenge, fireworks or not.

Her usual spot is a garden behind a house halfway along Regent Terrace. Not much to be found off-season, but when the house is full, there's always food overflowing from the bin. Not this evening, though. She has to go further afield.

On the far side of the road now, over the street from the houses, slinking along the edges. She's been kicked before. Humans scare her, the stink of them. The noise.

Nothing but leaves. Empty wrappers. No sustenance to be found here.

Her ears prick. There's a scream, a dull thud. Not too close, not a threat. She stops, poised to run, ready to seek shelter again. But as she's about to turn, it hits the back of her nostrils. She's caught a scent.

Blood.

Meat.

Fresh meat.

Now she's caught the trail, she's straight over the road, caution thrown to the winds, following her nose.

A long, wet trail, running across the pavement, into the gutter. Glistening in the streetlights. She starts to lap it up.

If she just looked up, toward the source of the blood, she'd see what had happened. But she doesn't. She keeps lapping up the liquid. The closest she's come for days to proper nourishment.

Another bang disturbs her. Then some barking. She raises her head. There's a dog approaching, hot on the scent. For a moment she stands, waits, wanting to see if it'll go or if she needs to move on. The draw of her meal is strong.

That's how the dog walker would have seen her if he'd looked. She's standing in front of the house. A silhouette. A shadow. She turns and flees, tail low.

Behind her, a trail of little paw prints.

Each red as blood.

12:00:35

No.

This isn't happening. I'm not here, not hanging over the railings face-down staring at the pavement. Going to try to look up.

It hurts. Try to move, to touch it. Cold metal. Wet iron. I lift my hand again, but it flops down.

I can't move.

Catch my hand in the light. Squint, my eyes closing fast.

Red. Covered in red.

I close my eyes.

1

"You won!"

"I won," I say, suppressing my grin. The victim's family are standing nearby at the door of court, and I don't want to rub it in. My client's mum might be delighted that his sentence has been cut by the appeal court from twelve years to eight, but judging by the mutterings and dark looks I'm being thrown, they're less than pleased.

"I don't know how you sleep at night," a man says, pushing past me to join the family. I pull my gown more closely around me, tipping my head so my wig obscures my eyes.

"Ignore him," my instructing lawyer, Jonah, says. He's not trying to suppress his smile. He looks delighted. "It's a brilliant result."

"We got what we wanted," I say. "Let me get changed and we'll get out of here."

"Drink?" he says, looking from me to our client's parents who are standing beside us. I nod, but they shake their heads.

"It's been a long day," the father says. "Thank you, though. We know he's still going to be in prison for a long time, but at least we can see the end of it now."

"I'll see you out of the building," Jonah says to them. He turns to me before he goes. "Daly's?"

I nod again, before skirting round the hostile group to get to the

robing room where I change quickly, folding my gown up and ramming it into my red bag along with my wig and my papers. Normally
it's my trusty wheelie bag, but not today; appearances at the Court of
Appeal are rare enough that they warrant the use of the bag that was
given to me by my first pupil master, my mentor, the top Queen's
Counsel in chambers, after the kidnapping trial that we did together.

He'll be pleased with today's result. I'm pleased, too. It all went off
exactly as I'd hoped. Better, even.

"Nice one, Sylvie," the barrister for the prosecution calls out to
me. I'm about to walk out of the main doors of the Royal Courts of
Justice. I turn to face him, moving back into the hall.

"You did well," he continues. I look at him closely, wondering if
there's a note of condescension lurking underneath. "I've heard a lot
of good things about you. Turns out they were right."

"Thanks," I say, my voice respectful. Maybe the condescension
is there, but to be fair, he's ten years my senior. And a QC with a
hotline straight to the Judicial Appointments Commission. If this is
going to be a good reference, I'm not going to fuck it up. "It was an
interesting case."

"Very interesting," he says. "Normally I'd say they should throw
away the key for kiddie fiddlers, but you made a compelling argument." He leans toward me, his face taking on a more familiar expression. "Rumor has it you've got a judicial application in the works. On
the basis of today, I'd say you're well in there." He pats my shoulder,
walks away. My heart pounds with excitement. One step closer to my
holy grail, the red sash and purple robes of the Crown Court judge.

Jonah has snagged a table and bought a bottle of wine. He pours me
a glass as I approach.

"That was great," he says once I've sat down. "You had them eating out of your hand."

"Not the way to talk about Appeal Court judges," I say, raising my glass to him. "They were very receptive, though."

"It was your skeleton argument that did it. You'd laid it all out so well. I'm impressed."

I take a sip of wine, but the warmth that's lighting up inside me comes from his words, not the alcohol. I worked very hard on this appeal. I knew how much was riding on it. Sure, I have to fill in the application forms, go through all the tests that are required in the process of trying to become a judge, but the better I'm doing in my real-life work, the greater my chances.

Taking another sip, I look around the bar, satisfaction seeping into my bones. There's a guy over there I recognize from pupillage, bloated now, years of drinking after work taking its toll. I know his practice is shit, bad cases for worse solicitors. Not like me, fresh from the Court of Appeal. I catch Jonah's eye and smile. Normally I'd temper my arrogance, exercise some caution in my self-satisfaction. Not tonight. Triumph is mine.

"So, what next for the unstoppable Sylvie?" he says. "Any more appeals up your sleeve? Crucial points of law?"

I shake my head. "I'm back in the youth court soon. Highbury Youth Court, to be precise."

He looks aghast. "What the fuck are you doing in there? I steer well clear these days."

"It's a trial, a multihander," I say, smiling at his confusion. "And I'm the judge."

Comprehension dawns on his face. "I always forget you sit as a district judge."

"Yeah, it's only part-time."

"Sensible move, too. Given your plan for world domination."

"Hardly world domination," I say, failing to hide my smirk. "I'll settle for ending up on the Crown Court bench full-time."

Jonah laughs. "I bet you're sorry there isn't a death penalty anymore. I can see you passing sentence now in your black cap: 'May God have mercy on your soul.'"

I laugh too, but a chill passes across me, the hairs on my arms rising in goose bumps despite the warmth of the bar. For a moment I'm miles away. Years away...

"Sylvie," Jonah says, and I'm pulled back to now. "Sylvie, do you want to have dinner? I was thinking it might be nice to hang out."

There's a question here that goes beyond food, and I contemplate it, looking him up and down. It would be fun. I can picture it now, the feel of his hands on me, the roughness of his beard against the softness of my neck. My thighs.

I shake my head. Not tonight.

"I have to get back," I say. "Someone's cooking me dinner at home."

"Ah, OK," he says, almost managing to hide his surprise, one eyebrow shooting up before he gets it back under control. "Nice."

I drain my glass and stand up. "Yes, it will be."

I decide to walk back to Oval. I could have left later, but as soon as Jonah asked the question, I knew it was time to go. It's not the first time we've ended up in a bar after a case, nor the first time that it's gone from there via dinner to bed. I can understand his surprise at my rejection. I'm telling the truth, though. There is someone cooking for me at home.

I nurse the thought of Gareth all the way across Waterloo Bridge and down Baylis Road. I can picture him now, chopping and sautéing, his face set in concentration. I've never met anyone who takes food more seriously. It puts my takeaway and microwave meal habits to shame. The first time he came down to stay, he looked through my fridge with disdain, filling a carrier bag with all the out-of-date sauces he found on the top shelf. I watched with growing horror, convinced that he was going to dump me for my nongourmet ways.

That was six months ago, and he's still here, still cooking. And my fridge is full of a much higher class of condiment. Not to mention wine. Friday nights in with the boyfriend might be a new departure for me, but they're certainly not a more sober one.

When I let myself through the front door, the scent of frying onion and garlic is thick in the air. I open the door to the flat and call out, but the extractor fan's on and there's no reply. Dumping my bag and coat, I go through to the kitchen. Gareth's standing with his back to me, stirring something at the stove. I walk behind him and put my arms around him. He jumps in surprise, jerking the hand that's holding a wooden spoon so that he flicks hot oil and onion onto me. I scream out and pull myself away from him, rushing to the sink to stick my arm under the tap.

He turns the fan off and the room falls quiet, the only sound the water rushing from the tap.

"You OK?" he says. "I'm sorry, you gave me such a fright. I didn't hear you come in."

"I'm fine, honestly," I say. "I didn't mean to scare you."

Gareth puts his hand out and takes mine, turning my arm this way and that to look at the damage. There isn't much, only a small red mark. He raises it to his lips and kisses the burn.

"It's not so bad," he says. "I've had worse." He waves his other hand at me, calloused from years of cooking. Asbestos hands.

I smile, move forward, and hug him again, but this time front to front. He puts his arms around me and we stand for a moment like that. I think about boyfriends before, how I wouldn't even let them stay the night, let alone give them the key and the run of my kitchen. I start to laugh, my face muffled in his shoulder, and he lets go of me immediately.

"You OK?" he says again, his voice filled with concern. I look at him blankly for a moment before I realize.

"I'm not crying," I say. "I'm laughing."

"Why are you laughing?"

"Because I'm happy," I say. "It's so nice to see you."

I change out of my suit while he finishes off dinner, shutting myself in the bathroom to redo my face. I'm relaxed with him; more than relaxed. Enough for tracksuit bottoms and a sleeveless top. Not quite enough for a makeup-free look, though I've gotten better from the early days, when I used to slide out of bed before he woke to slap concealer under my eyes. Compared to most, though, he's seeing the real me, as I emerge blinking into the light of a proper relationship.

"You look lovely," he says when I come out, handing me a large glass of red. "Good day?"

"Very good," I say. "I won the appeal."

"Wow, that's great."

"It really is. Just what I needed for my judge's application. I'll be able to talk all about it."

He raises his glass. "Congratulations. Here's to the future Lady Munro."

"I won't be a lady unless I make it to the High Court bench," I say.

"You will. I have no doubt that you can achieve anything you want."

Gareth drinks and I drink too, looking him straight in the eye. He's not who I expected I'd end up with, not some graying Lothario with an eye to a second wife. He's younger, fitter than me, lithe, and bright-eyed with all his own hair. Good with his hands, too…

"I don't know how I got so lucky with you," I say. "Still can't believe I ended up with my own private chef."

"No more than you deserve," he says. "I can't believe I found you, either. The person I've been looking for all my life."

I smile at him and he smiles back, the pulse between us warm and steady. I lift my fork and eat, relishing each mouthful. It's a chicken tagine, rich with spices—cumin, cinnamon, saffron—the bite of preserved lemon sharp against the sweetness of dried apricot, the tang of the green olives he's taken the time to pit, each one cut in half and half again.

"No one's ever cooked for me before," I say. "Not like this, at least. Normally it's a bacon roll if I'm lucky."

"I've got some bacon," he says. "I was hoping you might rise to the occasion and make me a sandwich in the morning."

"If you're sure you want to risk it," I say. I scrape the rest of the sauce up onto my fork before putting down my cutlery and running my finger round the plate, collecting up every last bit. Gareth laughs at me but I shrug, defiant.

"That was delicious," I say. "What's for dessert?"

In reply, he stands, moves over to me. He pulls me up to my feet and kisses me before biting my shoulder.

"You," he says, and takes off my top.

2

I wake before Gareth, watching the light grow round the edges of the blinds, gray to bright. He's snoring gently, flat on his front, one arm thrown across me. I'd have run a mile by now normally, slipping out from under the embrace, hoping to God the man of the moment didn't wake to find me making my escape.

Gareth's different, though. Ever since it began, it's felt right. We first met at a law conference I attended in Edinburgh six months ago, Sentencing across the Jurisdictions. We were all wearing name badges, milling round the lunch buffet. He was wearing chef's whites and a tall hat when he came over with a plate of mozzarella to top up the display. "Sylvie," he said, "that's a nice name," and as the delegates ebbed and flowed around us, we talked for a while, long enough to pique my interest and for me to hand over my number. It made such a change, to have interest from a man in his late thirties, hair and waistline still intact.

I put back my return to London and we had dinner the next night; the food good, the wine better. He kept my glass brimming over, my heart rate ticking over the edge. There was a buzz of intensity in his gaze, his eyes rarely leaving mine as I told him the bones of my life, the career at the Bar, my growing disillusion- ment with my corporate clients, how I switched to criminal law, became a deputy district judge. My dreams of becoming a circuit judge one day.

His stint in the corporate world had been even shorter. He'd lasted a few years at an insurance company in Edinburgh before his sister's death sent him over the edge and he jacked it all in to become a caterer.

"Life's too short to do a job you hate," he said, sitting back in his chair and swilling down some wine.

"Couldn't agree more."

"And it's going well. I've got my own business now. As you saw. We get a lot of conferences in. Weddings, funerals. The usual. Most of my work's in Edinburgh but I'm looking to expand south." He paused. "I'd be able to visit regularly."

I didn't reply immediately, letting his words sink in. Prodding them to see how the idea of it felt.

It felt good.

"Enough about me. Deputy district judge? What does that involve? Doesn't sound all that," he said.

"More fun than you'd think. I get trials, every now and again. Mostly Youth Court."

He made a face. "Fun. Robberies, I bet. Knives. Bit of county lines?"

"There's a bit of that, yes. Don't forget the cars, too."

He laughed. "Glamorous. Do you get to send any of them to jail? That would be my only motivation."

"Not sure that's quite the right attitude," I said. "Though to be fair, sometimes it's tempting. Anyway, yes, I can pass a maximum custodial sentence of two years."

I drained my wine, bored of work talk. I pushed my hair back from my face and smiled. "Anyway, this is dull stuff. That's not why we're here. We both know that."

We stared at each other across the table, but my eyes were the first to drop. I was flustered, on edge, a fizzing under my skin that could be the wine or could be something else entirely.

"We both know, do we? Go on, then. Tell me, why are we here?" he said, but he didn't wait for an answer, reaching over the table and taking hold of my hand, his thumbnail driving hard into my palm. I looked up in surprise, ready to protest, but he was smiling at me, a challenge presented. I leaned into the pain, smiling back. Bring it on.

Six months ago. I wouldn't have anticipated it lasting, but he's gotten under my skin. I roll over toward him, tucking my face under his shoulder before going back to sleep.

Later, I watch him dress, his back, the muscles moving smoothly under the skin as he pulls his shirt over his head. I stretch myself out in bed.

He bends down to kiss me. "That was fun," he says. "Are you free tonight?"

"I thought you were going up north today?"

"I was meaning to, but I can actually stay another night," he says. "If that's OK with you?"

"Of course it's all right. I'd love it. Shall we go out?"

"Why don't you cook for me? You could ask some friends round. It's about time I met your friends, don't you think?"

I sit up in protest. "I can't cook for you. You're a bloody chef." I ignore the second part of his question.

"Yes, and I do all my own cooking. I want the night off."

I mutter, not convinced.

"It's not an asking, it's a telling," he says with such a huge smirk that I throw the pillow at him. In response he grabs my arm, pulls me out of bed, and slaps me on the arse before pushing me back down and straddling me. "Maybe you don't need to get up just yet."

Despite the holdup, I'm in court on time, tripping into the robing room at Southwark Crown Court with a spring in my step, grateful for the eleven o'clock mention that's all I have to cover. There wasn't time for me to cook the bacon at home, so breakfast is a Coke and a cheese-and-ham croissant from Pret, and I wipe the crumbs off my lips with relish. The day moves fast, busy with emails and conferences once I'm back in chambers, and before I can stop to draw breath, it's time to leave. As I walk out to get the Tube home, my phone pings. Expecting it to be Gareth, I take it from my bag.

It's not. It's Tess. I think about Gareth's question to me earlier, about inviting my friends to meet him. She's the obvious candidate, my oldest friend from school. I come to a stop on the pavement, shifting sideways to get out of the way of the other pedestrians. Should I ask her? I've dodged questions from her for months about whether I'm going out with someone, reluctant to open it up to her scrutiny. To be fair, she and her husband, Marcus, have been going through a trial separation, and I haven't wanted to rub my happiness in her face. I don't think that sensitivity is the only reason, though. Am I scared to jinx it? Maybe I think she'll judge. She's had the husband and the nice house for years, even if right now they are on a break. Tess would be happy if I'm happy, though. I know it. Even if it's late notice, she'll come over the moment I ask.

I weigh it up in the balance, unsure still. Then I think about having to explain to her that I've been seeing him for six months and not mentioned it, and my heart sinks. I don't want to do it now. I'll sort out drinks with her soon, tell her the whole story. Then I can introduce them and it'll all be fine.

If he asks, I'll tell him that she was busy. I'll psych myself up for introducing them soon, maybe a nice dinner out with Tess, with Marcus too, when he goes back to her, stops being a dick. Not yet, though. I've been single too long to want to mess everything up by bringing them in too soon, exposing Gareth to a harsh glare.

Decision made, I mute the call, then go off light as a bird to buy the ingredients for a roast chicken dinner. No point trying to impress—I may as well just make something nice. It's not what he's stayed for anyway, let's face it.

Dinner is good. Gareth finishes his plate, a second helping too, licking his chops with relish.

"That was great," he says. "I love it when people cook for me."

The question springs into my mind as to who else might have cooked for him, other nights, other towns. I put it away. There's no need to become neurotic—it's far too chilled out for that.

"Glad you liked it. Come here."

He pulls me over to him and starts to kiss me, his hands moving across my back. Abruptly, he lets go, moving away from me.

"I brought something for you," he says, reaching into his pocket and pulling out a strip of black material.

"What is it?"

"A blindfold. I thought we could have some fun." Then he reaches into his other pocket and pulls out a pair of handcuffs, waving them at me.

It's cheesy, I know. Substandard Fifty Shades stuff, but it's Tuesday night and I'm bored of being serious. Gareth's funny and filthy, not bogged down with all the tiresome baggage of my friends and my nearly middle-aged life.

"That sounds interesting," I say, striving for a sultry tone. "What do you have in mind?"

In answer, he rolls his eyes, my attempt at sexy banter falling flat. He takes me through into the bedroom.

"Are you sure about this?" he says as he's about to fasten my wrists up over my head.

"Sure about what?"

"Sure that you want to be tied up? I could do all sorts to you and you couldn't stop me."

"I was rather hoping you would," I say, holding my other hand out for him.

"Seriously, though. You sure?"

"I'm sure. Please stop talking," I say. "This is exactly what I want to be doing right now."

After this, he doesn't ask anymore. And it's not long before I'm beyond saying anything at all, every sense heightened as my sight is darkened and the night begins.

3

Gareth leaves early the next morning to get back in time for an event in Edinburgh in the evening. I head off to work, going down to Holborn and into chambers, the clerks nodding hello at me. I've got two conferences and a pupillage committee call to make before working some more on the application form for becoming a recorder. Another reason to be in touch with Marcus. He's a successful QC and a part-time judge, and I want to ask his advice about the process as he went through it only a few years earlier. I've been putting it off, reluctant to look as if I'm taking sides with him in his separation from Tess, but maybe it's time I had a chat with her, got the all clear from her to speak to Marcus about it.

I'm not going to keep delaying it. I send Tess a quick text suggesting a drink. Opening my laptop, I look at the Judicial Appointments Commission website with a sense of total fear before taking a deep breath and making a start. The deadline is coming up and I don't have time to think, let alone check my phone for her reply. Every now and again I nurse the thought of Gareth, the way it felt the night before when he was bearing down on me. But I push it away. I can't afford the distraction.

By the end of the day I'm tired, my brain strung out and buzzing from the plates I've been spinning. I sit on the Tube home with my eyes closed, looking forward to an early night. It's been a fraught few days and I need a rest. Once I'm home, I change into tracksuit bottoms and a hoodie, scraping my hair back into a ponytail. I'm not expecting any visitors and Gareth is back in Edinburgh. I'm safe to be a slob.

Making a cheese omelet, I sit down to eat it in front of the TV, catching up on a box-set detective series. I check my phone every now and again, but it's quiet. Gareth must be working, and Tess hasn't gotten back to me yet. I'm surprised—she's normally quick to reply, but she's probably busy, too.

I clear up my supper and eat an apple, looking out of the kitchen window at the houses behind. A man is sitting at his desk working, a woman is washing up. There's the sound of children shouting before one of them bursts into tears and a door slams. I think about Tess and Marcus, their house with its secluded garden, no one overlooking it. Tess would never be seen dead in the tracksuit bottoms I'm wearing. When I spend time with them, I always feel like their wayward child, they my sensible parents in their spotless home.

What will they make of Gareth? I hope they like him. I wonder if it'll upset the dynamic to bring someone new into the equation. For as long as they've been a couple, I've been their third wheel, always welcome at their table. High days, holidays. Will their hospitality extend to him?

I find my phone and message Tess again. It's been nearly twelve hours now since I sent my first text. It was vaguely worded—Fancy a drink sometime?—so I go for something more specific. Drinks tomorrow night? Something I want to tell you about. xxx That should do it. It might be over twenty years since we left school, but some anxiety in me is always triggered when she doesn't get back to me. It's irrational, but I always worry that for some reason she's not talking to me, that I've done something terribly wrong that I just don't remember. I shake my head, trying to dislodge the concern.

Half an hour later and my phone is still silent. I flick through, checking the junk-mail folder in case Tess has emailed and it's gone there by mistake. Now that I've decided I want to tell her about Gareth, I really want to do it now. He's part of the future I'm planning, my new life in which I play a starring role, not understudy to my best friend. But there are no messages, nothing.

I put the phone down and go off and have a bath, wallowing as the last few days soak off me. I'm too tired to read, lying instead with my head underwater, listening to the banging of the pipes and the sounds of taps running from the flats above and below mine. I top the bath up with hot water, pushing the tap with my foot. I'm calm, relaxed, sleep hovering over my head, almost within my grasp.

The hot water finally runs out and it's time to get out, my fingertips wrinkled and dry. I look around the small bathroom. It needs a clean, detritus everywhere. Bits of Gareth will be here, too, his leavings of the night before. He used condoms and suddenly I'm struck with the thought that I should pull one of them out of the overflowing bin, squeeze the sperm out and try to inseminate myself.

I get back into the bath and put the showerhead up to the highest setting, standing under the cold water to rinse off my hair, wash away such thoughts. Once I'm dry and dressed, I get a rubbish bag and empty the bathroom bin out. After that I move through to the bedroom bin and empty that, too, scooting round the living room and the kitchen to pick up any more stray containers, bits of waste. I'll hoover and scrub tomorrow, get this place decent.

As I come back into the flat from putting the rubbish out in the bins, I hear my phone ping. At last. A doubt in me eases, an anxiety I was refusing to recognize. Tess has replied. She's not ignoring me. I'm going to be able to tell her about everything that's been happening, about the relationship with Gareth on which I'm pinning so much hope. There's a glowing future ahead. Not just a potential promotion, a boyfriend too. All the accoutrements of adult life.

The message isn't from her, though. It's from Gareth. Nice, but not what I wanted. But as I pick up my phone, ready to reply to him, it starts to ring. Tess. At last.

My flicker of relief is short-lived. It's nearly eleven now. Why hasn't she messaged? Tess never calls after nine unless it's an emergency. It's a rule she's had all her adult life, one of the many boundaries she put in place to counter the chaos of her upbringing, her mother who wasn't bothered by any such considerations. My finger hovers over the green button, held back by some strange premonition, some sense that whatever she has to say is going to change everything. I take a deep breath.

"Hello," I say.

"Sylvie," she says.

"Everything OK?"

"Everything's fine. I was too knackered to text," she says.

"Right. I was worried."

She ignores the comment. "The answer's yes."

"Yes to what?" I say.

"Yes to a drink tomorrow. The Eagle?"

"Sure," I say. "I'll be finished about six. I'll see you there."

She hangs up. I should be pleased. I've got the arrangement I wanted, the chance to tell her all about Gareth. But I can't shake off a feeling that something might be wrong, a shadow hovering in the corner of my mind.

4

I'm busy the next day, busy enough to keep my concerns for Tess at bay. Mostly. A long conference about a prosecution I'm leading, of a rogue landlord accused of corporate manslaughter following the completely avoidable death of one of his tenants from a carbon monoxide leak. Underneath it a drum beats, slowly, steadily. Relentless. Wine o'clock is coming, and Tess will be waiting, sauvignon in hand. I should be looking forward to seeing her, but I'm uneasy.

Her tone was businesslike the night before, cool. But there was a tremor below the surface, a string pulled too tight, vibrations running through the ether from her phone to mine.

It's lunchtime. Normally I'd be going to Pret, buying my usual avocado wrap and flat white, a bottle of fizzy water as a small luxury, a rebellion against all the reusable water bottles lined up on the desks around me. I'm not hungry, though, the disquiet I've felt since Tess's call the night before gnawing at my guts. I work through the rest of the afternoon, drowning out my concern with a deep dive into the fraud trial I've got lined up for the beginning of next year.

Finally, it's time to get to the pub. I make my way there slowly, still troubled, though unable to articulate it properly. I know it's irrational. In the worst case, she's going to say she's getting divorced from Marcus. I have to say, it wouldn't be the end of the world. I've seen some of their rows—they don't always bring the best out of each other.

I wait outside the Eagle for a few moments, unable to see Tess at any of the tables indoors, and then I see her walking down Farringdon Road toward me. From a distance, she looks entirely normal and my heart lifts, the worry that's clouded me since she called starting to fade. But as she comes closer into view, the clouds gather again. She's not smiling.

When she reaches me, she doesn't hug me but nods her head before going straight past me into the pub. It's still early enough that we manage to get a table near the window. Still without saying hello properly, she doesn't even stop to ask what I want to drink but goes straight up to the bar and places an order. I watch the barman uncork a bottle of red wine, take two glasses off the shelf, and polish them with a tea towel before putting them on the bar in front of Tess. She pays with cash, slipping the change into her pocket. She picks up the wine in one hand and the glasses in the other and starts back toward our table, then turns round and says something to the barman, who nods, noting it down on a pad.

"I've ordered some chips," she says. "I'm starving."

I take the glass of wine she's offering me. "OK," I say. A myriad of responses is running through my mind. I'm off carbs. I'm not drinking. I want white wine. But it's Tess, her scene that she's setting. Besides, I can see a bowl of chips on a table near us and they do look bloody good, crispy and golden. I never had that avocado wrap at lunch, after all.

Tess fusses with her scarf, her seat, twitching round as if she can't get comfortable. Finally, she leans back into the wooden chair.

"This is nice," she says. "Haven't been here for years. We really should have come out here more."

"I come here a lot," I say. "It's close to work, but not too close. Away from the fleshpots of Temple."

"I thought it would work for you."

I lean back in my chair, smile at her. "So nice to see you, Tess. I've got tons of news. Something really big has happened. Something exciting."

Tess's face doesn't change. It's as if she hasn't heard me. She doesn't smile back, even, but sips her wine. I'm already halfway down my glass. The silence hangs heavy, but despite her lack of response, there's no air of hostility. Just tension, crackling all around her.

"I've met someone," I continue, refusing to allow it to deter me. "He's lovely. It's an actual relationship. Imagine that—me, going out with someone."

Still nothing from Tess. She's staring ahead, her eyes almost glazed over. I'm struck with the urge to lean over, click my fingers in her face, yell at her. Anything to get her attention. I restrain myself, though.

At long last, she clears her throat. I lean forward eagerly, ready to catch whatever she might say. She doesn't speak, though, subsiding further into her chair and drinking more wine. I drink more wine, too, the valpolicella warm and fragrant in my mouth. I should be more edgy, but it's worked its usual magic. She clears her throat again, moistens her lips with the tip of her tongue. The red wine has left small marks at the corners of her mouth, and in the dim light of the pub it looks as if she's half smiling. She's not, though, her face grave.

"Sylvie," she says. "Sylvie, there's something I need to tell you."

"What do you need to tell me?"

"This is really hard," she says. "I don't know how to say it."

"What's really hard?" I say. "If it's that you and Marcus are getting divorced, you can tell me about it. Honestly, it's not like I'm your kid or anything." I laugh, but it falls flat. She's shaking her head.

"I have to tell you—" she starts to say but just then my phone beeps. Normally I wouldn't check it if I were out, but I'm pissed off now. It feels as if she's trying artificially to raise the tension, add a cliff-hanger to a situation that doesn't warrant it at all. Plus she's ignored me, my big announcement, the fact that my life has changed in such a major way. She's being way too mysterious, too hesitant, for what is surely just another recitation of Marcus's shortcomings, nothing important enough to warrant all this drama.

"Sylvie," she says, her tone sharp, and I look up, almost in apology. "Sylvie."

The phone is still in my hand as she starts to speak. By the time she's finished, I've dropped it, all thought of the message from work erased with the magnitude of what she has to say.

THE DOG WALKER

Terrible night for the dog, Hogmanay. I've tried everything—weighted blankets, CDs full of sounds of fireworks to desensitize him. Nothing works. He's been pacing all evening, shivering, licking at his lips in stress.

I hate it almost as much as he does.

He needs to go out, though. We always go for a wee walk before bed. He's stopped trembling and now he's pacing by the door. I can't win. He's still a bundle of nerves, though, not settling. I'll take him out now, I say to the wife. She's half-asleep, not complaining since it'll be me in the cold, not her. He jumps around me while I put my shoes on, my coat. Memory of a goldfish, that one.

He's pulling ahead of me, eager to get off the lead, but it's too dark. I don't want to risk him running off somewhere. We'll just do a pavement walk this time, go along Regent Terrace. I'll take him to Holyrood Park for a proper run round later.

Part hunting dog, that's what we've always said about him. He's normally good, unless he gets the scent of something. "Kenny, Kenny," I shout, but he's still pulling. A fox ahead, maybe, or a squirrel. He tugs so hard I let go, and he sprints off into the night before I can stop him. I pant after him, hoping to God a drunk driver doesn't appear out of the night, mow him down.

I get to the end of the terrace. I still can't see him. But then I hear a hideous growling, barking at some shape that's hanging on the railings at the front of the house. I walk round to him, closer, so that I can check it out.

Oh Jesus. Oh no. Oh fucking hell sweet Jesus no.

It's like someone's put rag dolls over the railings to dry. Giant rag dolls. All bent out of shape.

Not rag dolls, though. A body. Two bodies. Both caught on the railings—one doubled over, spikes straight through their guts, the other caught on their back, arms splayed backward, a spike protruding through their neck.

A river of blood.

I can't look but I can't look away and I watch Kenny licking at the blood, licking at the bodies, and then I start to scream.

5

"Things have been really difficult recently," Tess begins. I open my mouth to reply but she holds up her hand. "Really difficult. It's been hardest for Marcus. He's borne the brunt of it. But I know I've not seen you as much as I should, as well. I'm sorry."

I blink. I thought it had all been me, tied up with Gareth. Evidently not. "Remember when I cancelled on you a few months ago? When we were due to go out?" she continues.

"You mean when you told me that you couldn't be arsed to go out on the piss because you had to be up for a meeting, that unlike me you weren't prepared to show up hungover for work?"

Tess smiles when I say it, as if I'm joking when I remind her of her words. I'm not, though. I tried to shrug it off but her words had stung, hitting deep into my feelings of inadequacy, the girl-woman who never grew up. My eyes narrow as I look at her.

"I'm sorry," she says, reading my expression correctly. "I didn't mean to sound so judgmental. I thought if I pissed you off you wouldn't ask any more questions. It wasn't that I couldn't be arsed. I wasn't well. I'd fallen over, had some sort of fit."

"A fit?"

"A seizure. I came round on the floor, covered in bruises, my head splitting to burst."

"But you don't get seizures. I've never known you to have one. Never."

"No, that's the thing. I thought at first it was the medication I was on. I'd taken steroids for an ear infection. I thought it must be related. Or to do with the ear infection itself—labyrinthitis, or something," Tess says. She pauses to refill her glass.

"You didn't even mention that," I say. "You could have told me you were ill."

"I didn't want to make a fuss. Especially once I'd had the seizure. Anyway, the point is, it happened again a month or so ago, for a second time. On top of which, I've been having headaches. I haven't felt like myself. So I went to the doctor. I thought she'd tell me to get some more sleep, cut back on caffeine. But she took it seriously. Really seriously."

I've been pushing the chips into my mouth, one after the other, barely even waiting to finish chewing one before I've rammed another in, but I'm beginning to lose my appetite. I don't like what Tess is saying. A feeling of dread is building up in me, forcing my throat shut. The potato is turning into a solid lump stuck somewhere down my chest, and I swallow hard to dislodge it.

"Seriously? In what way seriously?" I say, the words coming out with difficulty.

"Enough to refer me to the hospital for a scan. That seriously."

I blink again. A scan? "What do you mean? Surely it's nothing. You're far too young."

She leans forward, takes my hand. All my anger is gone. This is Tess, my oldest friend, my closest confidant, talking about something I don't understand, that I don't want to understand. There's dread looming on the horizon, a sense that life is about to change irrevocably, and I don't want to know.

"I mean, that sounds like a complete overreaction if you ask me. A few headaches? Passing out? You're not epileptic—it sounds like you've just had a big reaction to the steroids. They're horrible things, steroids. Someone in the office had to take them once and they said it was a total nightmare. Terrible side effects." I can't stop myself talking now, words tumbling out of me helter-skelter. If I keep filibustering the danger will pass, the fear averted.

"Sylvie," she says, and there's huge warmth in her voice. Kindness too. I stop, looking closely at her, away. Tears are starting to form in the corners of my eyes and I brush them away, furious suddenly.

"What the fuck is it, Tess?"

"I had the MRI scan on Friday. There's a tumor."

"A tumor? What kind of tumor? Where?"

"We don't know yet. But there's a tumor, growing in my brain."

With those words, there's nothing else to say. I simply look at her, my hand gripping hers, clutching on as if it's the only way to stop myself from falling into the abyss that's opened now in front of me.

Seconds pass, minutes. I drink, drink again, trying to wash the taste of the words out of my mouth. I should be asking questions, saying I'm sorry, but I can't. There's a swooshing sound in my ears, a sense that my foundations are collapsing beneath me, crumbling away into sand. I know Tess is only my friend, not my family, not blood, but she's still part of me. It's more than family; I chose her. She chose me. We're meant to be getting old together, wearing purple. Upsetting our youngers.

I'm getting ahead of myself. It's a tumor, she said. There're lots of tumors. Not necessarily malignant. It doesn't have to mean death. I look up.

"There's so much they can do, isn't there? There are so many treatments. They're going to sort you out, aren't they?" My words are meant to be reassuring but there's a desperation behind them, the statements really questions, screaming out for Tess to lean over and tell me that everything is going to be all right.

She smiles, a twist to her mouth that I've not seen before. "As I said, it's early days. All they've identified so far is there's a tumor. They need to do further tests before they can work out what they can do. What treatment might be available. If any."

The last words are muttered so quietly I nearly miss them, drowned out as they are in the babble from the tables around us, the clinking of glasses and cutlery on plates. I look around me, filled with fury at the people surrounding us, all flushed and complacent, eating and drinking away as if the world isn't falling apart. I want to scream at them, tell them all to fuck off out the pub so that I can hear Tess properly, catch every last breath she takes.

"When are they going to do the further tests?" I ask. I refuse to acknowledge that treatment won't be possible. I'm not even going to address the comment.

"Next week, I think. Soon," she says. "They're getting on with it. Time is of the essence." She laughs, but it's a sound that chills.

"How is Marcus?" I ask. "He must be in pieces."

Tess pauses before she replies, drinks a little. "That's one of the reasons I needed to talk to you," she says. "He doesn't know. Not yet."

"He doesn't know yet? Tess, he has to be told. You can't keep this from him."

"It's hard. He's the one who wants the separation. We've done nothing but row for months. How can I dump this on him now? I don't want to force him to come back out of pity, or some misguided sense of loyalty."

I lean forward across the table, my hands clasped in front of me. "Tess, he loves you. OK, he said he was leaving, but you're only separated, nothing more permanent. This changes everything. It explains everything. No wonder you've been struggling, dealing with something as big as this."

She shakes her head. "He doesn't sound like he still loves me. He said he hated me. I can't even blame him, the way I've been behaving."

"Now come on," I say. "I was there, twenty years ago. Richer, poorer, sickness, health? This is the big one. The moment he knows about this, he'll be straight back. You're a team. You do everything together. You have to let him know."

"I can't tell him myself," she says. She's not smiling now, lines of tension running from mouth to nose. "He's not going to listen to me. He's shut his ears to me. He said as much, that I was always able to persuade him to change his mind about anything, however strongly he'd made a decision. He calls me his siren sometimes."

I don't say it, but I know exactly what he means. I always end up doing what Tess wants, too, whether by dint of her siren song or her sheer bloody-mindedness. I wonder how much determination he's had to build up to leave her. They've argued so many times in the past, but he's never done that before. Despite my words of comfort to her, I'm concerned about his feelings, how much they must have changed for him to make the move. She's not wrong that it's going to be difficult for her to get through to him, wax stuck firmly in his ears. But as soon as she does—

"Sylvie, I need your help," she says, interrupting my thoughts. "I need you to tell him. You're so close. He'll listen to you. Please, will you do this for me? It's going to be so difficult."

I look at her, so tense and miserable. Her hair, normally thick and luxuriant, is hanging lank and greasy around her shoulders, and there are a couple of flakes of dandruff on the shoulders of her navy jumper. She can't be ill. I don't want her to be ill.

I won't let her be ill.

"Of course I'll tell him," I say. "I'll call him now."

I pick up my phone, ready to dial, but her hand shoots out and takes hold of mine, fingers digging in hard.

"Not now," she says. "Later. Let's just enjoy this evening first, you and me. This might be the last time we can sit together like this, in a pub, drinking wine. I don't know what's going to happen. I'm scared, really scared. Can we just pretend for a bit longer that everything is normal? The moment that Marcus knows, it's going to be real. Will you play along with me, just for tonight?"

I can't think that alcohol is good for someone with a brain tumor. I should be telling Marcus, I should be stopping her from drinking, but instead I go up to the bar and order another bottle of red and some more chips, before returning to the table and Tess, the years blurring between now and then, all the times we've sat like this before, trying not to think that this is the last time we will ever be like this again.

"You're my best friend, Sylvie. Even better than Marcus, really. We've been through so much together. Linda, everything with the wedding…" Tess says some drinks later. I have to lean close to hear her, the words striking me like blows. Why has she mentioned Linda? We promised we never would, once it was all over. I'm about to interrupt but she keeps going, clutching at my hand with an iron grasp.

"It's never been quite right, you know. I mean, until recently, it's worked out. But given what it was based on…if he comes back to me, I'm going to ask Marcus to marry me again."

"But you're already married," I say, my brain struggling to keep up with Tess and the intense way she's speaking to me.

"A renewal of vows," Tess says. "You know, a confirmation of our marriage. Whatever you want to call it. I can wear my wedding dress again. But this time it'll be different. Don't you think it's a great idea?"

I sit, blinking. All I can think about is how difficult it all was the first time round. But she's looking so tense, wound up so tightly, all I can do is nod.

"And you'll be my bridesmaid again, just like last time?"

I open my mouth, but nothing comes out. "I…"

"It'll be just like last time," she says. "But better. Much, much better. Come on, say you will. I've still got your dress—I know it'll still fit. Come on, say yes. It'll be amazing."

I'm struggling to follow her shifts of mood. From dread that Marcus won't come back to her, Tess has leaped ahead to planning a whole ceremony of recommitment. But the look of misery has gone from her face, and I don't want to be the one to bring that shadow back.

"Of course I'll do it," I say. "Whatever you want."

6

I'm stuck to the pillow, unable to move my head. Something has trapped me. I'm between sleeping and waking, my heart starting to pound as I pull myself out of a dream in which I was caught under layers of thick, oleaginous treacle, my feet caught fast whenever I tried to move. With an effort I wrench my cheek free, and as I wake fully, I realize that it wasn't really stuck, but that it's coated in dried saliva. I need to stop doing this.

Yuck. I'm too old for hangovers. It's sapping my will to live. But as that phrase passes through my mind, fear strikes hard. Something terrible happened last night. Tess told me something and it's changed everything. I lie back, my head spinning, trying to piece it all together.

Her diagnosis. I remember that bit, the tight clutch of her fingers, the strain in her eyes. Not conclusive… I know that, nothing final as yet. Treatment may be possible. But from the expression on her face I know Tess isn't holding out a great deal of hope. My head spins again, my stomach churning with pure acid. I roll over onto my side, pulling the duvet close around me.

I agreed to tell Marcus. I remember that, too. My guts lurch and I sit up fast, reaching for my phone. Please God I didn't message him last night, I didn't tell him in some garbled, incoherent manner. I have a feeling I was doing something with my phone, but what exactly is completely lost to me right now. There's a number of notifications but I skip past them, pulling up my call history, my messages. Nothing to Marcus since well before yesterday evening. Relief seeps through me.

All the same, a sense of panic is rising. I've got to remember what Tess said, what I agreed to do. Tell Marcus, yes. But there was something else. I know that the conversation went on and on as we drank further and further down the second bottle, then the third. We should have stopped there.

"I want Jack Daniel's," she'd said when we finished the last of the wine. "I'm going to get us JD and Cokes. OK?"

I didn't argue. I was at the stage where I was happy to keep going all night, the small flames lit by the first glasses of red now a wildfire, ripping through me. Tess went to the bar and came back with the drinks, and we kept talking, through another, and another, until the bar shut and I came home, though how, I don't recall.

What the hell were we discussing? Her cancer. No, not that word. That wasn't the word we were using, still open to the possibility that the tumor might be benign, though I didn't think so, and neither did she. I know I agreed to something, to do something that Tess kept saying was incredibly important, that had to be done before she died.

"You're not going to die. I won't let you!" I do remember shouting that, so loudly that heads turned toward us, before Tess shushed me. I downed my drink in one, bolshie belligerent, before she brought me another and started to talk again.

My head's too sore and my tummy's too rancid. I can't think. I roll over to my other side, desperate to try to get comfortable, though there will be no comfort for some hours to come, not till this passes. I'm still drunk, my breath thick under the covers.

It's early, time enough for me to get to work, but there's no way I'll be able to make it. I'll have to work from home, once I can get out of bed. I click onto my calendar and check what meetings I have—nothing that can't be postponed. I send an email quickly to the office to say that I'm ill, hoping to goodness that no one was walking past the Eagle the night before on their way home, looking through the window, seeing me there, glass in hand.

As I'm about to put my phone down, a text comes through from Tess.

> *Thanks so much. I'm sorry to dump so much on you. Marcus, Linda, everything… It's so overwhelming. I'm grateful that you're willing to help. I know you're not keen on the idea, but it'll be really special. I'm sure you'll feel the same way soon. Also, I know you haven't told Marcus yet, but can you tell me when you do? Love you, Sylvie. You're the best friend anyone could want. xxx*

My mind's blank. What does she want me to help with? She must be meaning Marcus, right? I'm sitting up now, agitated. My heart was already racing as my body does its best to expel all the toxins I rammed into it last night, but now it's doing something worse, a weird syncopation. Jesus, I'm having a heart attack. I can't breathe all of a sudden, my heart racing harder. The acid from my stomach burns up my neck.

I need to be sick. Now. I throw my phone from me and run through into the bathroom, making it in time to vomit, the sick hurting my throat and making my mouth pucker. It does help, though. Once it's all out, I sit back on my heels, wiping my mouth with a clump of loo roll, tears streaming down my face from the force of the retching. I go into the kitchen and run myself a glass of water before returning to bed, tucking myself back under the duvet.

I pick my phone up again. *Help.* Help with what? I still can't work it out, what Tess means, hard as I try to remember. I refuse to address her comment about Linda right now. If I don't remember it, it's not real. The conversation didn't happen. There's too much roiling inside me, too much shame already without opening that locked door.

The phone pings. Another message from Tess. It contains a photograph, a scan of an older photograph, her and Marcus smiling at the camera. She's in white, and he's in a morning suit. The photo is nearly twenty years old.

For a short while I'm still in the dark, my memory occluded, the holes caused by JD and Coke as yet unfilled. I look at the picture blankly, trying to work out why she's sent it to me. And all of a sudden, there's no more bliss in ignorance. The promises I've made to Tess come flooding back, overwhelming me.

The renewal of vows. Not only have I agreed to tell Marcus about Tess's tumor, but I've agreed to be Tess's bridesmaid again, in a ceremony for her to renew her vows with Marcus. As if the wedding itself wasn't bad enough.

There was one more promise. I can feel it, looming over me. I tell it to fuck off, go away. She hasn't mentioned it. I must have been imagining it. A ray of light in the darkness. I have to tell Marcus. I have to be her bridesmaid. But she hasn't mentioned the worst request. And if she hasn't, I sure as hell won't.

Another beep. Tess again.

I know how much it upsets you to talk about Linda. Let alone think about getting in touch with her, finding out how she is. But it's time. Past time. You were drunk when you promised but I'm going to hold you to it. We are finding Linda and we are making everything right. x

I sit, head in hands, pinned beneath a weight of memory that I hoped I'd never have to confront again. The light's gone. Nothing here but dark.

AUTUMN TERM 1989

"He fancies you," she said.

"Does not."

"He does. He keeps looking at you when you're not looking. I saw him doing it in English. In history, too."

"Then why's he always such a shit? All he does is take the piss out of me."

"Like I said. He fancies you."

She jumped ahead of me, black suede boots kicking up dead leaves from the pavement of St. Stephen Street, the orange light from the streetlamp above glinting off the damp stone.

"And he gave you a cigarette, just then." Tess turned round, blazing triumph. "I told you so."

"He didn't exactly give me a cigarette. He was handing the pack round to everyone. I just happened to take one," I said.

"Same difference. Anyway, you'll find out tomorrow night. Shambles. You up for it?"

"I dunno…"

"Come on, Sylvie. He's the most popular boy in the school. You said you've never felt like you fitted in here. This is going to sort you out completely."

She was right. Apart from Tess, I didn't have any friends, never quite fitting in. That first day of term came back to me—I walked in new and shiny, chestnut penny loafers gleaming, heart pounding in my mouth. I wasn't quite late, but I was the last to arrive, and every face turned toward me as I went into the classroom for the first time. A snigger here, a snort there. My face immobile, I scanned the room, settling with horror on the one face I knew. Tess. A girl I'd seen only from a distance in the park, or at the odd disco I'd attended while at my previous school. She'd never spoken to me, sneered at me whenever she caught my eye. But that all had to change. With only six girls in the class and twenty boys, we needed to get on. Even if she was the only one who spoke to me, getting through sixth form would be hell without her.

Now she lit a cigarette, blew the smoke out toward me.

"Campbell says Stewart definitely fancies you, but he needs to see you're up for it. Tomorrow is the perfect night for it."

"I'm not even meant to be going out. You know they freak if they think I'm going to the pub."

"Don't tell them, then. Say you're staying at mine."

"I thought you were out with Campbell?"

"Only for food. We'll come to the pub after, I promise."

I sighed, nodded my acquiescence. Tess was always so much more grown-up than me, her eyeliner immaculate, the length of her skirt always just so. I tried rolling mine up to make it sexier but she sighed at me, curling her lip, and it made me feel about twelve. It would be nice to be a girlfriend, be part of her gang. We could double-date. I wouldn't feel so spare.

"I'll be there," I said, taking a drag on my cigarette, trying to look cool. Failing. I inhaled too deeply and started coughing, my eyes watering. Before I remembered I was wearing eyeliner, I reached up and rubbed them, a streak of black across the back of my hand.

"You can do this. He's really into you."

In the basement of Shambles, the following night. Stewart's hand had been up my top for the last half hour, his tongue down the back of my throat.

"Don't go home. You can come up to my brother's flat. He lets me stay there all the time. We'll get a carryout."

Before I could reply, his tongue was back in my mouth, awkwardly grappling with mine. I went along with it, uncertain as to whether I was meant to be enjoying it or if that was beside the point, when the man with the guitar started playing "American Pie" and Stewart let go of me so fast I stumbled. He started jumping up and down and singing indistinctly but enthusiastically, emphasizing *Chevy* and *levee* so much it was obvious he didn't know the rest of the words.

While the music played and Stewart was occupied, I took the chance to escape to the loo, feeling sober all of a sudden, out of place. It was quieter in there, the music not piped in, and I rested my head against the back of the loo door for a moment before emerging, pulling my skirt out from the back of my tights where it had gotten caught up. I looked in the mirror, checking my face, rubbing along my eyelids to straighten up the black eyeliner I'd applied so liberally at the start of the night. No lipstick left—most of that was now smeared across Stewart's face, mingled with sweat and lager.

A younger girl came in, from the year below. Karen, was that her name? No, Linda. That's right. I could hear Tess's voice in my head immediately. *What the fuck are you doing in here? Get the fuck out! This is for the upper sixth, not for you lot.* I told the voice to shut up, smiled at her. She was putting her weight on one foot, then the other, uneasy. Tess's reputation was formidable, and I was Tess's best friend. But I smiled, moving over to let her pass into the cubicle.

I had concealer and eyeliner in my pocket, lipstick too, and I got to work covering up the massive spot that was coming up on my chin. Looking more closely, I saw blotches of stubble rash from where Stewart had been kissing me, and I covered that up, too. His words were echoing in my head—*We can stay at my brother's flat... We'll get a carryout.*

"Do you know the time?" I asked Linda.

"Coming up for eleven," she said, her voice muffled by the loo door.

Not that late, then. Closing time wasn't until midnight, and there was always Fingers to go to, or one of the late-night Italians further up town.

When I emerged from the loo, Stewart was waiting, tequila shots in hand. He made me lean my head back and licked my clavicle, pouring salt onto the wet patch. Then he put a chunk of lemon in my mouth, skin first against my tongue.

"Stay still," he said. "Just wait."

I waited, my neck starting to ache with the weight of my head, the spins beginning to return as all the Stella I'd drunk started to make a reappearance with the noise and fury of the pub. I tried to speak but I couldn't, the lemon stuck still in my mouth. I rolled my eyes at him, urging him to get on with it, but he was shouting at one of his friends, almost as if he'd forgotten about me. After what felt like minutes, though it was probably only a few seconds, he turned his attention back to me.

"Here we go," he said. He leaned forward and sucked at my neck, hard enough to leave a mark, before tipping the shot down his neck and biting the lemon from my lips. I was relieved to be able to bring my head back down, the room swimming. He waved another shot to me, pouring salt onto the back of his hand for me and holding the other piece of lemon suggestively in his mouth. I knew I'd had enough to drink. I knew I should stop.

"I might not…" I started to say but he held up the hand holding the shot, pushed it at me again, using the other to take the lemon out of his mouth so he could speak.

"I got it for you especially," he said. "Don't be a lightweight. I didn't think you were like that."

I sensed the challenge in his tone. Not like the other girls. I took the tequila from his hand and drank.

"Any sign of Tess and Campbell?" I said.

"Fuck it, who needs them," Stewart said and pulled me to him, tongue in my mouth again. I thought about worrying, wondered about going home; it was still early enough, just, and I wasn't that drunk, but then the tequila hit and I couldn't deal with thinking about it anymore.

It was cold and I didn't have a proper coat so I clung onto Stewart all the way. I think he liked it, the way he kept hold of my shoulder, steering me along the pavement. There was an offie on the way and we went in, buying a bottle of the cheapest vodka, two packs of B&H. The man behind the till was about to take Stewart's money when he appeared to think twice.

"How old are you?" he asked. "I want to see some ID."

I froze immediately, splotches of guilt bleeding out on my cheeks. But he wasn't looking at me, he was looking at Stewart, and Stewart made a great show of pulling out a student card and showing it to the man, who gave it a cursory glance and nodded, ringing the purchase through.

"Not her, though," he said. I jumped, sure he meant me, but

when I looked up at him, he was pointing behind me, at Linda. I hadn't even realized she was still there. "Too young," the man said with finality.

Stewart nodded, taking the bag of booze and cigarettes from the man's hand. "We'll make sure she gets home all right. Thank you."

As soon as we were outside, he turned to Linda and hissed at her to fuck off. She looked defiant for all of about three seconds, maybe waiting to see if anyone else would stand up for her, but I stayed silent, and in the end she turned tail. Stewart started kissing me, and I couldn't be sure but I might have heard a sob. It went out of my mind, though.

Next stop chips, from L'Alba D'Oro, salt and sauce, and a short cut through Scotland Yard adventure playground. We sat on the massive tire swing, taking swigs of vodka and passing the bottle on. I was properly drunk by now, my words spaced and far away from each other. Tess kept coming into my head, leaving it again. It was all right, I was with Stewart. I hadn't been told to fuck off like Linda, I was all right and we were spinning spinning spinning round on the tire, heads back howling at the moon.

There might have been other people there with us by the time we got to Stewart's brother's flat, there might not. I was too drunk to tell. The chips had soaked up some of it, but I was topping up with swigs of vodka from the bottle and the world had contracted down to a small pinhole of light, Stewart's face almost within focus in front of me. He was laughing and somehow we were in a bedroom, me pushed back onto something soft, him hard above me, pressing down.

He got up, saying something about a condom, and I was nodding, not sure what he meant, *Kiss Me, Kiss Me, Kiss Me* by The Cure playing loud in my ears, drowning out his words, and then as "Just Like Heaven" started he was back, a rubbery smell on his hands, and I was pushed back again and this time he didn't get off. I was there but not there, watching it happen from a corner of the room, my legs bent against his back, his shoulders tense as he held himself up above me, and then it was over, and I was sitting up looking at the inside of my thigh, a smear of blood all down it.

"Did we have sex, then?" I was saying and he was still laughing at me, catching me in a quick hug before getting up and throwing a towel to me from across the room.

"Don't make a mess on the sheets," he said. "My brother'll kill me."

I sat, dabbing at my legs with the towel, looking at the blood. I'd felt nothing. Or maybe I had, but the drink had carried the pain somewhere else. I guess I'd said yes. I hadn't said no. It was time it happened, anyway. Next, Stewart threw me my clothes and I pulled my pants back on, my bra, but suddenly I was tired, really tired, too much excitement for one evening. *There'll be tears before bedtime.* Those words my mother would say were running through my mind, and there was at least one tear, a drip of water unexpectedly from my right eye, snot trailing from my nose, and I wiped it clear with the back of my hand, sniffing loudly.

"You OK?" Stewart said, sitting down next to me, and this was almost too much now, a kindness from him I hadn't anticipated.

"I need to go home," I said. "But I'm too pissed."

"You can stay here," he said. "It'll be OK. I can sleep in the other room."

"It's a bit late for that," I said. I looked at him and we both started to laugh. Maybe not what I'd planned, what I'd even wanted, but he was being nice.

"Are you my boyfriend, then?" I said.

"Yes. Yes, I'm your boyfriend." He was laughing at me but I didn't mind. He lay down next to me and we turned off the light. This felt more intimate than what had happened before, his breath steady, his body warm. I stared at the ceiling, willing it to stop spinning but happy. This was going to change everything.

7

Marcus refuses to meet me immediately. He's clearly pissed off that I haven't been in touch with him since he left Tess. I don't know what he expected, though. She's always had my loyalty. He's distant on the phone, elusive. I call repeatedly before he picks up, and even when I say that Tess has asked me to contact him, he grunts, shuts the subject down.

"I wouldn't ask if it weren't important," I say. "But there's something I have to tell you."

"Of course there is," he says. "But it'll have to wait. I'm up to my ears in a rape trial."

"When is it due to finish?"

"Thursday for closing speeches. Don't know how long the jury will take, of course. But I anticipate we'll send them out on Thursday afternoon. I could meet you then."

"Do you really want to leave it that long? It's important. I—"

He interrupts before I can say anything else. "You know what, Sylvie? Leave it. I'm happy right now. OK, I'm at a Premier Inn. But I'm not being endlessly criticized. I'm not being mocked, or gotten at for snoring. I'm not being yelled at, I'm not being ignored. I get to go to sleep, wake up, all without anyone undermining me or being nasty to me. I'm sleeping at night. Do you know how good that feels?"

"But, Marcus—"

"No, Sylvie. I don't want to hear it. We can speak on Thursday. If you need any help with work before then, call me, but leave Tess out of it. I will deal with that once this trial is out of the way."

He cuts off the call before I can say anything else. I'm surprised by the strength of his stance, but at the same time, part of me welcomes it. The thought of what I have to say hangs heavy on me. Once he knows about Tess's diagnosis, any peace he has will disappear. I send Tess a text to tell her that I've made the arrangement and that I'm going to be tied up in work myself for the next couple of days. Maybe I'm being delusional, but my hope is that if I keep not mentioning Linda, she'll forget about it. It's not good for her to keep dwelling on the past like this.

Head firmly in sand, I spend the rest of the day working on my application letter, thinking about who the best referees will be. I'm junior to be applying to become a recorder, a barrister for only seventeen years, but maybe the last three years I've spent as a deputy district judge will be of assistance. The youth court trial is the first multiday, multihanded matter over which I'll have presided, and my hope is that it will be sufficiently meaty that I'll be able to use it to bolster my claim that I'm up to the task of being a Crown Court judge. Also, I know that one of the defendants is being represented by a heavy-weight QC, who is in the same chambers as one of the members of the Judicial Appointments Commission. I know it shouldn't work this way, but on the off chance he could put in a good word, I want to make sure it all goes properly.

Work engrosses me. I don't want to think about any of it, the promises I've made. If I ignore them, they'll go away. I push it all out of my mind, only distracted when I get to the section of the application that relates to disclosure of character, where I need to fill out any relevant matter that might suggest I'm not of good character.

I'm sitting at my kitchen table, but my thoughts rush over twenty-five years back into the past: a beach, a fire. The screaming. The box of memory is tight shut, but Tess has shaken it up with one mention of Linda's name. I can feel tremors from deep within, a seismic rumbling as they threaten to emerge. After a moment I get a grip, push the lid back down further. No good will come from there. I get back to the form, running through all my competencies in my mind. I'm not a child anymore, a teenager desperate and hungry for love, for attention. I've got judgment, the ability to make hard decisions. Integrity.

Jumping to my feet, I stride to one side of the room, then the other. My agitation is growing, the past casting a dark shade. As the flames leaped from that bonfire, dancing into the night, my paranoia flickers up, sparks catching my skin. I take a deep breath, another, looking around the kitchen for something to ground me, anything to take me out from the past and back into now.

Five, four, three, two, one. Time to make my sensory lists, grounding me back in the present. Touch, taste, sight, sound. My breathing slows as I look round the room, take it all in.

Now smell. That's easy. The rubbish is full, overflowing from the sides of the bin, a sweet acridity lying in the air. I lit a scented candle earlier, masking the reek until I could be arsed to empty the bin, and this overlays the rot, sweet and roselike, almost convincing, but not quite, the artificiality suddenly nauseating me. A bitter gall rises into my mouth, the taste overwhelming me. I almost gag but instead go to the sink, rinsing my mouth out again and again until it's clear, nothing left but the residue of the municipal water, a chemical tang to overcome the seven sets of kidneys, bladder, urethra through which allegedly all London's water has passed.

Forget panic, I'm entirely in the moment now, again repelled by my lack of cleanliness, the state in which I've left the rubbish. I pull the bag out roughly from the bin, holding the plastic container down with one hand and tugging with the other. There's resistance to start with but it comes free all of a sudden, and I stagger, hitting my arm against the cupboard so hard that I drop the bag, spilling the contents, the sludge of uneaten meals spread wide across the floor.

The enormity of it all floods over me again. Tess's illness, Marcus. That whisper of a name: *Linda*. The ghosts of my past so rudely awakened. All the excitement I've felt about the next stage of my career is now under threat. A sob rises in my throat, a second, and I'm crying now, snot and tears, the way I used to cry as a teenager, as a child even, inconsolable. I rest my head against my knees, wiping the mucus down one side of my leg, my sobs growing in intensity.

It's only when the doorbell has been rung for a third time that I register the noise, the shrill chime cutting through my self-indulgent wailing. I try to pull myself together but it's gone so far now that I'm hiccuping with it all, my throat contracting as my breath catches. A fourth ring and I pull myself up to my feet, wiping my face on my sleeve, though it's sodden already. A fifth ring, lasting ten seconds, twenty, and I yell out with irritation, "I'm coming!", shuffling over to the door in the expectation of a parcel, a delivery for next door as usually happens.

I keep my head averted as I open the door, holding my hand out in the hope that I can minimize any eye contact, any human interaction, the slightest hint of someone asking if I'm all right likely to send me over the edge, and it's only when it's shouted that I realize a man is yelling my name.

"Sylvie. *Sylvie*," he says.

I don't want to look. My eyes are half-shut against the light, piggy from crying, the skin inflamed and tender. I blink, blink again.

"Sylvie," he says once more, and I blink once more, recognizing his face at last, and much as I don't want to, much as I wish at this moment that I had poise, grace, a modicum even of dignity, I start to cry again, all the strain of the last day bursting out of me as I stumble forward toward him.

"Sylvie, what on earth is the matter with you?" Gareth says, but he reaches out and catches me before I fall. He carries me through to the bedroom, placing me down gently on top of the duvet. "Are you all right?"

I think for a moment about telling him everything, all my fears, but the words won't come. I'm so tired, so drained with the shock of Tess's diagnosis, the ferocity of my hangover.

"I'm sorry," I say. "I'm sorry. I didn't expect to see you."

"I thought I'd surprise you," he says. "But by the state of you, I think it's a good thing that I came. Now, why don't you see if you can get some sleep and I'll sort out some food?" He pushes my hair back from my face, his touch still gentle, and I reach up and cover his hand with mine.

8

Gareth stays for the next few days, calming me with his solid presence. He makes soups, stews, food that's easy to swallow, to digest. He doesn't ask again what's happened, seemingly happy just to be with me and to see that I'm slowly coming back to myself. I don't have any court appearances due so I'm safe to hole up at home with him, shutting out the storm that's about to break.

The hours pass slowly, punctuated only by meals and afternoon naps, Gareth holding me close as we curl up on the sofa together. The time passes only too fast, though, and soon enough he has to return home and I find myself with Marcus in a wine bar, the lull truly over. Where Gareth's been the still point, Marcus is all movement, Brownian motion in corporeal form. I'm exhausted the moment I sit down opposite him.

"So you thought you'd just ignore me, take her side?"

"Come on, Marcus. That's not fair."

"You've ignored all my messages."

"You didn't send that many," I say. I need to calm down. The situation is too serious for this kind of tit for tat. "Look, there's something I need to talk to you about, Marcus."

"I think you owe me an apology," he says, shaking his head. "You've not always chosen her over me." I suppress the urge to slap him.

"Things change," I say. Marcus looks away, his cheeks flushed, before glaring at me. I look at his cross expression, fighting the urge to wipe it off his face by yelling *Tess has cancer!* at him. Restraint doesn't come easy to me but I'm doing my best to exercise it. My irritation starts to fade as I look at him more closely. I haven't seen him for the last couple of months, but now I realize how strained he was looking when I last saw him. He looks now as if years have dropped off him, his skin pink and smooth, his eyes less hooded, the crease between his brows less pronounced.

"You're looking well," I say, changing the subject, and he accepts the deflection.

"I feel well," he says. "Like I said to you before, it's like a weight's been lifted off me. I should have done this years ago. I mean, look where we are. We haven't done this for years, either." He gestures around him at the pub, the bottle of wine sitting between us, his packet of Marlboro Golds sticking half out of his jeans pocket. I nod my head at them.

"Back on the cigarettes, then?" I say, and he laughs.

"Only for a while," he says. "It's completely under control. Nice not to be lying about it, though. You know how much Tess hates smoking."

I nod my head. I do know. I think of all the times she used to yell at me, at Marcus, telling us it was a filthy habit, that we'd get cancer and die and it would be all our own faults. The irony of it hits me hard as a brickbat and I swallow.

"You OK?" Marcus says. "You've gone very pale."

"I have to talk to you about something," I say. "Not my judicial application. It's about Tess."

"If you're going to try and talk me into going back to her, you're on a hiding to nothing. We are done. Dead. It's over."

"Marcus, stop."

"We're like the proverbial parrot. It is not a live marriage; it is a dead one."

"Marcus," I say, louder, my hand held up, and this time he listens.

"What? What's so bloody important? She's sorry? Is that it?"

"We didn't discuss whether she's sorry or not. She was telling me something else entirely different. Marcus, she's going to need us."

"Why is she going to need us? I've left, goddamn it."

"You're going to have to go back."

"What the fuck are you talking about?" Marcus says. He sounds angry but there's fear in his eyes, flickering in his pupils as he looks from me to his cigarettes, to his glass, back to me again.

I lean forward, putting my hands on the edge of the table to steady myself. "She's got a brain tumor, Marcus. They've run tests. They need to run more. But there's no way this isn't serious."

His mouth opens as if he's about to speak but no words come out for a while, until he says, "I don't understand. What do you mean?"

"I mean that the chances are that she's got cancer. Tess has got cancer. She's going to need us, Marcus. She can't do this on her own."

Marcus bows his head, takes in a deep breath, exhales. Breathes in again. He looks as if he could get up and run any second.

"Marcus," I say, but he interrupts before I can say anything else.

"Are they sure?" he says.

I nod. "As I said, they need to run more tests. But there's definitely a growth in her brain. That's what she said."

He shakes his head, his expression bemused. "She's the fittest of all of us. All that running, vegetarian food. Never smoking. It doesn't make sense."

"It doesn't work that way. You know that."

He shakes his head again, shutting his eyes. "I just can't believe it. She seems so strong."

"She is strong. But so is this. She's really going to need us."

"How long has she known?"

"Not that long," I say. "She said she's been having some headaches, for a few months now, and she had a fit a couple of months ago, while you were away on circuit. She came to on the floor, all bruised up, not sure what had happened. Then she had another fit, so she went to the doctor and they arranged for her to have the tests. It's still early days… She doesn't know what kind of tumor or what treatment might be possible, anything like that yet."

Marcus picks up his glass of wine and drains it, fills it up again. I reach over and take the bottle from him and pour some wine into my own glass. I'm not sure I've ever needed it more, watching the life ebb from his face as he works through everything I've said to him.

"A couple of months," he says eventually. "All this time. While we were on holiday. Oh God, and I was so wrapped up in myself, worrying about work, thinking about what a cow she was being. It's not long after that I insisted on the separation…" His voice trails off.

I know what he's feeling now, the shame of it. Marcus wasn't the only one obsessed with work during that period. I had dinner with them around then. I should have been focused on my friends, but instead I was buzzing with excitement because of the new relationship with Gareth and, more importantly, because a rape trial I'd done had gone well and I'd been given the nod by the judge for the first time that I should get my application in for a promotion from district judge to take the next step closer to becoming a full-time Crown Court judge.

I didn't bother to notice how they were getting on, whether my friends were happy. I talked about the job application incessantly to

Marcus, asking his advice on how to complete the forms, whether he thought the judge was right and that I'd get through the interviews, the role play. Tess had spent hours cooking, and the food went cold on the plate in front of me as I ranted on about my career prospects, scents of garlic and thyme drifting off unnoticed into the night.

"I was too, remember," I say. "I wouldn't shut up about it all. You know that. I'm amazed she didn't get more pissed off with me." I go silent, thinking about how he left her shortly afterward. How little I'd noticed about what was going on.

"With us," he says. "I should have known better. It all makes sense now." He looks up at me. "Is it something that might affect her personality? Could it be why she's been so much crosser?"

"I guess it's possible. She did say the reason she was being so weird was because she was scared, that she didn't want to worry you. Or me."

He laughs but the sound is cold, brittle. "That's not exactly worked out, has it." It's not a question.

I shake my head. We sit in silence while Marcus drains his glass. The finality with which he places it down on the table at the end is clear, an end now to such frivolities. His jaw is set, his gaze steady. But the pink of his cheeks has faded, his brow no longer smooth. He'd come into the bar with a look of youth still to him, but he's leaving without it, gray now, tired.

"I'm going to go home now," he says. "She's going to need me."

"She is. I don't know what she's going to have to go through, but it's going to be shit. Completely shit."

Marcus pushes himself up to his feet. "Tell her I'm on my way home," he says. "She needs me. Nothing else matters. Nothing at all."

He strides out of the bar without looking behind him.

@BBCbreaking

Two bodies have been found impaled on railings early on New Year's Day in Edinburgh's New Town. Police were called to the scene just after midnight by a dog walker. The bodies have yet to be identified. More news as it comes.

12:01:25

Fuck. I'm screaming but I don't know if I'm making any sound, if anyone can hear me. The banging. My head's going to explode.

Pain. In my head, in my guts. Sick sick sick. Help me. Fucking bastards. I told them—

I told her no. It's all her fault. I'll kill her. Should be her here. Not me.

I know there's someone next to me. No movement, though. No breathing. I think he's dead.

Good. He deserves it.

They all deserve it.

Oh God…

If you make it stop, I'll do anything you want.

Everything hurts so much. Pain beyond words. I'm screaming but the bangs are too loud and no one knows, no one has seen.

Please. If you help me, I'll do whatever. Be whatever. I'll be good for the rest of my life. But please, take the pain away.

I can't move my hands now, my feet. So so cold. Everything cold.

Please, make it stop.

9

That's the last I hear from Tess or Marcus for a couple of weeks. I still wake sometimes in the night with a sense of dread, but it's fading. I'm happy to push it all out of my mind, ignoring the promise I made Tess about speaking to Linda, reopening the past. She hasn't mentioned it, and I'm guessing it was born out of panic, a loss of control without Marcus in her life. Now that they're back together, it's all fine. Gareth is up and down from Edinburgh, and I'm preparing myself for the youth court trial on which I'm hanging so many hopes of promotion.

"How long is it going to take?" Gareth asks me the night before the trial is due to begin while we're on the phone.

"Five days or so. It'll be quicker for me to decide on the verdict on my own than it is for juries. At least I don't have to agree with eleven other people."

"Fair enough. What did you say it was about, again? A robbery?"

"I don't know that I did," I say. "But yes, it's robbery—three boys, one victim. Robbed at knifepoint. Not sure I'm going to have the jurisdiction to sentence it if they do turn out to be guilty."

"Why not?"

"Because as a deputy district judge I only have the power to sentence people to twenty-four months. Any longer and it'll have to go to the Crown Court."

"Ah yes, I remember you telling me. Now I understand why you want to be a Crown Court judge. I've said it before. You want to be able to sentence criminals to death, don't you?" he says, laughing.

"You know perfectly well we don't have the death penalty. It's not like that," I say. First Jonah, now him. I'm beginning to get pissed off with this assumption of bloodlust.

"Come on, indulge me. I like the idea of you having that power. There's something very…seductive about it."

"Seductive?"

"Yes. It's given me an idea, as a matter of fact. I've never seen you in your wig, you know."

"Why would you want to see me in my wig? It's hardly seductive. Quite the reverse."

Gareth laughs again, his voice deepening. "Well, it depends on what else you're wearing…Why don't we switch over to a video call? It's been a while. You go and get changed and I'll see you in five."

He ends the call. I don't move for a moment, slightly stunned. I've always balked at dirty photos, having come late in the day to the digital revolution. I know from hearing some of my younger colleagues that it's entirely acceptable, but something in me shrinks at the thought. I pull myself together quickly, though. This is Gareth, after all, not just some stranger on the Net. He's seen everything there is to see of me. It's ludicrous to feel any reticence.

Besides, he'd told me this would be a prerequisite if we were going to continue in any kind of relationship. *It'll be hard to keep coming down to London*, he'd said. *The catering won't do itself. We'll have to improvise.* Improvise. That's one way of describing it. I strip out of my clothes at the kitchen sink, grabbing my wig out of my wig tin and shoving on a couple of layers of red lipstick. I'm about to turn on the computer when I stop, pick up the lipstick, and color in each of my nipples, before I dim the lights and open the laptop. It's showtime.

I'm still smiling the following morning when I leave the station at Highbury and Islington. Not even the grime of Holloway Road can dampen my spirits. I remember the years I used to trail up here as a pupil barrister, prepared to argue the most tenuous defenses imaginable in front of district judges who wore a permanent air of skepticism, one eyebrow always raised as they looked upon their courtrooms with world-weary despair. Now I get to raise my eyebrow in quizzical curiosity. I'm not the one having to argue; that'll be for the advocates appearing before me today.

In the side entrance and up the stairs to the youth court. Those hours I had to spend in the waiting room come back to me, the sadness of it, the time spent reassuring desperate parents as best I could that I'd do my best to keep their kids out of Feltham. I'm not sorry to be able to walk straight through to the judge's room at the back of the court, the court usher a damn sight more friendly than she ever was when I was here as a barrister. Though to be fair, she was always being harassed by lawyers trying to jump the queue and get their clients on next—it's no wonder she had boundaries of steel.

After getting rid of my bag and brushing my hair, I read through the papers until it's time to go into court. Everyone in the courtroom stands and bows toward me; I bow back. Even though I know it's the position they're acknowledging, the role of judge, not just me, Sylvie, a flicker of excitement runs across me, as it does every time. I can't deny that I like the feeling of power.

Two of the boys have been brought up from the cells and are in the dock; the other is already sitting in the court, his parents twitching beside him. I look through the notes on the case file. While all three had been on bail between arrest and first appearance, they were remanded in custody subsequently because they made a number of threats on social media against the complainant in the case, a boy in the year above them at school. Daniel Hall and Liam Asiedu have evidently remained on remand in custody, but it appears that Philip Presley, the third boy, was released on bail following an appeal to the Crown Court.

Both Daniel and Liam are being represented by the same barrister, a woman called Monique Price, in her late twenties, who is holding herself very still, shoulders braced as if against some assault. Looking further along the advocates' bench I can see why. Philip's family have pulled out the heavy artillery with their QC, David Lamb, the man I'm hoping to impress. His suit is beautifully cut, his silk tie muted but rich, his shirt starched and gleaming white. He looks the part, that's for sure. I straighten myself up, sucking in my stomach under the table. I catch his eye and he nods once, unsmiling. If he's finding Highbury Youth Court insalubrious, he's giving no indication of it.

The Crown Prosecution Service has instructed counsel. It's another woman, Jill Whitehouse, someone I've defended against a couple of times in the Crown Court. I'm relieved to see her there. She's very competent. She'll run it well. Though I still don't know what's being run, whether it's going to be a trial or whether they've managed to sort out a plea. From the tension I sense from the advocates, I'm not convinced that any arrangement has been met.

Looking behind the advocates to their clients, and the clients' families, the tension becomes even more apparent. There are two women sitting together, Liam and Daniel's mums, their partners, the boys' dads, at their sides. Philip's dad is clearly pissed off, continually checking his phone and his watch before whispering in a hectoring way to Philip's mum, a small, harried-looking woman who nods repeatedly as if to placate him. Philip himself is staring straight in front of him, his face rigid, while Liam and Daniel speak occasionally to each other, though never looking at him.

I'm normally hardened to the look of the defendants, so used to it after all my years of practice as a barrister that I rarely have much emotional response. Something about the look of these boys is getting under my skin, though. They seem so young, only fifteen.

So close to the age Linda was when she stood trial.

Not much younger than Tess and I were, too.

The prosecutor rises to her feet and opens the case. I clear my mind of all thoughts of the past and lean back in my chair, pen in hand, as I prepare myself to take notes.

10

She gives the bare facts. The three boys (all fourteen at the time of the offense) are charged with the robbery of a fifteen-year-old boy. It's alleged that a knife was involved, and it's an added complication that they all go to the same school. My feeling of reservation about my sentencing powers in the event of a conviction is strong. If all these facts are proven and the prosecution have gotten their evidence in order, it's a nasty offense. I shake my head clear… I'm getting well ahead of myself. I need to see what they all have to say.

Rather than paying attention to the prosecution opening, Monique, representing the two boys in the dock, has been looking back at them, her face showing concern. As soon as Jill finishes her short speech, Monique stands up, leaning forward against the desk as if for support.

"I'm worried about the perception here, ma'am," she says. "It seems to me to create an unfair impression to have my clients both in the dock while their codefendant is allowed to sit out in the body of the court with his parents."

I look from one to the other. I can't argue that she has a point. Jill stands up again for the prosecution.

"I would have no objection to Philip joining his codefendants in the dock," she says, drily. Monique nods.

"That would be one solution," she says. "Or else what I would suggest is that all three are allowed to sit in court with their parents, as is befitting a youth court."

Jill stands again. "While in principle I would be inclined to agree with my learned friend, I am concerned that in this case, where there is already evidence of attempts at witness intimidation, the complainant may not feel at ease giving his evidence. As I say, I would have no objection to Philip being placed also in the dock."

David butts in now. "I would have every objection to that, however. There is no justification for it. Philip is on bail and has caused no problems whatsoever in this case. I would argue that given we are fortunate enough to be presided over in this case by a professional," he says, bowing again in my direction, "there is no need to concern ourselves with the issue of perception. Our learned judge is more than capable of viewing a defendant with impartiality whether sitting in the courtroom or in the dock."

I look away as he says this, determined to keep my expression impassive although I'm flattered by his comments. Perhaps he's just saying what he would say in any case, to keep his client from being confined, but it seems to me that he might have a view already of my abilities, and that it's good. With an effort I bring myself back to the proceedings.

"I've taken note of Miss Price's comments on behalf of the two defendants in the dock, and while I appreciate the point that has been raised, I find that the defendants should remain as they are. On the most practical level, the dock is too small to admit of one further occupant. I find that it's preferable that we leave everyone where they are. The bench will put no interpretation on the seating arrangements but take the evidence into consideration as it's presented."

Monique appears unsurprised and looks back again at her clients, nodding at them as if in reassurance. David's face remains impassive, but Philip has leaned back in his seat slightly, more relaxed in his posture, though when he hears the victim's name being read out, he sits up again, tension running through him.

It's time for the first witness to be called, the complainant Ryan Collins. As he walks in, his head held high, I can sense the same tension from the boys in the dock. All the parents are glaring at him, but he goes straight to the witness box, takes the Bible in his right hand, swears to tell the truth, the whole truth, and nothing but the truth.

He looks so young. If the prosecution had asked for special measures, I'd have allowed him a screen. When I had to give evidence, I'd have loved a screen to block out Linda's face as I spoke. To block out Tess's intense stare at me as I testified, too, as she made sure I backed up her story.

The boy looks calm, though, unperturbed. No sign of the stress he must surely be feeling inside. I glance over at the defendants. All of them are looking at Ryan, barely blinking, lasers boring into him.

I've seen defendants facing complainants hundreds of times with no reaction of my own at all, but I can feel it getting to me, leaching under my skin. I've buried it down deep for over twenty years but now I'm there again, back in a courtroom in Edinburgh. I've seen that laser beam from a defendant before, felt its burn. I stood there in the witness box once, too, ready to give evidence against a classmate.

Ready to give evidence against Linda.

I'm miles away, my gaze going off into the distance. Not presiding over my courtroom at all. As Jill stands up to start the examination-in-chief, she clears her throat, pulling me back to the present. I blink, force myself to focus. I can't let the past start seeping into the present in this way. I know I've said I'll help Tess—but I can't let it jeopardize my future.

"Would you like to tell the court about the night in question?" Jill says, and I concentrate now, watching the boy's face closely, ready to take down every word that he says.

Ryan was walking home after dark that evening after a Boy Scouts meeting, he said, and was passing the petrol station on Camden Road when a group of boys in balaclavas, hoodies, and gloves approached him and pushed him against the wall. While one held a knife or other sharp, pointed object to his throat, the second searched through his pockets and took his phone and a small amount of cash, and another, the tallest of the three, stood back, laughing and egging them on, before coming forward to punch and kick him when he fell to the ground, then running away into the night. Given their heads and hands were covered, he couldn't make out any distinguishing features, other than that they were all slightly taller than him. From that, and their voices, he'd deduced they weren't much older than him.

He'd picked himself up off the pavement, blood dripping down his face, and started walking unsteadily up the road. Shortly after, he was spotted by a policeman on patrol, who rang for a car to collect him and drive him around the streets of Camden to see if they could find anyone who matched the descriptions that he'd been able to give of his assailants.

About half an hour after they started their circuit, Ryan saw three boys on the street together. He wasn't sure, but he thought they could have been the ones who robbed him, and he pointed them out to the police. He was told later that they had been arrested and charged. He didn't remember ever having seen them before and couldn't believe that they were at the same school as him.

"What effect did this event have on you?" Jill asks.

"I've gotten scared to go out on my own," Ryan says, lowering his head. He's not that small for fifteen, but not too big, either. "I don't like hearing footsteps near me—it makes me jumpy. I always try to get home before dark."

"What about Scouts? Are you still going to that?"

"No," he says, snapping the word out with an air of finality. There's a snort of laughter from the dock. I glare over but I can't see who it's come from. I shake my head, my face stern.

"Silence in court."

Ryan shrinks in on himself, his head lowering further and further into his chest. All his bravado has seeped out of him now; I expect he's exhausted from telling his story. Much as I resist it, I'm back in the witness box again in my head. I remember what it was like, how it felt to have gotten to the end of my evidence. Knowing that this was the easy bit over, draining as it might have been.

I watch Ryan leave the witness box, the way that he looks at Monique and Daniel on the way out. From the expression of fear on his face, it's clear he knows, too, that the worst is yet to come.

11

Given it's nearly half three by the time that Ryan has finished giving his evidence, I decide that we might as well finish for the day, so that he can rest before going into cross-examination the next day. No one argues with me. It's been a tiring day, stuck in the boxlike room with no natural light. I blink as I leave the court building, blinded by the sunshine. Philip is standing on the pavement with his parents, and I give them a wide berth as I head back toward Highbury and Islington station.

I'm shaken by the feelings that have emerged during the course of today. I haven't thought about any of this for years. But Tess has brought it all up again, poked the nest of snakes, and my ears are full of hissing. I did my best, that's all I know. But telling myself that doesn't make the hissing stop. *Linda Linda Linda* repeats in my ears until I put my earphones in and turn the music up as loud as I can bear.

Gareth's there when I get back to the flat. He called me the night before to say that he had a couple of days off unexpectedly if I wanted to see him, and I jumped at the chance. Even though it's not a surprise to see him in the flat, my heart still jumps. It's not just pleasure.

Relief too. He'll distract me, keep the snakes away. I'll be able to sink my face into his shoulder tonight and let his breathing drown out any whispers from the past.

"So it's going well?" he says.

"It's fine. Could go either way. The complainant's evidence was good, but we'll have to see."

"What do you think of the defendants?"

I bite back the reply that springs straight to my lips. *They remind me of what happened over twenty years ago.*

"Hard to tell. One of them has a very forceful QC. Time will tell," I say.

"Oh, I love it when you talk work," Gareth says. He pulls me over to him and kisses me before unbuttoning my shirt and removing it, carefully undoing each cuff before pulling my hands free of the sleeves. He reaches behind me and unhooks my bra.

"Now, where's that wig of yours?" he says. "I liked what you did with your wig box last time."

I blush, nipples tightening at the memory, and all thoughts of the trial go out of my head. Linda too.

Later on, we're lying in bed when my phone beeps. I pick it up, expecting it to be a message from the pizza company to confirm the delivery that's about to arrive. It isn't, though. It's Tess.

> *Thanks so much for telling Marcus. Sorry for radio silence. I've been all over the place. It's so weird—it's like something's come unstuck. I can't stop thinking about Linda. And Stewart. What happened. What we did. We need to sort this out.*

"Shit," I say. "Shit." I sit bolt upright, taking the covers with me.

"Oi," Gareth says. "It's too cold for that. Come on, get back into bed." He tugs at my arm.

"I can't," I say.

I get up, throwing on my dressing gown. Gareth's right, it is cold. November's struck without my noticing. I sit down on the side of the bed again and look at my phone, trying to work out if there's any way I can put Tess off thinking about this anymore.

"What the hell is going on?" he says.

"It's complicated," I say. "I'm not really sure how to explain."

"Try me," he says. "A problem shared and all that. I'm a good listener."

I take in a deep breath. "My best friend has just been diagnosed with cancer."

"God, I'm so sorry to hear that."

"Yeah, it's shit. It's come as a complete shock."

Gareth takes my hand and strokes it. "That's really shit."

"You know, there's nothing I wouldn't do to help. She's my oldest friend. We've known each from school. It's years."

I get up, stand by the window, looking out between a chink in the curtains. The room's in half darkness but I can't talk about it if I'm looking at him.

"Something happened when we were at school. Something bad. I've done my best to forget about it—we both have. Or at least, I thought we had. But now Tess keeps mentioning it."

"Mentioning what?"

"A girl called Linda."

"What about a girl called Linda?" Gareth says, his questions hypnotic in the gloaming.

"Someone died, Gareth. A boy called Stewart. And she went to prison for killing him. She wasn't even eighteen. I never spoke to her again. I don't think Tess did, either. The last time I saw her was at the trial."

"Trial?"

"She was tried for his murder," I say. "She'd hit him over the head with a plank of wood."

"Wow," Gareth says. He's shifted across the bed, leaning his back against its head. "She was convicted of murder?"

"Not in the end," I say. "Culpable homicide. She hadn't meant to kill him."

"Right," he says. "What did you have to do with it?"

"I was there," I say. "At the party when it happened. So was Tess. We both ended up having to give evidence."

"What evidence did you give?"

I go over to the bed and sit down. "I can barely even remember now," I say. "I've done my best not to think about it for all this time. It was terrible. Stewart had been my boyfriend. Not that it was a major relationship, but still…"

Gareth doesn't reply. We sit in silence. He's within an arm's length of me. I could reach out and touch him. But I don't, trapped in my thoughts as they spiral out, taking me back there again.

"When did all this happen?"

"A long time ago. A lifetime. Over twenty years. I've tried so hard to forget it. But now I'm going to have to dig it all up again."

My phone beeps again.

> *Sylvie, are you there? Sylvie, you promised. You have to help me. It's like I won't get better if we don't sort this out.*

I fling my phone away from me onto the bed. Gareth picks it up, reads the message.

"What does she want you to sort out?" he says.

"I don't know," I say. "But I'm terrified to find out."

THE CAMERAMAN

Big house. Nice. End of the terrace. There's a couple of embassies along here, I think. Or there were. Party let, this one, so they've told me.

Bottom to top, the boss has told me. So I start with the bodies. Not a good sight, I have to say. A woman, facedown, spikes protruding through her abdomen and out of her back. I home in on all the details, trying not to focus myself too closely on the screen. I'm good at compartmentalizing, but this is raw. So much blood, soaked into the ground all around her, running down onto the pavement.

That's where I start. On the gutter, the first trace of blood, following the flow up to the railings where the bodies are to be found. I make sure I include the little paw prints running off out of the pooled blood. Past the woman, a long flow of fabric in which she's draped. Then the man.

He's fallen onto his back, a spike through his neck, pointing up through his Adam's apple, another lanced through his thigh. Hanging off to the side, like a piece of game, waiting to age.

My gaze has lingered on them long enough. Time for a tour of the house.

Grand. That's my first thought. When I go in, whitebooted and suited, I walk down to the basement before switching the camera back on. Kitchen, gym, storeroom, a slow panning round every space. Up the stairs to the ground floor, the huge, ornate dining room, still filled with the detritus of a party, glasses and empty bottles lined up along the side. It's not out of control, not destroyed. But it's clear that a good time was here to be had last night. Until it stopped.

Upstairs now. The first floor. Even grander. One of those rooms that takes the whole width of the house. Again, evidence of a party, but not one that was out of control. Chairs all upright, neatly placed. Glasses here and there, a few bottles. No cigarette ends, though, no real carnage.

A woman, sobbing. A man beside her, holding her hand. A female police officer sitting next to them. I skirt the camera around them, trying not to intrude.

A master-bedroom suite to the back, the bed unmade, clothes strewn across the floor. The most mess I've seen.

Up the stairs again. Another bedroom. Another unmade bed. More clothes.

Now the place they're most interested in. The roof. Through an open door and up a solid ladder, the sort that's attached to a hatch that pulls down when it's opened. I climb up it, filming as I go. The roof space has been converted, though it's very plain, unlike the rest of the house, a plywood floor, plywood walls. At the end, there's a hatch, already open.

I climb out. a couple of forensic examiners are going over the scene. I raise my hand to them in greeting but we don't speak, merely nodding. It's a slate roof, the pitch going in a C shape around where the hatch comes out at the bottom, in the valley of the roofs. I pan the camera over all sides, concentrating most on the roof that slopes up to the front of the house, where the bodies were found below.

The forensics officer gestures to me, showing me the route I can climb up. I go carefully up the side, before getting to the top.

That's when it hits me: the height, my unsteadiness with only one hand free, the drop all the way down below.

The corpses, bled out into the ground, spikes sticking out of them. My hand shakes, the camera too. I sit down, fast.

It's too far to fall.

12

Gareth leaves before I've had time to wake up properly, kissing me on the shoulder before letting himself out of the flat quietly. I'm groggy. Telling him about Linda the night before stirred up so many emotions in me that it was impossible for me to sleep for hours, probably not until about four, and even then my slumber was uneasy, full of nebulous shapes flickering in and out of focus and a sense of impending doom. I'm glad I've got the trial to distract me.

Ryan is back in the witness box, but this time he's going to be cross-examined. He was pretty solid during evidence-in-chief, leveling his chin up and keeping eye contact with me when required. I'm interested to see how he responds to a more hostile line of questioning.

Looking at him now, it's clear he's nervous. He's chewing at his lip and pulling at his sleeve as if unsure what to do with his hands. The QC is leaning back in his seat, a small smile flickering across his face in pleased anticipation, a well-groomed spider waiting for his prey. A chill runs down my spine, a little trickle of cold. I remember that look, the way that the defense advocate waited for my answers, sure I'd trip and ready to catch me out as soon as I did. I didn't know what to do with my hands, either. I'd bitten my nails so much while I was waiting to get into court that two of my fingers were bleeding, the pain only a small distraction from the terror I felt.

Linda's advocate had been so harsh, so determined to prove that I was lying…

The questioning of Ryan has begun. I snap my attention back to now. Monique is doing her cross-examination calmly, with none of the gleeful malice that radiates from David Lamb. She's not going down a hostile line. She seems understanding, and Ryan visibly relaxes, his shoulders lowering from round his ears where they were fixed. She's not trying to trip him up, but rather reinforcing how impossible it is that he could have made an accurate identification of the boys involved in the robbery. It was dark, the situation was stressful, it all happened so fast—how can the boy possibly be sure that the three people who held him at knifepoint are the same as the three people who were picked up forty-five minutes later by the police?

"When you got into the police car straight after the robbery to look for the suspects, you were very stressed?"

"Yes," the victim said.

"You hadn't been able to see their faces during the robbery?"

"No."

"And given you described them as wearing balaclavas and gloves, you couldn't even tell what skin color they might be?"

A long pause. "No."

"So you can't say with complete certainty that these three boys were the ones responsible?"

"It must have been them. They were the only boys we saw in the street when the police drove me round in their car," the victim said, his words pouring out before the defense solicitor could stop him.

"Yes or no answers, please. The boys may have been out in the area not long after the incident you describe, but you can't say with complete certainty that it was these three boys."

"No. But I'm sure it was them, all the same."

The prosecutor sighs audibly and gets up to reexamine.

"Please remind the court how long it was after the incident that you spoke to a policeman," Jill says.

The victim looks grateful that he's being addressed by someone on his side. "I ran into the policeman about five minutes later, coming round the corner. I told him what had happened and he put out a call on his radio. It didn't take long for a car to arrive, and I got straight in and we drove round till we saw them. They just looked right. There wasn't anyone else around that looked the same."

"No further questions."

Jill sits back down and David prepares to stand up, ready to question Ryan in his turn. Ryan's face has tightened, his lips tense. He's balled his hands into fists. If he were to hold one out in front of him, I'm sure it would be shaking. I wonder if I should give him a break, suggest that we have a twenty-minute recess in which he can prepare himself. But when I look over at David, I know that's not the right suggestion to make. I have to harden myself against any feelings of sympathy that might cloud my judgment. I shift my gaze to the defendants, Philip and the boys in the dock. They're tense too, they're shaking. It's their futures at stake, after all.

David stands. He looks at Ryan in the witness box, fixing him with an impassive gaze. Ryan looks stunned, a rabbit caught in a cobra's stare. I can see his right arm jerking slightly, up down, up down, in time with the clock at the back of the courtroom, which is ticking now so loudly I'm amazed I haven't heard it before. A few weighted seconds more and David begins.

"You told the court that you didn't know these boys were at the same school as you, is that right?"

"Yes."

"So you're certain you'd never seen them before?"

"Yes."

"Until these events, you didn't know their names?"

"No."

"You're absolutely sure about that?"

"Yes."

David nods. He's smiling, and while Ryan seems slightly to have relaxed, I'm on the edge of my chair, noting down the full exchange. David shuffles through some papers on the table in front of him before picking something up.

"Could this be handed to the witness, please?" he says, giving the item to the usher who takes it over to Ryan in the witness box. Ryan takes it, and it's as if his body shrivels, his shoulders rounding in on themselves, his cheeks blotching red.

"Please could you describe the item you are holding to the court?"

Ryan clears his throat. He opens his mouth, closes it again. Finally he manages to speak. "It's a photograph."

"A photograph of what?"

"A photograph of a school football team."

"Is there a date on the photograph?"

"Yes. Autumn 2017."

"Do you see yourself in the photograph?"

"Yes."

"Can you point yourself out to the judge?"

Ryan holds the photo up toward me and points. It's too far for me to distinguish the details but he seems to be pointing to a figure in the center of the group that has been arrayed in three rows for the camera. As he points, the tremors in his hand become apparent.

David goes through his papers again before pulling out a second photograph and handing it to the usher to give to Ryan again.

"Now will you describe this photograph, please?"

"It's another photograph of the school football team."

"Are you in this photograph?"

"Yes." Unprompted, Ryan turns the photograph round and points to where he's standing. Rather than in the middle this time, he's on the edge.

"Is Philip in this photograph?"

"Yes," Ryan says, speaking so quietly now that I can barely hear him.

"Is there a date on this photograph?"

"Yes. It's Autumn 2018."

"Is Philip in the earlier photograph?"

"No."

"Is it right to say that you were the captain of the football team in 2017?"

"Yes."

"Is it right to say that Philip was captain of the football team in 2018?"

A long silence. "Yes."

"Is it right to say that you were demoted when Philip joined the team?"

Another silence, longer still. "Yes."

"And it's correct that you were very angry about this demotion, shouting at Philip in the locker room and telling him that you'd have revenge on him for stealing your place?"

Ryan looks as if he's about to cry, his head bowed. The prosecutor, Jill, is biting her lip, her eyebrows furrowed. I'm trying not to let any surprise show in my face, any judgment. This is elementary stuff. I can't believe it got past the police only to come out at this stage of proceedings. Monique's brows are also furrowed, but she doesn't look as tense, clearly working through the ways in which she can turn this to her clients' advantage. David isn't smiling but there's a calm satisfaction to him. He knows what he's doing.

"That's not what happened," Ryan says. "No."

"I put it to you that it's exactly what happened. You were resentful of the fact that Philip played better than you and took your spot in the team."

Ryan lifts his chin, takes a deep breath. "No. He didn't play better than me. He threatened me with a knife the day before the trials and he said that if I played better than him, he'd shank me. I didn't have a choice."

Philip is shaking his head. I catch a look of surprise on David's face before he smooths it over. "And this is the first time you'd thought to mention this?"

"Yes," Ryan says. "I was scared. I thought he'd do it."

"Are you seriously expecting the court to believe that this happened?"

"Yes," Ryan says. "I'm telling the truth."

He's crying now. The usher passes him a box of tissues and he blows his nose, snorting loudly. I can feel a constriction in my throat, too, a tightening of the muscles round my mouth. Shadows of the past are falling on me fast, the moment I was asked if I resented Linda, the fact that she'd stolen my boyfriend... I hadn't cried, though. I'd held my head up. *No!* I'd said, adamant.

I'm sure it was the truth.

David's speaking again. I pinch my thigh to bring myself back into the moment. I've missed the beginning of the question, but Ryan is crying even harder now, shaking his head.

"I'll ask you again," David says. "I put it to you that you're not telling the truth when you suggest that Philip threatened you."

"I am telling the truth."

"And that you had good reason to dislike Philip as he had out-played you and taken the captaincy from you."

"No."

"So when you saw him and his friends out and about that night, you decided it was a good idea to make up a story about them?"

"No." Ryan is standing bolt upright now, his hunch gone. He looks as if he's going to explode with rage.

"You weren't held up at knifepoint at all, were you?"

"I was!"

"This whole story has been a lie from start to finish, hasn't it?"

"No!" Ryan says. Then he turns to me. "Are you going to let him speak to me like this?"

I raise my hand, slowly. "The defense are entitled to put their case to you," I say. David nods.

"I've had enough," Ryan says. "I'm telling the truth and I'm not having this."

With that, he pushes his way out of the witness box and storms out of court. I realize my mouth is open in surprise and I shut it, not wanting to show so much emotion, but everyone in the courtroom looks equally shocked. The prosecutor rises to her feet.

"The Crown would ask the court to rise for a short while," she says, "until we have located our witness."

I nod. "Yes, briefly," I say. "I'm keen that we should make prog-ress, but I understand that this issue needs to be addressed." With that, I stand, bow to the court, and go into the small room at the back. I'm still reeling with surprise at the boy's actions. Part of me is almost impressed. I know how he must have felt. There were points during my cross-examination all those years ago that I nearly told Linda's advocate to fuck off before storming out, too.

I managed to restrain myself, but I can see how Ryan might have lost control.

The prosecution are going to have to sort it out, though. I hope it doesn't take too long.

13

At least it gives me the chance to check my phone, though the moment that I switch it on, I wish I hadn't. I'm already twitchy because of Tess's message the night before, the one I've managed to ignore, and seeing her name flood the display now as it lights up does nothing to calm my nerves. She's left three voice messages and sent four texts. All variants on Call me, only one mention of Linda, but the persistence is scary. I message her saying, In court all day, hoping it'll put her off, at least for a few hours.

I'm going to have to face it at some point, though, make a proper decision as to what to do. After I gave evidence in the trial in Edinburgh, I got on a train south, and I barely looked back. Only once in twenty years, until I came up for the conference and met Gareth. I thought I'd outrun it, but it was always at my heels, the shadow to every move I took.

Another beep from my phone but I turn it off without looking at it. I've got enough to think about as it is. I've never had a situation where the main prosecution witness has stormed out, and I need to work out what to do. I don't have long to think, though, before the court clerk comes through to get me back into court.

"The witness won't pick up his phone," the clerk says, "nor is he to be found at his home address. The defense wish to make an application to have the case thrown out."

"Naturally," I say. "They could give it a minute, though."

She laughs and I smile in response, the smile still on my lips as I walk back into court. Philip is staring at me, his face ferocious, and I smooth the expression off my face immediately.

David stands up and starts with no preamble. "I understand that my learned friend is going to ask for an adjournment so that her witness can be traced." I look over at Jill and notice the dull red staining her cheeks. She's angry, it's obvious, but she doesn't try to stop him.

He continues. "I am completely opposed to this adjournment. The defense should not be prejudiced by the prosecution's inability to keep their witnesses in order."

Jill stands up. "As my learned friend says, I am certainly going to ask for a short adjournment so that we can find our witness and persuade him to return to court."

David snorts. I raise an eyebrow. I don't want to have to challenge him, but if pushed, I will. The thought flits into my mind, too, that his behavior might actually be a test, to see how well I rise to the challenge of managing him, someone so clearly senior to me and potentially influential on my future career. I put my chin up.

"Have you made any progress at all in locating him?" I say.

"Not as yet, but it may be that he's still in the Underground. Police officers will attend his address if you are minded to grant a warrant for his arrest, so that if necessary he can be compelled to attend."

"Of course," I say. "I'll give you the rest of the day, but if he doesn't attend tomorrow morning…"

David shoots a look at me that's so suffused with rage that I begin to worry that he's not testing me, that he really doesn't think this is reasonable. I turn to him.

"I appreciate your indication that you won't support the adjournment, Mr. Lamb, but I really have no choice in this matter. Given the age of the witness, it's not entirely surprising that the pressures of cross-examination should have gotten to him."

"I'd remind you of the age of my client, ma'am," David snaps back and I raise my chin higher. Good reference or not, I'm unimpressed about being addressed in this way in my own courtroom. His chin is raised, too, and for a moment it's a standoff between us. Internally, I start to quail but then I remind myself, I'm the one with the judicial position at this moment, not him. I open my mouth to take charge, but before I can speak, I'm interrupted by a loud sob, then another.

It's Philip's mother. She's sniveling, tears streaming down her face. Philip's father puts his arm around her. He's looking angry now, too.

"For God's sake, can't you see what it's doing to her?" he says.

Another flashback. Another decade. Stewart's mum, Linda's mum facing each other across the public gallery in the court in Edinburgh. *For God's sake, won't you tell us the truth?* Stewart's mum begged as Linda stood in the dock. The cry dragged at my heart then. Haunts my dreams sometimes even now.

Another sob. Back into the present.

"At this stage, court will adjourn until three o'clock this afternoon. That will give the witness time to return and for any further examination to be carried out," I say, standing up smartly and bowing before getting out of the room before anyone can argue with me further.

There's only so long I can hang around in the airless rooms in Highbury Youth Court. I decide to go out for lunch, figuring if I go far enough away from the court building, I'm not likely to run into any of the participants. I know there's an Italian restaurant along

St. Paul's Road, and given it's still early, I decide it's worth a go to get a table.

I'm welcomed into Trullo with open arms and sent up to a table at the end with a long bench on one side and a chair on the other, its back to the room. I choose the chair as the table next to it is occupied by a couple of women with young kids who are bouncing up and down on the bench, and I don't want to be too close to them.

Selecting a pasta first course and a lamb chop for my main, I pull out my phone again. I've been thinking about the whole Linda situation as I've walked to the restaurant, and I've changed my mind again. Brain tumor or not, it's a can of worms that Tess should leave shut. Watching Ryan give his evidence has only served to remind me of how fraught it all became, how much our own futures hung in the balance at that point, too.

The pasta arrives and I eat it greedily, sucking up the strands of strozzapreti, the choker of priests. Was Ryan telling the truth? Was he the victim of Philip's behavior, or Philip of his? I know the truth lay somewhere between for Tess and for me, for Linda too. It was all very well for Tess, though. She didn't give a shit about where she was going to go for university. She wasn't trying to escape years of unhappiness at school. Everything always slipped off her, her sleek, impermeable surfaces. She cried and the court believed her. Me? Less so.

I know I'm flip-flopping, changing my mind all the time about whether to help Tess or not. I want to help her. I know she's going to have to go through a lot. But despite my sympathy, resentment is rising inside me. It's not just her life she's potentially fucking up; it's mine. All my hopes, all my dreams. I've had a career path planned for years; I'm nearly at the moment when everything is going to come to fruition. I'm fucked if I'm going to let Tess destroy it all, brain tumor or not.

I pick my phone up and finally reply to Tess.

No. I'm not doing it. It could kick off a huge mess. You're not thinking it through—remember what you did? It could fuck everything up. I can't do this.

My rage has put me off my food, delicious as it might be. Probably for the best—pasta always makes me sluggish. I normally avoid carbs at lunchtime to keep myself sharp. Pushing my plate to one side, I pour myself another glass of water. The noise from the restaurant, the people around me, slowly begins to permeate into my consciousness.

It's filled up as I've been ruminating, shrill now with the sounds of conversation. A woman behind me is laying down the law about the specific way that her chicken should be served; a man is boring on about his latest work crisis.

"But how can you be so sure he won't come back?" a woman says, close to me.

"How would I know?" This voice younger. A boy. The question doesn't sound sincere. It sounds mocking, a jeer in his voice. A voice I've only heard once before, confirming his name and address.

I freeze, tucking my head down in front of me as if engrossed in my phone.

"That's quite enough of that," a man says, his voice resonant. Mellifluous. The voice of a trained advocate. I sink further into my seat. Not just any man. David Lamb, the QC representing Philip.

"You'll look after him, won't you?" the woman says. I can hear now how much emotion is running through her, her words trailing off at the end.

"Of course he will," another man says. "Dave'll do anything for his godson."

If I could make myself invisible, I would. This is beyond embarrassing. I try to reassure myself, though. I don't need to do anything about this. If there's a personal connection between one of the defendants and his representative, it's not the end of the world. David Lamb is extremely senior. Extremely experienced. He should surely know how to maintain his professional independence.

Godson, though. That word has set my teeth on edge. That's close. Very close. I start to type into the search engine of my phone before stopping myself, opening a private window. Then I look until I find guidance from the Bar Standards Board. Has David considered whether his connection with the client is so close that he might find it difficult to maintain his professional independence?

Other words are making themselves heard, snaking through my mind. The sneered question, *how would I know?* The question that preceded it. *How can you be so sure he won't come back?* There aren't many possible interpretations available here. I take in a deep breath. I need to do something. But what? If I challenge them now, I run the risk of becoming a witness in the trial over which I'm meant to be presiding. I can't believe they've been so careless as not to check their surroundings before speaking so openly.

Then I think about it. I'm a near middle-aged woman in a black suit, sitting on her own, back to the room. I'm invisible. Nothing interesting about me. I'm just a part of the furniture as far as they're concerned. A jag of anger spurts up in me. Subsides. I'm not challenging Philip. I'm challenging David Lamb. And his influence is huge. It'll be the end of my career.

My palms are prickling now, my heart pounding loudly in my ears. I need to stand up, challenge them. Recuse myself from the trial, make a statement to the prosecution. I'm about to do it, ready to stand. David starts to speak again.

"Don't worry," he says. "I'm going to make sure everything's all right. I'm not going to let your boy destroy his whole future here. I'm not going to let him go to Feltham. It's not going to happen."

I freeze again. The conflict builds in me. After all, what have I heard? Philip was asking how he would know if the complainant would come back to court. A question that does not imply knowledge. I might *think* I heard a jeer in what he said, an implication that of course he knew perfectly well, but that's my interpretation. I don't know it for a fact. He hasn't said explicitly that he's threatened Ryan.

And David—he's a professional. Being a godfather to someone doesn't necessarily confer a closeness of relationship that might impair someone's judgment. David is affluent, successful. Personable. He's the kind of person who likely has lots of godchildren. I doubt he'd even remember Philip's birthday. He's probably been pulled in to do the case as some favor and is resenting every moment of it, treating it purely as a job and no more. If I go throwing accusations of lack of professional independence around, it's going to cause huge offense. I simply don't have the evidence.

My choice is made. I reach into my bag and take out my earphones, plugging them into my ears so that I can block out any further revelations. I don't want to upset anything. I just want to eat my lunch in peace.

An hour later I've had pudding, coffee, another coffee, and two glasses of water. I've stretched the meal out for as long as possible to avoid any confrontation with Philip and his family. But I'm desperate for the loo. Surely they'll be finished by now. I don't want to glance over my shoulder, just in case they're still here, so I pick up my phone and switch the camera onto selfie mode to sneak a glance.

They've gone. My body subsides, able finally to relax. I signal to pay the bill and go downstairs to find the loos. I'm halfway down the stairs when I'm nearly knocked over by someone bounding back up toward me. He pulls himself short, holding his hands up in apology, before going straight up. I've pushed myself into the corner of the stairs and my hair has fallen over my face so I don't get a good look, but I know it was Philip.

What's more to the point, does he know it was me?

14

Three o'clock and we're back in court. There's no trace of recognition in Philip's eyes as he looks up at me in court. David doesn't seem aware that we've been in the same restaurant, either. I'm going to let it go. Any suspicions I might have are just those, suspicions, and the thought of what might kick off if I were to go on about it is too much for me to contemplate.

The complainant hasn't returned and the prosecution asks for one further adjournment, to the following morning. David stands to argue and I hear him out before telling Jill that I will grant her one further adjournment, but that after that, the case will have to continue, complainant or not. I go home and switch my phone off, not wanting to deal with Tess or anyone else.

I'm feeling better the next morning, more human. More able to deal with Tess. I put my phone back on and my instinct's correct—she's gotten the message.

> *OK. Come round anyway tonight. Let's talk about New Year, the vow renewal. I'm excited about that.*

She doesn't mention Linda and I take from this that she's gotten my point. This is one situation we do not want to disturb. I text my agreement to the plan and make my way to court with a clearer mind.

Ryan has not turned up.

"There's no reply at his address, or on his phone," Jill says on behalf of the prosecution. "I won't be applying for a further adjournment. The complainant has given his evidence in any event so I would submit that the case can continue."

David shoots to his feet. He looks furious. "This is entirely unsatisfactory," he says. "His evidence was not complete. He made a very damaging allegation about my client, and I did not have the opportunity to test it in cross-examination."

I look back through my notes for the moment when Ryan suggested that he was threatened at knifepoint by Philip on an earlier occasion.

"My notes clearly indicate that you challenged the complainant on this point and put it to him that he was not telling the truth."

David continues, ignoring what I've just said. "The learned judge has now heard this allegation, and much as I do not seek to imply that she will be unable to put it from her mind, the perception of justice is everything. I would urge the court therefore to call an end to this parody of a trial and order a retrial in front of a new bench, where all the evidence can be tested properly as justice dictates."

His expression is as pompous as his words, and my hackles go straight up. If he's able to put his own godson at a professional distance, I can easily put one piece of evidence out of my mind. I'm not going to put a halt to proceedings.

"In my previous remarks, I made it clear that the evidence to which you refer was, in my view, properly tested in cross-examination. The case will proceed," I say. "Any evidence that was not thus tested will be erased from proceedings. I invite the prosecution to proceed."

If looks could kill, I'd be stone dead. Philip, his dad, and his barrister. Beyond that, his codefendants in the dock. The look on David's face says clearly that this is going to be appealed straight to the Crown Court, but there it is. I'm sure of my position, in this at least.

Now we're on to the police interviews, no comment all the way from all three defendants, all of whom were represented during the interviews by the duty solicitor. Checking the paperwork, I can see that this is the firm still representing Daniel and Liam. Philip's parents must have arranged their new representation shortly after this. I shuffle through some more of the papers and the explanation presents itself. They'd all been remanded in custody, until an appeal had been lodged at the Crown Court for Philip which had led to his release on bail with a number of stringent conditions. It's no wonder he looks bright-eyed and bushy-tailed in comparison to the slumped shoulders of the other boys.

I repress a shiver of sympathy. I've seen this so many times, the change that the first time in Feltham Young Offender Institution wreaks on the boys who end up in its maw. They start out terrified, and maybe the first time they're brought to court after being remanded there, they're still able to speak about it, how much they dislike it, the way it affects them. But by the time we reach the third or fourth hearing, they're lost in a world beyond my comprehension, their barriers up so high they're impassable in the short time available for consultations.

Liam and Daniel have this look now, a deadness round their

eyes as if they've lost hope, their expressions as gray as their track-suits. Philip's in a gray suit, by contrast, his hair neatly trimmed and brushed into a side parting. Despite the daggers he's looked at me, the tiresome way that his QC has behaved, I do feel whole-hearted sympathy for him. For all the boys. I'd be fighting for my life, too.

It's exactly what I did.

Philip is due to give evidence first. He takes the stand, swears on the Bible to tell the truth, the whole truth, nothing but the truth. David begins to take him through his evidence.

The examination-in-chief is designed to show Philip in his best light. Not only does he have no previous convictions, but his academic achievements are outlined to me, also his position on the school football and debating teams. I try not to react when football is mentioned, my face impassive. Anyway, it's not relevant. I wish he'd get on with the night itself, but I'm not going to rush him. There's no need for me to give the defense any unnecessary grounds for appeal. David will already feel he has enough to undermine a conviction if that's the way it goes.

Perhaps David can tell that he's losing my attention, but he pivots the questioning smartly onto the night in question. Yes, Philip knows Liam and Daniel from the football club, yes, Ryan too. Not to speak to, Ryan. He's in the year above Philip and the others. Philip knew vaguely that Ryan had been the football captain and that he'd lost his position when Philip came onto the team.

"I'll lose my place as captain soon, too. It's the way it goes," he says, his face open, innocent. "But Ryan didn't take it that way. He was furious."

"In what way was he furious?" David says.

"Furious enough to threaten me after he was demoted. He said he'd get me back. My friends, too. Now look at us," Philip says, open-ing his hands out to the court in demonstration.

He's good, I'll give him that. His whole demeanor is that of out-raged innocence. Ryan was good, but Philip is even better. David asks if there was any time when he challenged Ryan before the foot-ball trials that won Philip the captaincy.

"No way," Philip says. "I wouldn't want to be captain if I hadn't won the place fair."

That piece of evidence dealt with, David takes him back to the night again. Very simply, he was hanging out with a couple of friends from the football team. He gestures behind him as he says this. They had kicked a ball around in the park and were walking up the hill to go to the corner shop to get some Coke and crisps when they were arrested. That was it, simple. They had nothing to do with any rob-bery. None of Ryan's belongings had been found on them, and it was nothing to do with them.

Jill cross-examines him, but it doesn't get far. He stonewalls her at every turn. He's not lying, he's telling the truth, why would he need to rob anyone? *I've got an iPhone 11.* For a boy of his age, he has a remarkable level of sangfroid.

I lean back in my seat to evaluate him. He knows how much is at stake for him right now. It's no wonder that he's giving it this level of focus. The way that his friends look must have had its impact on him, too, the Feltham effect. I'd be doing everything I could to pre-vent myself from going inside, too.

Besides, he has a point. If they stole Ryan's phone, where is it now? It wasn't found on any of the three codefendants. The prosecu-tion haven't brought up any other corroborating evidence. It's Ryan's word against the three boys, and he couldn't even be bothered to stay in court.

Philip finishes his evidence and sits back in his seat beside his parents, clearly relieved to have gotten his testimony out of the way. We have a short adjournment, and Daniel follows to give his evidence, almost a carbon copy of Philip's. He'd been present, too, when Ryan lost his temper with Philip and said that he'd get him back for stealing the captaincy from him.

Philip nods along as Daniel speaks, smiling when he manages to bat away Jill's cross-examination. As Daniel returns to the dock, there's a definite sense that it's all over now. Only Liam left to go, and that's going to happen tomorrow morning.

At this rate, the boys will be acquitted by lunchtime.

HOGMANAY 1989

I could tell Tess meant trouble the moment I walked through her door. Her eyeliner was as thick as my little finger, black lines swooping from the inner corner to meet the wing flicked high from the upper lid. Her eyelashes were so thick with mascara that they looked fake, and her lipstick was a perfect shimmer of iridescent purple.

She handed me a drink as soon as I came in. I lifted it up and smelled it before taking a sip; the spirits hit so strong at the back of my throat that I coughed.

"Drink up," she said. "Don't be a wuss."

I took another sip before putting the glass down and looking more closely at what she was wearing. A tight black dress that stopped some inches above her knee, thick black tights, black boots. Not far off from my outfit, though my skirt was considerably longer than hers. I had just left my parents' house, after all. I rolled the skirt up at the waistline until it, too, sat above my knees.

"Do you have that belt you said I could borrow?" I asked and she nodded, handed it over to me, a thick elastic corset with a silver zip down the middle. I sucked my tummy in and zipped it up, making sure my skirt wasn't bunched up stupidly over my bum.

"Nice," Tess said. "It suits you."

She led me upstairs to her bedroom where she sat down on her bed, a small compact mirror in her hand, and she painted on a further layer of eyeliner, her eyes glittering darkly from inside the black kohl. Even though she was my best friend, at that moment she looked completely strange to me, like someone I had never met and would in all honesty cross the street to avoid.

"You look fierce," I said, laughing, though it didn't feel like a joke.

"I feel fierce," she said. "This is going to be my night. I'm unstoppable. I'm going to get smashed, stoned, and shagged. You just watch me."

"That sounds like a plan," I said, laughing again. Campbell had dumped her only the week before but she seemed to be getting over it.

We pulled our coats on and left. The plan was to start at Stewart's brother's flat for drinks till it was time for the bells, when we were going to go up the Tron for the annual glandular fever fest that was the mass of kissing that went on. I'd gotten off with a couple of boys last New Year but I hadn't enjoyed it much, the crush of the crowds overwhelming as the fireworks exploded overhead and nameless hands groped at me under my coat. It felt completely different to know that I'd be going up with Stewart, my actual boyfriend. It was the first New Year I'd been loved up. The first I'd ever actively looked forward to.

Back at Stewart's brother's flat. Stone Roses on the stereo and a can of Stella thrust in my hand by someone. I found Stewart standing at the kitchen table, Campbell beside him, Linda on the other side. They were doing tequila slammers. A bottle of Jose Cuervo sat on the table, and Stewart was sloshing ginger ale into three tumblers. He put the bottle down and all three took their glasses before covering the top with one hand and slamming them on the table before throwing their heads back and downing the contents in one. Campbell let out a huge belch and Stewart jeered at him. Linda in the meantime was holding onto the side of the table, an expression of concentration on her face, her eyes screwed shut. It didn't look like she'd be fit for many more.

Stewart caught sight of me in the doorway and waved, a shit-eating grin splitting his face ear to ear. "Sylvie! Have a slammer!"

I stood beside him as he sloshed out the drink into the three cups. Linda had opened her eyes by now but she shook her head vehemently at the suggestion of another one, so Stewart gave me her glass. I was semi-pissed from the drinks I'd had already, and the tequila hit me nicely in the gut. I turned round to Stewart and pulled his head to mine, giving him a long kiss. He tasted of booze and fags, a staleness already to his breath. He kissed me back but pulled away after a moment.

"Sylvie, about tonight."

"What about tonight?" I said.

"I've been talking to these guys about it, and we think we should have a competition."

"What kind of competition?" I said, pulling myself away from him. The warmth in my gut was subsiding fast, a chill setting in.

"How many people we snog, of course! It's traditional!"

"I, well, I'm not sure I—"

"Don't be such a spoilsport. You're gorgeous. I bet you'll win," Stewart said, just as Tess made her entrance. She poured herself a shot, necked it.

"I'm the one who's going to win, Stewart," she said.

The fireworks proper wouldn't start till the bells, but there were random rockets firing off as we walked up from Broughton Street to town. The streets were full of people, the pubs throbbing with music as we passed. *Happy New Year* shouted by every next passerby. I'd passed the point of pissed now, carried along on a wave of other people's emotions, smiling with Tess as she grabbed a man in a tartan tam-o'-shanter and stuck her tongue in his mouth.

"One," she yelled in my face, triumphant. I shook myself free of her. I'd grabbed a bottle of Baileys from the side at the flat and I took a long swig, the sugar hit swiftly followed by the alcohol.

Stewart grabbed me and spun me round, high as a kite on drink and the headiness of freedom. He'd already grabbed a couple of girls en route to Princes Street but they'd rebuffed him, laughing all the time. I knew this wasn't where the main action was, though. That would be on the Royal Mile, thousands of people all thronged together to bring in the New Year. We were on Princes Street now, getting closer to the Mound, and it was more and more crowded. I held tight onto Stewart with one hand, the Baileys with the other. Campbell and Linda were close ahead of us linked arm in arm, and Tess kept bumping into me on my other side.

Every now and again we'd stop as one or the other found a willing recipient of their kisses. Tess had nicked a tartan cap from one of her victims and she wore it now at a jaunty angle, her eyes still glittering darkly underneath. Stewart's eyes were glittering in the same way, and when they turned to us, I could see febrile excitement in Linda and Campbell's faces, too, currents of energy sparking between them all.

I was there and not there, so numb with drink now that I'd left my body, floating somewhere above my head as we forced our way through the crowds and up to the top of the Mound. I had a vague memory that we were meant to be meeting some more people outside the Carwash, the pub at the top, but I didn't care what we did, where we went, happy to be pulled along on the tide of energy that was holding our little group together. Stewart was stopping every couple of yards to accost a different group of girls, Tess too, Linda and Campbell all joining in, and I stood at the heart of it all, Baileys in hand, watching the fireworks explode in the sky above.

Finally we were up at the top on the Mound, pole position on the steps by the pub. There were more faces I recognized, people from school, girls from the year below, boys who'd left already, but it was all blurry, all spinning, the thud of music from the pub behind me pounding through me so hard the sound waves had solid form. On and on it pulsated, insistent, hard, and I realized it wasn't music, it was Campbell, his hands on my waist as he ground his erection into me in time to the music. I wanted to pull away but I couldn't, the crowds too tightly wedged in around me, and when I turned my head to protest, he took it as a come-on and started to kiss me, the angle awkward, my neck stiff.

I didn't kiss him back but I didn't stop him either, my mouth open but slack. I was leaving my body again, floating higher and higher until I was up in the sky with the rockets, branching flowers of purple and red and golden light streaming down around me. I watched as Campbell's hands ran over me, grabbed and squeezed at me, as if it were happening to someone else. He had his hand down the back of my skirt, squeezed in underneath the corset belt, and I knew it would be uncomfortable, digging into my tummy, but again it was happening just over there, out of the corner of my eye, not directly to me.

I turned my head away from him and drank more Baileys, relishing the sweet flavor pulling me back into myself. I was seriously drunk now. If Campbell weren't holding me so tightly, I'd be on my knees. I didn't want him holding me, though, now that I was back to ground. His hands were too hard—it was hurting me, the way he was pulling at my belt and trying to reach down through my tights. It was too much, the booze sitting in my tummy and the pressure he was putting on me. I started to struggle, trying to break away, but by the way his breathing got heavier on my neck, maybe he thought I was getting into it, grinding him back.

There was a pulling at my arm, an insistent tugging, and for a moment I thought it was more of Campbell's assault, but it kept going, and in the end I turned my head to the left. Tess, her face tight with fury. When she saw I was paying attention at last, she jabbed at my arm, vicious. My sensations might be numbed through drink but I felt that all right. There'd be a bruise in the morning.

"Fucking slag," she hissed. "What the fuck are you doing?" Even through all the bangs, the music, I could hear her, such was the force of her fury.

"Nothing," I said, but my mouth wasn't working properly, the word refusing to come out. I started to laugh, but the laugh got caught up with a sob and then I was crying, the sky spinning around me.

"You're shit-faced," she said. "Oi, Campbell. Get the fuck off her. She's off her head."

Somehow this must have been enough to persuade Campbell to let go because I was free now, no longer held in his grip, and as I'd thought I would, I stumbled, started to fall, but there were so many people around that they broke my fall and then someone was hanging onto my arm, pulling me up, steadying me against them, and it was Tess, the anger gone from her face.

"You silly cow," she said. "You know you can't handle Baileys. Come on, let's get out of here."

She pulled me behind her, not stopping to snog people anymore. It was like walking through tar, the crowds so thick that at a couple of points we were actually picked up off our feet and pulled with the sway, this way and that. I knew it was frightening but I didn't feel it, my viewpoint again somewhere above my head. Tess was shouting and swearing but I felt safe because I was with her, away from Campbell's predatory hands.

At last, we were out of the crowds, down the side of St. Giles near Parliament House. It was quieter here, only a few people standing there as if to catch their breaths before returning to battle. There was a couple getting off with each other, a boy and girl, leaning against the statue of Charles II that stood in the middle of the car park.

"Get a room," Tess jeered. Now that we'd stopped, everything was spinning properly around me, lights dancing in my eyes while my vision slowly dimmed. I was about to be sick, I knew it, and I dropped down to my knees on the cold pavement, breathing in deeply to see if I could avert it, though the waves of nausea were mounting.

"Seriously, get a fucking room," Tess shouted again. I looked up to see the couple disengage, turn around to seek out the source of the insults.

"Go fuck yourself," the man said. Even through my sickness there was something familiar about his voice and I looked up, moving my head slowly. It was Stewart. I could see his face wavering in the dark in front of me. Behind him, Linda, pulling at her clothes, zipping up her coat.

I jerked my head inadvertently and the movement was too much, a wave of nausea flooding up on me again and this time taking me down as I spewed what felt like gallons of Baileys over the granite pavement. Stewart and Linda was a problem that I knew I'd have to confront sometime, but it would have to wait.

"Fucking hell, that's disgusting," I heard a voice say somewhere above me, but I didn't know whose voice and I cared less. Nausea gripped me again, and this time I fell headlong into its depths.

15

I go straight to Tess's house after court finishes. There's a layer of nerves running under me about what she might want to discuss, but superficially, I've decided to take her word for it that tonight is only about the vow renewal. She hugs me as I go in and pours me a glass of wine before we both sit down in the kitchen. I start talking to her about the case but it's clear she's not that interested, flicking through the magazine on the table in front of her, saying *uh-huh* and *yeah* without looking up at me.

I persevere for a while longer, describing the conflict I'm feeling about Philip's guilt, Liam and Daniel's prison pallor, set against the fact that Ryan's been so traumatized he's run out of the courtroom.

"Why are you so bothered about it?" Tess says, finally looking up. "If you don't believe them, find them guilty. If you don't believe the defendant, acquit them. Isn't that your job?"

"I suppose," I say, slumping back into my chair. I'm tired, wired with the thoughts of all the evidence I've heard today, not ready to engage with Tess about her plans for the reconfirmation of her and Marcus's vows. I'm still in court, still sitting behind the wooden desk, breathing the recycled air in the windowless room, not ensconced in one of Tess's new designer dining chairs, the subtle scent of Pomegranate Noir from a Jo Malone candle burning somewhere in the kitchen.

Tess keeps going. "Anyway, I don't want to talk about your work. Not today. I want to talk about how we're going to do it."

I'm only half listening, my thoughts still full of it all.

"Sylvie," Tess says, and she's practically shouting. "Will you pay attention to me?"

"Sorry, Tess. Sorry," I say. "There's just something about the case. It's gotten to me."

She looks at me, her eyes narrowed. "I don't know why you care so much," she says again, "though I know you're always obsessed about work."

With that, I realize why I'm so preoccupied. Dissimilar as they may be in many respects, this case has still taken me back over twenty years. Tess, in court, telling the jury what she'd seen, what Linda had done. When I'd argued, asked how she could be sure, she'd leaned to me, one hand clawed tight on my wrist, and she'd narrowed her eyes. *I don't know why you care so much.* For a moment I feel completely cold, my fingers curling into my palms, but then Tess smiles and the warmth returns to the room.

"I'm sorry," I say again. "I'll pay attention properly. What do you want to show me?"

"Well," she says, and settles back into her chair. "I've organized loads already. It's going to be perfect. I've got carte blanche to do exactly what I want."

Marcus has agreed to everything Tess wants to do, she says. She opens her laptop and runs me through everything she's booked so far.

"I've found this amazing house on a holiday booking website, a special luxe one for big house parties. It sleeps twelve so at least some of us will be able to sleep there, and it's not as if there's any shortage of tourist accommodation in Edinburgh."

"When are you planning on doing this?"

"Hogmanay, of course. It'll be brilliant. We haven't done New Year in Edinburgh for years."

Thoughts of New Years past fill my mind but I push them away. I'm looking forward, not back.

"Where's the house?"

"Regent Terrace," she says, pushing the laptop over to me. I admire the photographs of the imposing house with its four stories, three windows wide. The big front door is a glossy green and the railings at the front are resplendent with decorative spikes, painted black. There's an ironwork balcony across the first-floor windows, and along another low row of spikes at the front of the roof.

"It looks impressive," I say.

"Doesn't it," she says. "I looked at bars and restaurants, that kind of thing, but I thought it would be too restrictive. It'll be far more relaxed having a house party."

The thoughts of New Years past are becoming more intrusive. I push them away, even harder this time. "I've never found house parties that relaxing," I say.

"This'll be different," she says, laughing at me. "I'm not meaning a load of cans of lager and some crisps if you're lucky. This is going to be much classier. Canapés, bowl food, champagne. A good view of the fireworks, and only a quick stagger up the stairs to get to bed. Nothing like the debauchery of our youth."

"Canapés? Bowl food? Do you mean we're going to have to cook?"

"Don't be daft, Sylvie. I'll get a caterer. Look—they've got a list here on the website. They can sort it all out for me."

She clicks on a tab of the website that advertises the house, opening a page with photographs of smoked salmon blini and miniature Yorkshire puddings. There's a list of links to various caterers. I skim through it out of force of habit, not expecting to see any names

I recognize, but then Gareth's company jumps out at me. White Rabbit Catering—because we can always pull something out of a hat, he explained to me—is at the bottom of the list. I can't help but let out a surprised snort, though I try to suppress it.

"What?" Sylvie says, never one to miss the smallest of tells.

I take in a deep breath. I was going to have to tell her sometime, I guess. Might as well be now. "You know I said I've been seeing someone," I say.

"Oh yeah?" She's back looking through her magazine now, not much interest in her voice.

"Yeah. Bloke called Gareth Quarry. Thing is, he's a caterer. This one," I say, pointing to the link on the web page.

This gets her attention. "You mean he's this caterer? What are you doing going out with an Edinburgh-based chef?"

"We got talking when I was at that law conference a few months ago. I did start telling you before."

"Right," Tess says, distracted again. She's staring off into the middle distance as if she's doing some kind of calculation in her mind. "Do you think he'd do the food? Would he be good enough?"

She still hasn't registered what I've said. Time was, me going out with someone would have her all ears. But she's completely fixated on the screen in front of her, the information contained therein.

"Yes," I say, "he is good enough. The food at the conference was excellent. His cooking is fantastic."

"That's great," Tess says. "Can you ask him for me? I think there's going to be about twenty of us in total. Maybe he can send me some menus? I know he's based up north but maybe if he's down seeing you sometime soon we could do a tasting."

"I'll tell him," I say. "I'd love you to meet him anyway. I think this one might be serious." She still doesn't react, but I try not to take it too personally. I'm wryly entertained to think there'd been a point when I hadn't wanted to mention him to Tess in case she got too overexcited about it. I shake that thought off, too. She may be obsessing over this stupid ceremony, but it's better than obsessing over her health. I glance over at the laptop screen. Aside from the website relating to the house in Edinburgh, there are five other tabs open. The Mayo Clinic, the NHS website, three for brain tumor charities. I need to engage myself fully in it.

"What are you going to wear?" I say, injecting as much brightness into my tone as possible.

She turns to me, enthusiasm radiating off her. I've made the right call. "Now that's what I call a really silly question," she says.

"Why's it silly? Aren't you going to get something new? Maybe something in purple like they do in that Bridget Jones film?"

"Honestly, I do wonder sometimes if you're not the one with the brain tumor," Tess says, shaking her head.

"OK, maybe I'm being stupid. I have no idea what people wear to renew their vows, though. I've never been to anything like it before."

"I'm going to wear my wedding dress, of course. I can still get into it, you know," Tess says with a broad grin.

"Of course you can," I say, striving for the same brightness. There's a shadow on the horizon, but I'm doing my best to ignore it.

"And you're going to wear your bridesmaid dress," she says. The shadow's turned into a solid object, knocking me out of any brightness into a dark gloom.

"Seriously? But…" I start. Stop. I've never told her how much I hated it. I smiled my way through the service, doing my best not to look down at the shiny mauve fabric that encased me like a sausage skin. That was then, though. Perhaps I've learned enough about boundaries over the years to be able to tell her no.

"That's really not going to work," I say. "It won't fit me anymore, and besides, it never suited me that well. I'll get something new for this… We can go shopping together. It'll be fun."

"Sylvie, no," she says. "That really won't work for how I want it to be. This is going to be like our wedding, but better. It's really important to me that we're all wearing the same thing. It gives it the right sense of renewal, like a reset."

The gloom isn't lifting. But then, a spark of hope. "I'm so sorry, though, Tess. I've no idea where it is. You know how many times I've had to move. I haven't seen it for years."

"That's because it's here," she says triumphantly. "I saw it looking all sad and wilted in your wardrobe a few years ago and I thought it needed some TLC. I've had it cleaned—it's all ready. Why don't you come and have a look?" She leaps up and marches out of the kitchen, turning round to beckon me on behind her before she skips up the stairs two at a time. I follow, leaden-footed.

If I'd realized I was going to be undressing in front of someone I'd have worn better panties. A better bra, too. Tess makes a face as I peel off my jacket and shirt. Mismatched, washed out. Saggy.

"I thought you said you'd gotten a bloke," she says. "You're going to have to make more of an effort."

"He's not in London at the moment," I say. "No one's going to see."

"You might get hit by a bus tomorrow," she says. "Then everyone would see."

She's right, but I can't be arsed to argue. I take the dress that she hands to me without focusing on it, trying to let its appearance skim over me. Unfortunately, this tactic only serves me until I look behind myself to try to find the zip, pulling it up until it sticks halfway. I can't pull it up any further. Wincing, I look at my reflection. I last wore the dress in my twenties, when I was still lithe and relatively taut. While I've kept myself around the same size, gravity has taken its toll, and what was stretching it back in the early 2000s is now fit to bust, the contours of my tummy molded in harsh relief in shiny purple fabric, the tops of my breasts thrusting obscenely against the sequined crumb catcher.

"I look like I'm going to burst out of it," I say, pulling in vain at the zip. "It's not going to do up any further."

Sylvie moves in behind me and tugs at the zip. It catches at my skin, but she ignores my yell and keeps going until it's fully done up. It's so tight I can hardly breathe. I'm starting to panic, I feel so constricted.

"You look lovely," she says, so kindly it's as if she almost means it.

I try to wheel round and glare at her, but my movements are restricted by the dress. Rather than an angry swoosh it turns into an uncoordinated hobble, somewhat undermining the effect. My mouth's open to tell her to fuck off but once I see her, the words die on my tongue.

"Wow," I say. "You look amazing."

It's true, she does. Her wedding dress cost a fortune at the time, and it looks as good as new. Its pristine condition isn't really the point, though. It's how much it still suits Tess, how well it fits her. Soften my focus a little and she could pass for the bride she was then, the only significant difference being a better haircut and softer highlights. She moves over next to me and we face the mirror side by side. The comparison is not kind to me. Nor was it back in the day.

16

"Wow, look at you both!" Marcus says, walking straight into the spare room. I didn't hear him coming up the stairs and I jump when I hear him, stepping backward so fast in the dress that it makes an ominous creaking sound. I breathe in again. I don't want to rip it— it's bad enough as it is.

"Get out," Tess shouts. "You're not meant to see this." She's nearly shouting, but her voice is more upset than angry.

"Sorry, sorry," he says, and I hear his footsteps retreat out of the room, the door shutting behind him gently, as if he's taken extra care not to slam it. Constrained by my too-tight skirt, I hobble over to the bed and perch on the side of it.

"You OK?" I say to Tess. She's standing immobile, still facing the mirror. I peer over her shoulder and see that her eyes are tight shut. Her shoulders start to quiver as if she's about to cry. I'm about to haul myself up and hobble back to her when she spins round and comes over, sitting on the bed next to me. There's a tear trickling down her left cheek. She raises her hand and wipes it off abruptly, smearing mascara across her eye.

"I wanted to surprise him," she says. "I didn't want him to know that I was going to wear this."

"I bet he barely noticed. He was out very fast," I say.

"Still. I just want this to be perfect. Like the wedding was."

I reach over and put my hand over hers. After a moment she turns her hand over, wrapping her fingers through mine. "It will be perfect, Tess. You've put so much work into it. How could it not be?" Her fingers tighten until the pressure is almost unbearable, before she lets go, her hand falling back into her lap.

"It was perfect, the wedding. Wasn't it? Everyone had such a brilliant time."

"Of course it was," I say. "We all loved it." There are other things I could say, other comments I could make, but I hold them in. We're looking at the same view through completely different prisms, hers colored with rose, mine black as night. But just as I never told her how much I hated the bridesmaid's dress she made me wear, I've never told her how much I hated her wedding, either.

"I'm so lucky I get to do it all again," she says. "It's going to be amazing."

I stand up, careful not to rip the beastly frock. "Right, can you undo me, please? I'll take this with me, go and get it taken out by a tailor. It definitely needs something done to it."

Tess takes hold of my hand again, her nails digging into my palm. "It's perfect," she says. "You mustn't mess with it. I don't want anything changed. Nothing at all."

"It's way too tight," I say. "I'll end up splitting it halfway through the evening."

"It's all in your head," Tess says. "Honestly. You look fantastic. I know you think I'm being unreasonable, but I'm sure it'll bring bad luck if anything is different."

I'm about to tell her to stop talking such bollocks, when it all comes crashing back to me: her diagnosis, the tumor, her illness. The real reason we're going through this, the shadow that's turning it from farce into near tragedy. "I'll cut out some carbs," I say. "That should do it. It's not that far off, after all."

"You don't need to cut any carbs," Tess says, all smiles now that I've surrendered. "It fits just as well as it did. I promise you—you always think you look terrible, but you never do. You're gorgeous. And it's as good as new. I even had a tear fixed on the back that I found. You must have been giving it some on the dance floor."

The smile stays fixed on my face but inside I feel a cold chill seeping down from my neck. I know it was ripped. I remember the moment only too well. "Great," I say, forcing myself to speak. "Can't remember that happening at all. I guess I was pretty pissed by the end of the night. We all were."

"Speak for yourself," Tess says. "I was stone-cold sober. Remember?"

"God, Tess, of course. I'm sorry. I totally forgot."

"I wish I could," she says.

Guilt claws at me. Tess had been pregnant at the wedding—of course she hadn't drunk. Only early days, but she'd been so happy, so excited about it. So sad when she'd miscarried the pregnancy shortly after the wedding. Another memory I've buried deep under a mountain of shame.

"Still, at least it means I have lots of clear memories of the night," Tess says, smiling. Perhaps it's my imagination, but I'm not sure the smile reaches her eyes, the irises glinting a cold, cold blue.

I reach round to my back, trying to unzip the dress. I get hold of the zipper in my right hand and try to pull it down, but again it catches in my skin. The pain is sharp, unpleasant. I gasp, trying to free myself, but I only make it worse, embedding the zipper more deeply into myself. It hurts even more.

"Tess," I say. "Can you help me, please?"

"What's the problem?"

"I'm stuck in the dress," I say. "I can't get out of it."

"Hang on," she says, but she doesn't move. I can feel my heart starting to beat faster, my chest squeezed in by the bodice. I want to take in a deep breath but all of a sudden I can't. It feels like the dress is getting tighter, if anything, wrapping itself round me anaconda-like, ready to swallow me whole. I pull again at the zip and this time it's driven fully into my flesh, the pain sharp and relentless. I cry out and this time Tess stands up.

"You're bleeding," she says. "I hope it doesn't stain the dress." She takes hold of the dress and pulls it away from my skin hard. I cry out again.

"I had to get it free," she says. "The blood's getting everywhere. It's going to get on my dress, too, if you're not careful."

I want to shout at her, but I can feel her fingers working against the zip and I'm too desperate now to get out of it to care about what she's saying to me. Her words may have a heat to them, but her fingers are cool and it's soothing, the movements almost rhythmic as she tries to get a purchase on the zipper, and even though she's pulling horribly at the fabric, causing it to strain dangerously tight over my bust, I'm so relieved she's helping me that I just stand and let her get on with it.

At last, I'm free. As soon as she's unzipped me, I step out of the dress, leaving it puddled on the floor, and go over to the mirror again. I crane over my shoulder to look at my back—there's a gouge in it, blood trickling down. The dress is off, at least.

"You could have helped sooner," I say, pulling my clothes back on. Tess looks blank for a moment before she replies.

"I was miles away. Thinking about the wedding. How lovely it all was. I've been so lucky to end up with the love of my life."

Again, my anger seeps out of me. "Yes, it really was lovely."

"Wearing this… It's bittersweet. It's what makes it so hard, you know. The idea that I'm going to leave him," Tess says, and she starts to sob, covering her face with her hands. This time I sit back next to her and put my arm round her, holding her close to me.

"You don't know that yet," I say. "You don't know for sure how bad it is. You told me that. It might be OK. You mustn't give up hope."

She cries a little more, tears running wet down my neck as I hug her, before she pulls away and wipes her face with the back of her hand. The mascara that she'd smeared earlier has been entirely washed away. Then she smiles, her lips still trembling.

"I haven't given up hope," she says. "But I'm very aware that this could be it. It's changed so much, how I look at everything in my life, as if someone has given me a lens which gives such new clarity, it's a miracle I could see at all before."

I sit back and watch her, unsure how to respond to this. There's a purpose to her words, though I don't know what it is.

"It's really brought the past home. That's why I'm making such a fuss about it all."

The purpose is emerging, and I don't like it. I haven't shut her down, much as I'd hoped I had. "About what?" I say.

"Oh, Sylvie. You know what. I can't believe you haven't been thinking about it all, too. I'm sure that's why you're so bothered about this trial you're doing."

"What are you talking about, Tess?" I say, though I know, and she knows I know, and the words are redundant.

"Linda," she says, a stone dropped in a still pool, the ripples spreading far before they cease to move. "It's time for amends."

"I don't think that's a good idea. I told you," I say, trying to keep my tone measured, control the tremor I can feel underneath the surface.

"It's been so long," she says. "It won't do any harm to us. It might make all the difference to her."

I look at Tess, unclear as to whether she realizes what she's saying. It might not do her any harm, at least not in the long term. But even if it makes her feel better, it could destroy more for me than she can begin to comprehend.

"I'm serious, Tess. It's really not something that I think we should do. It was terrible, I know. But it's past. She's been out of prison for a long time. The last thing she'll want is for us to bring it all up again, I'm sure."

She looks at me, eyes still crystalline. "If I'd been convicted because two girls had told lies about me, I'd want to know about it, too. I'd want to know they were sorry. They were going to do something about it."

"I'm just trying to protect you," I say. "This could start something off that goes completely out of control. Don't you have enough on your plate?" I'm hoping against hope my reluctance will be enough to put her off. But I don't dare look at her again, afraid that she'll catch me in her blue gaze and never let me go.

17

By the time we get downstairs Marcus has made supper, a curry bright yellow with turmeric, fragrant with spices.

"I've done some reading," he says when I come over to look at it. "Turmeric's really good for cancer."

"He's bought a book," Tess says from the kitchen table where she's sitting. "Done some research on the internet. Thinks he knows everything." Her tone is fond, though.

"You like curry, anyway," he says.

"I do," she says, and we sit around the table and eat. The food is delicious, but my throat is too tight to eat. Tess hardly speaks, pushing the lumps of chicken around her plate with her fork, but she doesn't make any more digs at Marcus, either.

I get up to clear the plates from the table. Marcus and I are standing at the sink about to start washing up the pans when there's a loud thump. Marcus calls out in alarm, and I turn to see that Tess has fallen off her chair onto the floor. I run to the table, pulling the chairs away from around her. Her muscles have stiffened and her back and head arch back in convulsions that pulse through her body. She's lost control of her bladder, urine spreading in a dark pool on the floor.

"Help her," he says. "I'm going to call an ambulance."

I kneel down beside her, checking there's nothing on which she can hurt her head, and after only a few seconds more, her body relaxes. She lies on her side on the kitchen floor with her eyes closed. I put my hand on her shoulder.

"Tess. Tess, can you hear me? Are you OK?"

She opens her eyes and looks at me, expressionless. She doesn't focus on me, doesn't seem to see that I'm there.

"Tess," I start again when I'm interrupted by Marcus. He runs over to Tess and takes hold of her, pulling her up against him as he kneels on the floor beside her in the pool of piss. I back away, realizing that my suit trousers are soaked through with it, too.

"The ambulance is on its way," he says. "They'll look after you."

Tess struggles up into a sitting position, still leaning against Marcus. "I don't need an ambulance."

"You bloody do," Marcus says.

"I don't. I'm all right," Tess says, speaking so quietly I have to strain to hear her. She takes in a couple of deep breaths and pulls herself up more, her back straight. "I don't need an ambulance. Please cancel it, Marcus."

The doorbell rings as she says this. She turns to me, her eyes more focused now. She knows where she is, at least.

"Sylvie, please can you tell them to go away. I'm all right. I really don't want to see them. I don't need to go into hospital."

I stand undecided, trying to catch Marcus's eye. Eventually he stops looking at her and glances over at me. He shrugs, nods, a tiny movement, but big enough that I get the message. Once I've persuaded the paramedics to leave without checking Tess, I go back down to the kitchen. Marcus has maneuvered Tess onto the sofa and she has her feet up, wrapped in a blanket, while he perches on the arm, holding her hand. He's put paper towels down on the floor, yellow stains leaching vividly onto the paper against the white.

I hover in front of Tess. "When is your next appointment?" I ask. "You'll need to tell them about this."

She sighs. "I'm going to see him in a few days. I'll tell him, I promise."

"OK. I'm just worried about you, you know."

"I know. It's OK. Look, Sylvie, I'm knackered. Do you mind going? I just want to collapse in bed now. I'll call you tomorrow." Tess turns away onto the sofa, burying her head in a cushion.

"See you soon," Marcus says. He doesn't look up, but stares intently at Tess, his face as troubled as I've only ever seen it once before, the time when she lost the baby soon after they married. I feel a clutch of sadness in my chest. I raise one hand in farewell and leave, but it's not till I'm nearly home that the image of them together passes from the front of my mind.

All I want to do is strip my piss-stained clothes off me and stand under a hot shower until I've washed the evening off me, the patina of grime from Highbury Youth Court. But as soon as I arrive home, Gareth messages me, asking if we can FaceTime. Or rather, as he calls it, can we sexy time. *It's been days, babe*, he says. *I'm getting hard just thinking about you.* I'm tempted to emulate the sex-line workers of the eighties, breathing heavily about the skimpy knickers I'm wearing while in reality I do the ironing and make a cup of tea. I won't be able to get away with that on video, though.

"I'm sorry, Gareth," I say, "I've had a shit evening on top of a long day. I'm sorry."

"What happened?"

"It's Tess," I say. "She had a seizure while I was there. It was awful… I didn't know what to do. Marcus called an ambulance, but she wouldn't go with them, said there wasn't any point as she's going into hospital early next week for scans anyway."

"That must have been scary," he says, the louche tone immediately gone from his voice. Now he radiates concern.

"It was. It's made it very real," I say. "Before, it was just words. They've found a tumor. They need to do scans and make a full diagnosis. But now I see the real impact of this. She's really ill, Gareth."

"It sounds like it," he says.

"I feel terrible about it. I'm desperate to help, but I don't know how. There's nothing I can actually do."

"It's horrible feeling so helpless," he says.

"Yes, it really is. I mean, I'm going to be her bridesmaid again for her renewal of vows thing. That's something," I say. Then I remember the conversation I had with Tess earlier. "Actually, that's what I wanted to ask. Would you be able to cater the event? On Hogmanay? She's renting some deluxe holiday let in Regent Terrace that lets you do parties. I told her about you."

"I'd love to," he says, sounding genuinely pleased. "It would be great to cook for you properly. And your friend. I've got a couple of bookings already that night, but I'll move things around so I can be there myself."

"Thank you," I say, and for the first time I feel some of the gloom lift. Knowing I can be of practical assistance eases the feeling of futility. "It's good to know I can help. She brought up Linda again, too."

"Ah. Why?"

I take in a deep breath. "Well. It's so difficult. There's something I didn't tell you. It's…possible that Linda may not feel that Tess and I were entirely straightforward in our evidence. It was all so heated. There were things Tess said, things she might be regretting now… but she wants us to track Linda down, make amends. It seems to be really bothering her."

Gareth looks grave. "I mean, I can see why you wouldn't want to go digging up the past. But if your friend is dying…"

"I know. There's nothing else I can do. I'm just going to have to get on with it."

With that, the conversation drifts to an end. I make myself a stiff drink and try to force away all the thoughts that are shoving their way through my mind, forcing past all the barriers I've had in place for so long.

THE CRIME SCENE MANAGER

God only knows how we're going to manage this one. At least two points to secure, the railings outside where the bodies are caught, and the roof. I'm assuming they've fallen off the roof. Looks like it, when I look up, checking the path of the trajectory. We'll have to get a specialist onto that.

I'll get the tent put up over the bodies. We've gained access from the basement now, through the side kitchen door. The basement area's full of blood, the pavement too. I'm no medic but it looks to me like it wasn't necessarily the fall that killed them as much as the loss of blood. Though mind you, once you've been impaled through the neck or stomach, there's only one way it's going to end.

It's shut up the new officer, the cocky one who was banging on about what an interesting change it'd make from the usual stabbing. The usual. Don't make me laugh. He looks about twelve. Mind you, they all do. Anyway, he took one look, turned pale green, and had to remove himself from the scene.

At least he had the sense to do that. He knows I'd have ripped him a new one if he'd puked on my crime scene.

We've put the tent up, cordoned off the street. I'm going to have to call in some specialists for the body removal. Thinking maybe the fire brigade. It's a toss-up which is the best way to do it. If they were still alive, it'd be a no-brainer. Cut the metal and transport the whole thing, impalement and all, straight to hospital. But now they're dead…

We need lots of photographs. Lots and lots of photographs. A video, too. Not just the scene out here, but inside, too, and the roof. What the fuck were they doing on the roof anyway?

Scratch that—stupid question. Hogmanay, fireworks, one of the best views in the city up there. I'll bet their blood alcohol level's sky-high. The rest of their mates must have been off their faces, too, given no one noticed these two were even missing. Let alone impaled.

What a fucking mess. I could do without this. Shit start to the year.

18

It's a relief to be back in court the next day, to pack away my fears for Tess and turn my attention to the case. All we have to get through is Liam's evidence, and then it'll all be over. He comes out of the dock to the witness box and it's clear immediately that he's jittery, picking at the sleeves of his jumper which hang down over his hands. His mum is his appropriate adult, sitting on the bench next to him, and I watch her watching him, her lips tight as if she's stopping herself from telling him to stop fidgeting.

His solicitor, Monique, starts to question him. I have my pen poised but I'm not expecting to take any notes. All I'm going to hear is the same story that Philip and Daniel have already told me. It's a setup, a revenge. But it turns out that this is not what's happening.

"I'm changing my plea," he says as soon as he's taken the oath. "I'm going to go guilty."

Another moment where I need to control my expression. I look at Monique and she looks as shocked as I feel, her hand held up as if to stop him. I open my mouth to challenge her when Liam speaks again.

"Don't blame her," he says, pointing to Monique. "I didn't tell her I was doing this—only just decided to. It wasn't anything to do with Daniel, either. We met him afterward. But Philip and I did rob Ryan. And threatened him before, to make sure he played badly."

Uproar. Philip starts shouting, his father yelling something incoherent, too. I look over at Liam. Despite the outburst around him, his eyes are steady. There's an air of calm to him even if he's veering dangerously off script. I can't believe he's only fifteen. He's pure adult at this moment.

"Liam, we should take a moment to consult," Monique says. "There are procedures that we need to follow if you're going to change your plea. Please, will you stop for a moment so we can speak?"

He shakes his head. "Look, Daniel, I'm sorry it's gone this far," Liam says, ignoring Monique's question and addressing himself to his codefendant in the dock. "I can't let this happen anymore. You shouldn't be here at all. Let alone inside with me. I should have said something at the start."

I hold my hand up to stop him and open my mouth to speak but he plows on. "I was out with Philip. I know him from football. We were in the team together. Though you know that—you've seen the photograph. Anyway, we'd been out, kicked a ball around. But we were bored. Philip wanted us to do something. We were hanging round near the shop, and he said he had something to show me. A blade. He pulled one out of his jacket. I thought he was joking but he was dead serious."

David's face is tense. He's scrawling a note on a piece of paper and thrusting it to the solicitor behind him.

Liam continues. "Philip hates Ryan because Ryan's a better player. That's why he forced him to play badly. That's why he wanted to do him over when we saw him on the street. It was just me and Philip. I shouldn't have gone along with it but I did. I'm sorry. But Ryan's confused when he says there were three of us there. Daniel wasn't there. Just me and Philip. Philip was the one with the knife. Philip said we had to deny everything, but if you're going to believe Ryan, you've got to believe that Daniel wasn't involved. I don't give a shit about Philip, but Daniel's my friend and this isn't fair."

His words have poured out, one after the other, a relentless indictment of Philip's behavior. I've been like a rabbit in headlights but now I unfreeze, holding my hand up and telling Monique to take instructions from her client before this evidence goes any further. David stands up and addresses me, ice in his voice. "Might I suggest, ma'am, that you take back control of your court? This is outrageous behavior. I expect you to put this outburst out of your mind, ma'am. This is not evidence which you should consider, particularly as it has not been put to my client."

I nod, though I'm fuming at how patronizing he sounds. To be fair, the situation has gotten out of hand. I tell all three representatives that we need to have a discussion in judge's chambers once Daniel and Liam's representative has spoken to them both, given the turn the case has taken. I then retire, relieved to have a break for a while from the high drama of the situation. Something about it has left me profoundly uneasy, more shaken than it ought.

While I'm waiting for them to sort out the mess that's taken over the trial, I check my phone. Various messages from Tess and Gareth, a juxtaposition of filth and family arrangements that makes me laugh despite the stress I'm feeling, and a message from Marcus suggesting we meet for a drink after work this evening. We have things to discuss, the message says ominously. I text back—El Vino's 6 p.m.—and receive a thumbs-up in return. I don't ask what. I don't want to know. There's enough to deal with here.

The QC's scorn of me has gotten under my skin a little, the thought of my application to the Crown Court bench in my mind. If I don't get the situation under control, he could easily let the Judicial Appointments Commission know how badly this trial has fallen apart, scuppering my chances. So much hangs on whether we can salvage something from this mess. If the whole trial has to be vacated so that a new district judge can take it over, it's going to look shambolic on my part.

That's not what's shaken me, though. It's something more profound than that. The look in Liam's eyes as he finally told the truth, protecting his friend. The look of integrity. That's what's wrong. I have weighed myself in the balance and been found wanting.

A gentle tap at the door, and the defense barrister and QC come in, followed by the prosecutor. Monique, David, and Jill. Monique is flushed, David's color's high, too. I hope he's not going to have a stroke in my office. Jill is looking cross. They shut the door behind them in the small office space I have to myself, and all three start to talk at once.

"I'm going to take Liam's comment as a guilty plea."

"I insist that the trial is vacated and the prosecution sort the case out properly."

"I apologize for my clients, but they have very strong feelings about this."

I hold my hands up, quieting them down. I gesture to them to sit down in the hard wooden chairs, before I let battle commence.

Over an hour later, the lawyers leave my chambers and go back into the courtroom. It's a messy compromise but it'll have to do. Liam will be warned that the evidence he is giving is leading him straight toward being found guilty and he will be invited formally to change his plea. Philip will be called back onto the witness stand when the trial resumes the following Monday so that he can give a response to the allegations that have just been made about him. I will disregard the evidence given by Ryan that was not properly tested in cross-examination. But I've no doubt that David's going to appeal if I convict Philip, regardless of how the rest of the trial plays out.

We adjourn for the day, even though there are still another forty-five minutes left of court time. It's safe to say that we've all had quite enough.

19

Marcus is already at El Vino's. He's sitting at the same table as the last time and he waves as I approach. There's a bottle of red already open and poured into each of the two glasses. I sit down with relief and pour a good amount of the wine down my throat. I'm tempted to say that we must stop meeting like this, but his expression is so grim I don't feel it's remotely appropriate.

"That was quite the day," I say instead.

"What happened?"

"It was a three-hander in the youth court. A robbery. The victim stormed off before he'd even finished giving evidence. It was looking as if they were all innocent until the last codefendant got in the box and started confessing left, right, and center. Plus he totally implicated one of his codefendants."

At least it brings a smile to Marcus's face. "Chaos. I love it when that happens."

"Maybe in retrospect. It wasn't so much fun at the time. And it didn't look so entertaining to the codefendant's parents. Or his representative. They've got a QC. David Lamb."

Marcus's face twitches and too late I remember that they're in the same chambers. "That's too bad, Sylvie. He's pretty influential with the Judicial Appointments people. I hope he's not going to give you a bad reference."

Fear clutches at me, the idea that my future career could be jeopardized by this stupid trial. Then I calm myself. It's not my fault that the boy went rogue with his evidence. But try as I might to be dismissive about what Liam's done, it nags away inside me, the integrity he showed in the face of such pressure, not caring how badly it might turn out for him as long as his friend was all right. How badly Tess and I behaved in comparison.

"It wasn't that bad," I say. "It was more on the defense solicitor losing control of her client than anything to do with me. He can't hold it against me if I convict his client."

"Wanna bet?" Marcus says. He's not smiling but I laugh anyway, determined to make it into a joke. "Anyway, I wanted to talk to you about Tess."

"I thought that was what you wanted to talk about," I say. "Should you really be out? Is she OK on her own?"

"Her mum is down for the weekend," Marcus says. "We're hoping to God that Tess doesn't have another seizure. She doesn't want her mum to know what's going on yet. She'll tell her when she has to, but she doesn't want a fuss."

I nod. I know that's not what Marcus means, but I don't need to contradict him. We both know that the real issue with Tess's mum is not that she'll care too much, but that she'll care too little, caught up as she always has been in her own affairs. Literally so, on many occasions.

"What brings her down?" I ask.

"Spending time with Tess, of course," Marcus says. This is something I can't let pass, and I raise my eyebrow. He laughs. "Yeah, fair enough. There's a big party over in Glasgow at the end of the month and she wants to go shopping."

"Is Tess going to tell her about the vow-renewal ceremony?"

"I fucking hope not," he says. "Do you remember what her mother was like at the wedding? She'll be in an even bigger meringue this time, to make doubly sure she upstages poor Tess.

"It was amazing to see you both in those dresses again," he adds. "Neither of you has barely changed at all."

"Thanks," I say. "You know how much I hated it before. Can't believe I have to wear it again." I finish my wine, and a certain recklessness takes hold. "She's even mended the tear. Remember?"

He's still for a moment before he nods, once, the movement slight but still there. "Yes," he says. "I remember." Our eyes lock and all the noise and bustle of El Vino's falls away, the last years, too.

If it hadn't been a leap year, perhaps their wedding might never have happened. But Tess had been planning forever how she wanted her perfect wedding to be, and Marcus fit the part of the groom perfectly. He was smitten enough to be thrilled when she proposed on the 29th of February that year, and had readily gone off up Hatton Gardens with her the following day to find her a diamond that met her four C requirements. But Tess then seemed to turn into a monster, truly fulfilling the cliché of the demanding bride, and Marcus became more and more demoralized. We'd hide in the upstairs of Inner Temple Library, sharing muttered conversations about how much he hated the seating plan and I hated the dress.

To hand it to her, it was a miracle of organization. She pulled together a full late-summer wedding in just over six months, getting not only her first choice of venue but her first choice of church, too, a last-minute cancellation at St. Giles's Cathedral in Edinburgh. It was a spectacular service, marred only by the fact that my arse looked huge in the purple frock. We'd been taken out in coaches to a stately home near the Firth of Forth where we'd all gotten hammered—except for Tess, as she so firmly reminded me yesterday.

If Tess was abstaining, though, Marcus had drunk enough for two. He'd jumped up on the stage to take over the mic from the wedding singer at one point, giving a rendition of "Can't Take My Eyes Off You" which had been excruciating as opposed to excruciatingly funny. Tess had been visibly pissed off. The row only happened later, though, once we all got back to the hotel in which we were staying. ("My mum suggested we stay at hers," Tess had said, "but fuck that.")

She and Marcus traveled separately in a limo and so arrived back before the rest of the party in the coach, which made a couple of stops along the way to let people out in various parts of Edinburgh before we got to George Street. I went upstairs to my room to change out of the purple monstrosity, and as I passed the door to the suite on the way up, I could hear incoherent screaming and crying. I thought about knocking on the door, but I was too pissed, and I didn't want to get involved. Tess had bollocked me enough during the day variously for smiling too much and not smiling enough that I really didn't feel that I could be fucked with it.

It took three goes but I finally got the entry card to work and got into my room where I took my shoes off with a sigh of relief. There was a bottle of champagne in an ice bucket and I tore the foil off in one go, desperate to have another drink after the stress of the day. As I was trying to pull out the cork, there was a bang at the door. I staggered over to open it, and as Marcus pushed his way through, the cork popped out of its own volition, hitting him on the forehead and exploding all over my dress.

He took the bottle out of my hand, pouring a long draft down his neck and grabbing me with the other hand. I turned away from him, getting out of his grasp, before he caught hold of the back of my dress. I moved away again, hearing a ripping sound. I swore and he let go, sitting down at the edge of the bed and putting his head in his hands. "Fuck," he said. "Fuck."

"We're not going to."

"No?"

"No," I said. It was tempting. If she hadn't been so awful for the last months, if I hadn't been so drunk, if *he* hadn't been so drunk. If they'd never been together in the first place... But I wasn't going to go there. Nothing good would come from that.

"I feel so trapped," he said. "I told her I didn't want to go through with it last week. That's when she told me she was pregnant."

I sat still, the room spinning. I knew what Marcus had said was important, but I didn't know how to process it. She couldn't be pregnant. She'd have told me. It didn't make sense. But I was drunk and knackered so not much was making sense, really.

"You'd better go back," I said, and he groaned. "I can't."

"I think I'm going to be sick. Please, could you just go."

He left with no further argument. I threw the dress off me onto the floor and curled up to sleep without taking off my bra. When I woke, it was long past nine and I only got down to breakfast by the skin of my teeth.

It didn't take me long to regret not only breakfast, but the fact I'd ever been born. Tess was beaming, brandishing her wedding ring like a blade. And her news, the pregnancy she wanted to share with everyone after she was married. I looked from her to Marcus, his rictus grin, a hostage smiling under duress. I thought of his hand on my arm, his attempt to pull me into an embrace, and I lowered my head, unable to meet Tess's gaze.

"I never wanted to think about the wedding again," Marcus says. "The whole idea of it brings me out in a rash."

"Me too."

"It's not even that," he says. My hand jerks involuntarily, spilling my drink. We never speak of it. "It's the whole thing. Her manic conducting of this insane orchestra playing a nightmare bridal symphony from hell."

"It wasn't that bad," I say, with no conviction at all.

"It fucking was," he says. "It took me months to get over it. Let alone how shifty I felt. I've never told her the truth about where I went off to after our row."

"Maybe you should have told her."

"You could have done it, too," he says. "She's your best friend."

"I would have," I say. "But the pregnancy. The miscarriage… I thought you and she had sorted things out after that happened. I didn't want to upset everything."

We fall into silence. I look around the bar, at the tables of barristers and solicitors knocking back red wine, prosecco, rinsing the taste of the working week out of their mouths. We've finished our bottle now and the way the conversation's going, I could do with a lot more to drink.

"Shall I get another one?" I say.

"I'll get it," he says, but I shake my head.

It's been nearly forty years since women weren't allowed to be served at the bar here, but I still take a perverse pleasure in going up. Besides, I need to catch my breath from the oppression of Marcus's misery. Dislodge the stone of guilt that lies heavy in my gut.

20

I thought the conversation we'd had already was bad. It was nothing to the conversation we have when I get back to the table, elbowing pin-striped men and women out of the way, my reluctance to sit back down with Marcus growing the closer I get to him.

"I've been thinking about what you said," Marcus says when I get back to the table. "The miscarriage. There's something you don't know."

I look at him, eyes narrowed. "What don't I know?"

"Haven't you ever wondered why we don't have kids?"

"Not really. Tess told me she wasn't interested and neither were you. Can't say I've given it much thought. You know my view on kids."

"True. But it's not as simple as that. I mean, neither of us *is* that interested, but there was a period of time when we tried for a while. About a year."

"Tess never told me," I say.

"It wasn't something we wanted to talk about," he says. "We were trying not to let it dominate our lives."

I nod.

"In the end we went for tests," he says. "Tess was fine. It was me that was the problem."

I raise an eyebrow.

"I've got a very low sperm count," he says. "It's impossible that I could get anyone pregnant."

There's a long pause after he says this. For a moment I don't understand why he's felt the need to share such intimate revelations with me, but my throat constricts as the implications fully dawn on me.

"So you couldn't have been the father? Is that what you're saying?"

"Of course that's what I thought," he says. "We had a huge row. That's when she told me."

"Told you what?"

He pauses for a moment to drink the rest of his glass of wine. He puts the glass down and looks straight at me. "She wasn't pregnant, Sylvie. Tess was making it all up because she was terrified that I was going to ditch her right before the wedding. She pretended to have a miscarriage afterward to put an end to the charade."

"Are you sure?"

"Yes, I'm sure. It took me a while to believe that this had been the lie, rather than that she'd cheated on me. But I did believe her."

I'm in shock at the revelation. "Faking a pregnancy to make sure a marriage goes ahead? That's not great."

"It isn't," he says. "I forgave her, though. We moved on."

"So why are you telling me now?"

He looks away from me, over into the far corner of the bar, but I don't think he's aware of anything that's happening in front of him.

"If she's lied before to stop me from leaving, who's to say she isn't lying again?"

"You mean…"

"I mean, maybe this whole brain tumor story is a lie?"

He tops his glass up and drinks. I sit in silence, stunned, unable to think of anything to say in reply, the acrid smell of Tess's urine after her seizure yesterday evening suddenly strong in my mind.

"No," I say. "That's not possible. Who the hell lies about having cancer?"

He shrugs. "She lied before," he says.

"It doesn't mean she's lying now. Think about it. The situation is completely different. If you'd jilted her at the altar, it would have destroyed her life. I'm not saying she did the right thing, but I can understand why she might have done that. Maybe she even thought she was pregnant. This is completely different, though."

We sit for a moment in silence. I'm sifting through my memories of that time, of how guilty I've felt ever since that I presented a temptation to Marcus. All this time I've blamed myself, thinking how terrible it was that I should have let him into my room when she, my best friend, was pregnant and alone in hers. Some of that weight of guilt shifts now. But it was all so long ago…

"I shouldn't be so negative," he says. "I'm probably in denial. I desperately don't want it to be true. I'd rather she was a liar than have cancer. None of this means anything in comparison to what she's going through. What she's about to go through."

"It's unimaginable," I say. "No one would lie about something like this. Look, I think we need to be more positive. Focus our energy on the vow renewal. It's fair enough she wants to have something to look forward to."

"I'm happy to do whatever she wants," he says. "Even if I am moaning about it. It's good to get the chance to do it again properly, I suppose."

He's got his most sincere expression on, eyebrows knit just so.

"I'm happy to do what she wants, too," I say. "Even if it does mean wearing that dress I hate so much."

Marcus laughs now, a little too long, a little too loud, but it's clear the spell of gloom that had him in its clutches has passed. His eyes are clear now, no trace left of the suspicion he voiced.

"It's good we get to start again, turn over a new leaf," he says. The smile fades. "I wish she wasn't so obsessed about the past, though." A jolt in my chest, my hands shaking.

"She's been talking about something that happened when you were both at school," Marcus continues. "She says she wants to come clean. She seems really bothered about it. Linda. Apparently you're going to help sort all this out? She was throwing the word 'amends' around a lot."

I drink my wine down, nearly a whole glass in one go. "I keep hoping she's not serious about it."

"She's deadly serious, Sylvie. To be fair, she might be dying. I suppose it focuses your mind."

"I don't even know where to start with it all," I say.

"You said you were happy to do what she wants…"

I sigh. "I am. It's just…this is really complicated. I've tried to tell her. I think it's one of those things that's best left alone."

"Scared of what you might dig up?" Marcus says. His eyes are narrowed. "She said you'd both been key witnesses in a court case that ended up in a verdict of culpable homicide. I don't want to jump to any conclusions, but it would be inadvisable, shall we say, for you to have any gray areas lurking in your past when you put your judge's application in."

I can hear blood pounding in my ears above the pub noises. Only Marcus's face is clear to me now, every spider vein on his cheek visible, the pores of his nose. Despite the tension I feel, I can't help but think that age does not become him, a coarsening there of the features that were once so fine.

"What are you trying to say, Marcus? I don't think I'm quite sure what you're getting at."

He darts his tongue into the corners of his mouth, both stained dark with the wine. "I don't think either of us can imagine what Tess is going through right now. It's terrible."

"It is."

"I've put all of my issues aside to be back with her," he continues. "All the petty disagreements and grievances. It's worth it. I would really appreciate it if you would do the same."

"Who says I'm not?" I say. I've controlled the panic I felt at the mention of Linda's name, but I can feel it seeping back.

"This whole amnesty business," Marcus says, speaking slowly but clearly. "Tess needs this from us. From you. If you can't deliver Linda, I'm going to have to give her something else."

"Something else?"

"Something else, Sylvie. Maybe information that neither of us want her to have. Like you never telling her I made a pass at you."

He's looking down at the drink in his hand, not at me. No fucking wonder. If he caught my eye right now I'd burn through his eye socket straight to his brain. Despite all the noise of Friday-night drinks around us, I can almost hear him breathing, I'm focusing so hard.

"Are you trying to blackmail me for something you did, Marcus?"

"Don't be silly," he says. "I'm just looking out for my wife, that's all. For some reason, she's in need of a big gesture. Probably she wants to get some control back in her life. You know what she's like. This tumor business, it's terrible for anyone. But for someone like Tess? The uncertainty is killing her."

He looks up now, and I can see that there are tears forming in the corner of his eyes. "I know it doesn't always look like it, but I've always loved her. She can make it very difficult sometimes, but I really do. I don't know how we're going to deal with it if it comes to the worst."

"It's awful," I say. "I can't imagine what she's going through. What you're both going through."

He leans forward and reaches for my hand. "I'm sorry. I didn't mean to sound threatening. It's just…I want her to have something else to focus on, so she doesn't drive herself mad diagnosing herself and coming up with worst-case scenarios. Whenever I see her on her laptop, she's looking up brain cancer charities, or the Mayo Clinic. That's why I'm happy to go along with the vow-renewal event."

"Well, yes," I say. "Me too."

He leans even closer, holds my hand even tighter. "And that's why I want you to try and find this Linda person and get her to talk to you both. It's really bothering Tess, whatever this is about."

I pull my hand away gently, not wanting to appear antagonistic. Or intimidated. My mind is whirring, though, working through all the permutations of carrying out Tess's request.

"I'll do my best," I say. "I don't particularly want to. It doesn't bring back any happy memories, looking at what happened at the end of school. But I'll do it if it'll keep Tess happy. You know I'd do anything for her."

He nods. "Thank you. I do know that. It's so weird, given how long I've known you both, that neither of you has ever mentioned until now that something so big happened to both of you at the end of school."

"We said we'd never talk about it again," I say. "Though it's funny, it's probably why both of us ended up doing law. We'd seen what it was like at firsthand, being part of a trial. We have more in common than we know, me and Tess. Even without discussing it, we came to the same decision. Though unlike me, she gave up when she got married. It was such a surprise when we met up after graduating. I didn't think I'd ever see Tess again after we left school. But here we are."

"Here we are indeed," Marcus says. With an effort, he changes the subject. "How's your judicial application going? Have you completed it? They haven't approached me for a reference yet but I'm not on top of the timings."

"I'm nearly done," I say. "Hoping Lamb won't put the boot in after the trial this week. I have to say, it all feels a bit trivial in comparison to this, though."

He leans forward again, but this time he takes hold of one of my hands in both of his. "I won't let you think that," he says. "You have worked like a dog all the way through to get to this. It's been your ambition to be a Crown Court judge for as long as I've known you. You can't let anything get in the way of it."

My mouth twitches. I control it as quickly as I can, but he's caught the movement. He looks at me coolly, dispassionately. I can almost see the pattern taking shape in his mind as understanding dawns.

"Will raking up the past with Linda get in the way of it, Sylvie? Is that what you're scared of?"

I try to keep still, not react at all, but Marcus knows me too well. He shakes his head once, twice.

"Jesus, Sylvie. This isn't good. Was the evidence core to her conviction?"

I nod.

"OK," he says. "That's really not a problem. I mean, she might not like that you were a witness, but presuming she's come to terms with everything that happened, she can't kick up a stink. As long as you were telling the truth, the two of you."

A pause. One beat. Two.

"Ah, Sylvie. Don't tell me... You were telling the truth, weren't you?"

It's not a question. It's a plea. I sit, helpless, not knowing what answer to give, the weight on the past heavy on me. He drains his glass, and I take that as a sign to make my farewells and go. I've had enough for one night.

21

The evening is crisp and cold. I decide to walk home after saying goodbye to Marcus outside El Vino's. My head is thumping, a pounding at my temples. I stop and put my hand to my forehead. Is this how it begins? Do I have a brain tumor, too? Then I stop, berate myself for my stupidity, my narcissism. Of course I don't have a fucking brain tumor. I've got a boozed-up head and too much guilt in it, that's all.

I set out along Fleet Street, walking in the direction of Waterloo Bridge. The view from the bridge will calm me, the lights reflecting all the way down to the Eye and beyond as far as I can see before the Thames bends and goes out of sight. I turn and look over in the direction of Blackfriars, London Bridge, before I keep stomping south. I'm not calm... The walk hasn't worked. I'm as tense as I've ever been, different issues thrusting their way up on top of each other, clamoring for my attention like a classroom full of toddlers all hyped up on sugar.

The trial has taken an unexpected direction, but I know for a fact it's going to be appealed afterward, and that bastard QC is going to make sure everyone knows it was my fault that the witnesses went out of control. The way that Lamb looked at me as he left my chambers was unsettling, to say the least. I know my position is under threat. Add to that Tess's obsession with finding Linda, and what that might lead to… It's a lot for my head to handle.

I've paused to look for one last time over at Tower Bridge, lit up in the distance, but now I turn and walk with purpose, heading down past the roundabout, the giant IMAX cinema looming above me, before crossing under the bridge and turning right onto Baylis Road, keeping south down past the Imperial War Museum, then along Walnut Tree Walk where I'd lived for a while in my early years in London. My thoughts turn in time with my steps: worry about the trial, worry about the judicial application, worry about the past and the implications of finding Linda. Worry too about Liam's integrity, the cost to him of telling the truth and how it didn't put him off. I am worth less as a person than I'd hoped, than I've tried to pretend for all this time.

Underneath it all, insistent, however much I try to silence it, is the thought of Tess's illness and what it means for me to confront the possibility of her dying. Not being here anymore. We've been friends for so long, ingrained so much in each other's lives, that it's simply unthinkable to consider that she will be gone. I do understand intellectually what she's told me, that any firm diagnosis is some way off, likewise any prognosis or treatment plan, but I can't push away the sense I have now, incredibly strongly, that very soon she's going to die.

My stride falters. I stop walking, looking over at Kennington Park, though not seeing it, not registering the dark shape of trees looming ahead. I'm seeing Tess and me through the years, laughing, crying. Bitching about each other incessantly, tearing each other down. Building each other up. Betraying each other sometimes in the most fundamental way; forgiving or forgetting, sometimes even both. Our friendship has gone on so long now she's blood—blood or not. With that thought, something crystallizes in me. Just as I always have, I will do what she wants. And not only being her bridesmaid.

I'll find Linda, and if she lets us, we will talk to her. We will explain ourselves, we will ask what she has done with all these years since we last saw her as she was taken down to the cells following the imposition of the prison sentence for the culpable homicide of Stewart, my ex-boyfriend, the boy she said assaulted her, the boy we denied having touched her, both lying in our own ways.

I take in a deep breath. I know this has the potential to destroy my career. If I'm forced to admit publicly that I lied in court, it's the end to any judicial ambitions. It's the end to any further practice, quite honestly. She could make a complaint and instead of sitting on the bench, I could find myself in the dock, facing a charge of perjury. If not worse.

That final thought spurs me back into movement. Tess wants to control the narrative, and given her condition, I see that I have little choice but to let her. I need to find Linda and then see what damage could be done. What further damage I can prevent.

I'm on the final stretch home now, down Kennington Road, past Oval Station, past the huge Georgian houses subdivided into multiple flats, rows and rows of doorbells lined up by the front doors. Sometimes I wonder how I've succeeded in compartmentalizing myself. I think I'm a good person, generally, law-abiding, tax-paying, good at recycling, kind to the dogs and cats I pass in the street. But I'm someone who has lied and cheated, let one woman go to jail for a crime she probably didn't commit, fucked all the wrong people, and I've managed to push this all down into a place that's hidden in me, so buried that I've gone years without giving it a second's thought.

Now I'm at the end of my street, and I pause again. There's something stirring inside me, something I don't like at all, an uncomfortable sensation of guilt, tentacles of it stirring up from the deep. There's been no space for this for years, any thought of it immediately pushed down by my ambition, my desire for professional fulfillment. But now, in the face of Tess's impending death…

"I have no idea how you go about finding someone," I say a few minutes later to Gareth. He's called as I go in the house, and tired as I am, drunk too, the idea of talking to someone friendly, someone on my side, is too much to resist. "I haven't seen her for years."

"Google," he says. "Social media. There's lots of ways. What's her name?"

I open my mouth to respond, shut it again. "Linda. Linda something. It's on the tip of my tongue, but I can't actually remember. My mind's gone blank."

"Really?" Gareth says. "You don't remember?"

"It was a long time ago," I say. "I've spent a lot of time trying to forget the whole thing. It was really traumatic having to give evidence."

"It must have been traumatic for her, too," Gareth says, "being on trial for something so serious."

"It must," I say, squirming in my chair. My skin's tingling, prickling with the heat of shame. I'm glad we're not on video call, that he can't see the blotches that are beginning to emerge on my face, my chest.

"Look, I know I'll be able to deal with it. Maybe I'll even find her this weekend. I'll give it a proper go in the morning."

"Good luck," he says. "If you think I can help, just let me know."

"I will," I say through a yawn that splits my face nearly in two. "Look, I'm sorry, but I'm knackered. Can I call you tomorrow? I need to get to sleep now."

"Sure thing," he says. "Sleep well."

I don't go to bed, though. I don't even put the light on. I sit at the kitchen table in the dark, turning it all over in my mind. It was only a few weeks ago that I was all set to make a break from Tess at last, get myself out of the clutches of her demands and the memories of the past. But there's no escape now. There never really was. Tess, our shared history, it's deep in my bones. To get rid of it I'd have to cut it out with a knife, great pieces of flesh, slicing down until the blade hit the bone, taking chunks out of the living, growing tissue till I got to the marrow and scraped it out, scrap by scrap...

There's a poem I read once, back when I was in my teens and such things had the power to embed themselves as deeply as this friendship. *I'm just a blotter, crisscrossed with the ink of words that remind me of you.* I might hate Tess sometimes; she might hate me. There might be secrets about each of us that if known, if fully spoken, would cause us to gouge each other's eyes out, but the idea that she might go and leave me here to live without her fills me now with a horror deeper than the fear of losing any career or professional advancement. One day soon she's going to be gone, out in a puff of smoke, and in that void I will have to find a way to carry on. There'll come a day when I pick up the phone to call her, share a thought that's just occurred, a joke I know only she will get, and at the end there'll be nothing, only silence, and at that thought I fill with dread, falling into a bottomless abyss, no way to break my fall.

I *will* find Linda, goddamn it, I'll talk to her, I'll tell her, we'll share our stories. Maybe she's forgiven us by now, maybe she'll understand how much we didn't understand at that time, how stupid we were, how young. Maybe she'll be angry at first, unforgiving, but when she sees how ill Tess is, how sorry we are...

It's late, I'm tired, cold, my legs cramping as I sit unmoving on the hard wooden chair. I should get up, go to bed, tuck myself into warm covers, and let sleep take away this sorrow, but it's as if I'm pinned to my seat by a force so strong it renders me immobile. And as I sit there, my sadness is chased away by growing terror, an intimation of impending doom so strong it's clear that I should get up, leave this place, break off all contact with anyone I've ever known and eke out a new existence somewhere far away.

This fear transfixes me for what feels like minutes, though it's probably only a few seconds, and when it passes I slump down, head on hands at the table, wrung out with exhaustion now and empty. I press my forehead against the laminate table, cool, unyielding, and I cry.

SPRING TERM
January 1990

"She's coming over," Tess said, jabbing me in the ribs with her elbow.

"She's not."

"She is, look."

We fell into silence as we watched Linda approach across the playground to where we were sitting on the steps in front of school. She hadn't made eye contact with either of us, but she was striding in our direction with a determined jut to her jaw.

"I can't handle it," I said. "I've got nothing to say."

"Let's go then, as soon as she gets to us," Tess said. "That'll show her."

I nodded. The moment that Linda was within a few feet of us, I jumped to my feet, pulling Tess up by the hand, and we walked away past her, one on either side. I almost brushed into her with my shoulder, so keen was I to show that she was nothing, no obstacle to me, but I balked at the move at the last minute, pulling away so sharply from her that I turned my ankle and nearly fell.

"I wish she'd just leave us alone," I said.

We sat in the back of English while Mr. Marsh explained the finer details of "The Love Song of J. Alfred Prufrock" to us. Normally I'd have been well into it, teasing the imagery and finding a way to relate it to my own life (oh yes, measured out in pints of Stella, so profound), but this time I couldn't engage. I stared at the back of Stewart's head so hard it was a wonder it didn't explode there and then under the force of my gaze. We weren't back together. He'd reassured me it was nothing, that Linda had taken advantage of his drunkenness. I was trying to believe him, but it was hard. Whenever I saw her, I got wound up again.

I needed to put it out of my head. I was missing him a lot, and my social life had taken a hit since we'd started going out. It seemed churlish still to be hanging onto the grievance.

Tess poked my arm and I became gradually aware that Mr. Marsh was demanding my attention. "Sylvie, Sylvie," he was saying, "why does he fear to eat a peach?" I snapped back into myself, pushing the thoughts of Linda away.

After the class, Tess took me to one side. "You need to get over this," she said. "You always look so miserable whenever you see Linda, but we're not going to get rid of her, so it's time to get over it. Come on, let's go out Friday and forget all about it. I'll look after you. It'll be great."

Eleven o'clock the next Friday night and Tess was being as good as her word. She'd been stuck at my side since the start of the night. She'd lent me her favorite skirt, made me up, done my hair, poured vodka down my neck and handed me a new cigarette the moment I put the old one out. We were sitting at the side at one of the tables, watching the dance floor fill up as Mudhoney came on the speakers.

"I'm going to get a drink," I said, standing up, but she pulled at my arm.

"I'll get it," she said.

"I haven't bought a drink all night," I said. "It's definitely my round."

"I want to," Tess said. I looked at her, eyes narrowed. She could be nice. But this was overkill.

"Why are you doing all this, Tess? Why are you looking after me so much?"

"I'm being nice," she said, shouting in my ear over the yelled refrain. Mudhoney were tired, I was tired too, the music resonating through me, shaking my core. It was the bass, cranked up to the max, and I shook in time to its beat. Maybe she *was* just being nice. It wasn't that unusual. Even so, I stared her down and made my way over to the bar, ordering two pints of snakebite and black and two shots of vodka. The barman caught my eye and I knew he knew, but neither of us could be fucked with the dance of it, the question asked for ID that I would answer with a flourish of my laughable forgery.

The pints were full to the brim, the meniscus threatening to burst with an evil purple glow. I took a large slurp from each of them before picking them up, the shot glasses too, and carrying all four carefully, I made my way back to the banquette where Tess and I were sitting. As I approached, I saw she was no longer on her own, but that Campbell was sitting next to her, a proprietorial arm around her shoulder.

"Sylvie, I was there too, you know. It was only a joke. But you got well into it. I mean, you got off with loads of people. I really don't see why you can't forgive Stewart," he said, yelling through the music.

Maybe it was the vodka. Maybe it was the hit of the snakebite. The room shifted, a crack opening up beneath my feet, and with it a fear that I was about to fall. I had to grasp hard onto the tabletop, the tacky metal surface the only solidity I could feel. That wasn't what happened, was it? Perhaps I was misremembering? I looked at Tess, expecting her to shake her head, tell Campbell he had it all wrong, but instead she looked steadily back at me, her expression somber, sad, as if she had looked into my soul and seen it for the wanting, pathetic scrap it was.

"Sylvie, you were so out of it," she said. "It's hard to say that it was all Stewart's fault, you know. As Campbell says, you definitely looked like you were well into getting off with everyone. I agree with him. I think it's time to let go of it. Stewart's going to join us soon. Why don't you give him another go?"

My certainty was slipping. I'd been so sure, but maybe I'd gotten it wrong. Maybe it was easier to blame Stewart than face up to the fact that I'd been keen, too.

"No one's judging, Sylvie," Campbell said into his pint. "We all love a slapper round here." He reached his hand down Tess's top and grasped hold of her right breast, squeezing hard enough that she gasped before slapping his hand away.

"Speak for yourself," she said. "I'm no slapper."

Her words stung, but perhaps she hadn't meant what she said to be an attack on me. I washed the sting down with the last of my snakebite before swallowing what was left of my pride.

At that moment, Stewart came over. He looked at me with one eyebrow raised. I could have resisted but I didn't want to. I wanted my life back to the good version again, the one where I was going out with the most popular boy in the school, where I had status when without him I had none. I nodded. He sat down and took my hand.

It was as if nothing had ever happened.

"You're back together, then," Linda said, pushing past me in the pub toilet. I jumped. I hadn't seen her come into the pub that night;

otherwise I'd have made sure not to be in the same place as her. At least I wasn't on my own. Tess was with me. It was a month after I'd been persuaded to get back together with Stewart, and by now I knew exactly what to believe about what had happened between him and Linda on Hogmanay.

"What's it to you?" I said, not meeting her gaze, shouldering my way up to the mirror to apply another layer of black eyeliner.

"Nothing," she said. "I didn't take you for such a pushover, though."

"Pushover? What the fuck are you saying?"

She shrugged, found her own space by the mirror, and taking out some lipstick, painted her mouth a vivid shade of red. Her voice was steady, her hand less so, and the lipstick skated off up the side of her lip. It should have been funny but something about it caught at my throat, crimson rising in her cheeks as she tried to wipe off the residue. Only once she'd cleaned it up did she turn to me.

"I wouldn't have forgiven him so easily," she said. "I'd have run a fucking mile."

"You weren't fucking running anywhere. That was the issue," I said. "If you'd just left him alone, there'd have been no problem in the first place. You could see how drunk he was. If you hadn't been all over him, none of it would have happened."

Linda shook her head, rubbed her front teeth with her index finger to ensure the lippy hadn't gotten there, too. "Is that what he told you?"

"It's what I saw," I said. "He looked hammered when you let go of him."

"Oh, Sylvie," she said, shaking her head. "He's done a real number on you." She turned back to the mirror, straightened her hair. I glared at her reflection, Tess too. She might be the year below but she couldn't have seemed less bothered by it. "Is that seriously what you think you saw?"

I opened my mouth to reply, but the certainty I'd felt just a moment before ebbed away from me. If anyone had been hammered that night, it was me. I had seen the two of them together, that was for sure, Linda with her back against the statue, Stewart close in front of her, his dark head bearing down on hers. I had seen him turn, tell us to fuck off. Linda had pulled away, I remembered that too, pulling at her clothes. But after that, my mind was blank. I'd started to throw up, and after that wasn't aware properly of my surroundings for a long time.

"Stewart told me," I said. "Tess backed him up. Tell her, Tess. They're not lying to me, Linda. I know it was you who tried it on with him. Everyone knows you're a complete slag."

She laughed, and a chill passed across my scalp, all the hairs tightened for a moment.

I looked at her, mute with disbelief. Defiance too.

She shook her head from side to side, hard lines etched down from the corner of her mouth. I could see then how she'd look in twenty years, a heaviness to her movements. The look passed and she was young again, her lips trembling as if she was about to cry.

"Believe what you want, Sylvie. There's nothing I can say that will get through to you, you're so sucked in by them all," she said, turning away from me as if to leave the bathroom, but then she took three steps and stood right up in my face, hand tight on my shoulder. I could smell her breath, thick with fags and booze. I stepped back but she kept hold of me.

"Get the fuck off me," I said, but she didn't let go.

"Just you wait," she said. "One day it'll be you. You'll be shit-faced and he won't wait for you to say yes, either. He'll be on you whether you like it or not. Let's see what happens then."

"Is that what happened?" I said, unable to hold the question back.

"Ask Campbell. He was at the flat Stewart took me back to when I could hardly stand up. After we saw you. He took me back and fucked me on the coats still left on the floor. I was so out of it, I let him. But I never said yes. And I didn't want it to happen. Not that way." As she said it, she let go of me, stumbling backward on her heels.

"I don't believe you," I said.

"Of course you don't," Linda said. "Of course you fucking don't." With that, she stalked out of the bathroom. The door shut behind her.

"*Do* you believe her?" Tess said.

"No. Stewart wouldn't do that."

"Well then. We'd best get out. They'll be worried about us."

"I'll just finish putting on some eyeliner."

"Well, get a move on," she said, moving in close to me. "Don't let that Linda upset you."

"I won't," I said. I was touching up the flick on my left eye as I spoke, not looking at Tess's reflection, but it seemed like her eyes flickered and something passed across her face. I didn't ask, though, and she said no more.

"Babe, baby," Stewart said when I got back from the toilets. "Where have you been for so long? You shouldn't leave me on my own like this. Someone might try and snap me up."

I sat down next to him, pulling my chair close to his. Shambles was packed. We were right at the back of the bottom section, the room full of sixth formers spilling over into the upper areas, too. I looked around, trying to see where Linda was sitting, but she was nowhere to be seen. Perhaps she'd left. I hoped so. I didn't want to see her again, didn't want to have to worry about whether what she said was true or not. I looked around the table, Tess and Campbell holding hands, Stewart with his hand on my thigh, his voice at my ear, a warmth beating from him. This was right, this was good. I wasn't going to let anyone spoil my perfect setup.

22

Gareth messaged me during the night so it's the first thing I see when I wake, far too early on Saturday morning, and check my phone.

You sound miserable. Come and see me. I've got an event so I can't get down but you could get on the train and be here by lunch. I can help you with social media shit. xxx

At first I smile at the thought but dismiss it. Scotland—it's miles, I don't have time, a myriad of excuses. Then I think about the number of times that Gareth has trekked down to see me. On a National Express coach, too. He's right—I can jump on a train at King's Cross and be there before I even know it. I look around the flat, the pile of washing-up, the bigger pile of laundry, the detritus of the week. I consider my options. Stay here and clear it up, fighting off all the anxiety I'm feeling about Tess, her health, the way she's acting, or escape for a couple of nights and leave all this behind.

It's not much of a choice. I go straight for my overnight bag and throw some clothes into it, stopping only to change out of the suit I'm still wearing and into my jeans. I know I should wash but I can't be fucked. Maybe Gareth and I can shower together when I arrive, soaping each other languorously before falling into bed together. I shake my head, knowing well I'm being ridiculous. More likely we're going to spend the afternoon squashed together over the screen of my laptop going down wormholes looking for the biggest mistakes of my past.

Still, anything has to be better than the desolation I felt last night. I clean my teeth quickly, scrubbing away the film of red wine still left from the glasses I sank with Marcus. There's acid in my stomach but the thought of the journey north is neutralizing it, the sour taste vanquished by a quick shot of espresso before I run out of the door. I'm on the Northern Line up to King's Cross before I remember I haven't even told Gareth yes.

As soon as I've bought the ticket, I message him and then I hover by the announcement board waiting for the platform number to come up. It's the first time I've come to King's Cross since the renovation works. I remember it differently, a modernist block of concrete, low-roofed, an air of squalor seeping around it. Now the glass ceilings are high, daylight streaming in rather than the yellow fluorescent glow it used to be. Then the most sophisticated food available was from Upper Crust, if you didn't want a Maccy D's. Tess and I had always wanted the Maccy D's.

The platform comes up—Number 5—and I head over, memories of the last time I did this journey starting to come up now that I'm out of the new part and back in the bit I recognize, the InterCity 125 high-speed train not so dissimilar from the ones of my youth. I'm in First Class, though, a sop to age and hangover, not like the orange-seated smoking coaches of the couple of journeys that Tess and I took together when we were still at school.

I sit down and wait to be given a coffee, a bottle of water, and marvel at the luxury, unthinkable then. We were just seventeen, the last trip we took during the May half-term before the end of sixth form, the party at the beach, and the death that changed everything. I remember it now as if it were yesterday as the train pulls out of the station and makes its way through north London. The Arsenal stadium might be different, new and fancy with its Emirates branding, but the tower block for London Metropolitan University is still there, still lowering gray as we move beyond Holloway Road and up until we're out of London and heading toward Peterborough.

The carriage is nearly empty. It's eight o'clock, too early for the stag and hen dos, no business travel needed today. I pull out my phone and take a selfie against the antimacassar emblazoned with the operating company's logo. I'm on the train. I send it to Gareth and lean back with my eyes closed, tired now from the exertion that's gotten me here.

After the trial, my parents moved away immediately from Edinburgh, unable to cope with the flickering looks of the people they knew as they passed them in the street. Not that I'd done anything wrong, let's be clear, but the association itself was bad enough. I moved with them, an incomer to Bath, a town cruelly similar, the beauty the same, but empty of all my friends, my foundations of history. Once I escaped to university I never went back, nor north of the border to the only place I really called home, until Sylvie's wedding, and then only the one trip.

My trip up to the conference at which I'd met Gareth was the first time I'd returned on my own since I was in my teens. Perhaps that's why I was so open to him, emotionally receptive as my defenses were assailed by nostalgia, memories. The journey didn't have the same impact as this, though, arriving on a plane, going straight into a taxi to the conference center at the Sheraton. It could have been anywhere. This train ride, though…

The rocking motion of the train and my own exhaustion combine and I fall asleep, head slumped against the side of the seat, and it's only as we're approaching Berwick on Tweed that I jolt awake, my timing perfect. I've deliberately chosen a seat on the right of the carriage, and I watch the coastline unfold beside me, the quick sighting of the little ruined house on a tiny inlet, the island of Lindisfarne far off in the distance. We had a school trip there once, carting down in a coach with a packed lunch and a pack of Capri Sun. That was before I had any friends, when the evil duo of Carole and Caroline, queens of the hockey pitch, bullied me and wouldn't let anyone sit beside me on the way home.

Tess had saved me from all of that. She took me, a girl still scarred from the bullying of the all-girls' school, and built me up into someone with confidence who could attract boys and talk to anyone in the room, rather than someone who hid away and avoided any confrontation. Sure, she'd been a little cavalier in her methods sometimes, but she was right, I was oversensitive. I'd taken all those relationships too seriously—Stewart, Campbell, all of it—too much to heart.

The fear I felt the night before is now gone, replaced by bravado. I'm not scared that confronting the whole Linda situation is going to fuck up my career prospects. She doesn't really know anything. Nothing she can prove, anyway. It was such a drunk night, everyone was so confused about what was happening. She doesn't need to know how much of a lie I told. I can fudge it, make sure she only knows that maybe I wasn't as sure as I told the court I was about what I saw. If I tell her I'm sorry, it'll be OK. I'm sure of it. It was so long ago.

Gareth meets me off the train and we walk down to his flat in the New Town, not far from where I used to live with my parents. The past has me in its grip—I'm seventeen again. I stop him on Dundas

Street and run into a newsagent's to buy a pack of cigarettes, hit by an urge I haven't felt in years. I light one up as we walk down the hill, Fife in the distance over the Firth of Forth, and I turn to Gareth and laugh.

"I can't believe it's been so long since I've been here," I say, "though it feels like no time at all."

"Are you sorry you left?"

"Of course. Though at the time, there wasn't much choice. My parents just wanted to get out. The trial was very stressful. Everyone knew what had happened."

I fall silent. The urge to laugh has passed, the urge to smoke, too, and I stub the cigarette out on the pavement, grinding my foot against it and kicking it into the gutter. I'm silent till we've walked up the long flights of stairs to his flat on the top floor, overlooking the rooftops and gardens at the back of the street.

"This is lovely," I say, and it is, homey, full of plants and books and a large gray cat who winds itself around my ankles. "Your view is amazing."

"I know," he says. "I'm very lucky."

I put my stuff down and he makes a coffee, then brings it over to me.

"Here you go," he says, handing it to me, "though you look like you could do with something stronger."

I smile, my mouth twisting up at one corner. I haven't gotten it past him, then, the stress I'm feeling. "It was a weird night last night."

"How so?"

"I had a drink with Marcus. It was intense. He pretty much said he thought Tess might be faking the cancer."

"Wow," Gareth says. "That's big. Why would he say something like that?"

I know I shouldn't say any more, betray Tess's secrets like this. I can't help myself, though. "She faked being pregnant before they got married. I think he might have been going to call the whole thing off, but of course he couldn't after that. Then she faked having a miscarriage."

"Sylvie," Gareth says. "That's appalling."

I look up at him. His expression is grave. Part of me wants to agree with him so strongly that I end up making excuses for her. "It sounds worse than it is," I say. "I think it made sense to Marcus in the end. I really don't believe she'd fake this, though. I mean, she had a seizure on the floor in front of me."

His face stays set in the same grim expression for a moment longer before he shrugs. "I suppose."

"She wet herself, Gareth. You're not going to fake something like that."

He shrugs again, ending the discussion. Sitting down beside me, he talks me through setting up profiles on Facebook and Instagram.

"I can't believe you haven't joined social media before," he says. "You're a total anomaly. I literally know no one else who hasn't signed up. Even if they left afterward."

I shrug. "Never fancied it," I say. "Maybe because of all this. I didn't want to have to deal with anyone from school again. Once I left, that was me, out. When Facebook first came along, it was my idea of hell. Tess signed up and I think she contacted a few people from school, but I didn't want to know. Once I started being a district judge, it was even more sensible to steer clear. If I go saying anything about any of my cases, or indicating any prejudiced opinions… Well, it would be foolish, put it that way."

He nods, clicking away at the computer. "You can have proper privacy settings. You don't have to have lots of friends, either. But

I think this is a better way to find her. Apart from freaks like you, everyone's on Facebook now." He leans back into the sofa on which we're sitting. "There you are."

He passes the computer over to me and I look at what he's done. A profile in my name, a recent photo of me that isn't too revolting, my school and university listed in my personal information. I look more closely and see there's a box for relationship status that he's completed as It's Complicated. I slap his arm, laughing, but a little stung that's what he's thought to say.

"What would you call it, then?" he says. "Am I your boyfriend?"

I open my mouth, but I can't think of a response quickly enough. Truth is, I don't know what he is. I shrug. Smile. "Fair enough. I *am* complicated."

"You said it."

I look back at the computer screen. "What next?"

"You make friend requests. Here, I don't know who your friends are." He pushes the computer over to me.

I search for Tess, a couple of people from chambers. I put Marcus's name in, not expecting him to have a profile, but his photograph pops up. I make a friend request of Tess, not the others as the option doesn't offer itself.

"I told you it's got good security. You can't just accept requests from any old fucker," Gareth says. "I really can't believe I've met one of the last people in the world not to have Facebook. Quite remarkable."

I mess around on it for a while, uploading a couple more anodyne photos, clicking Like on a couple of interests. That's not why I'm there, though, and I know it. I'm putting off the inevitable, circling in to land anywhere but where I'm supposed to be.

"Aren't you going to look for Linda?" Gareth says.

I shake my head. "I know I should. But I'm scared. Why would she want to talk to me?"

"You've promised Tess, you told me."

"I know, I know. There's no need to remind me," I say, more crossly than I mean to. I subside back into the sofa. "Sorry. This is really stressful."

He rubs my back. "It must be," he says. "I know it's hard to go back. I'd hate to have to do it. But you did promise… Look, I'll do it for you if you like. What's her surname?"

I look at him, as blank as when I tried to remember before. I can't understand it. Something as huge as this, such a big event that it caused me to leave Edinburgh and never return, and I can't remember the full name of the person who ended up in prison for it.

"I must be blanking it out because it's so hard?" I say. Though I don't mean it to, it comes out as a question, the tone rising up at the end of the sentence. I'd hoped I would have remembered by now, but my brain has been doing a good job of protecting me. Perhaps too good.

"Maybe," Gareth says. "Or maybe you've had no cause to think about it once it was done and you've just forgotten. I mean, you wouldn't be delving back into this if it weren't for Tess, would you?"

I shake my head without turning. Shame is creeping up my cheeks, a prickly heat. "It's terrible, isn't it? I haven't given it a thought for years. I buried it away and that was it. It's been so long…"

"Is Tess going to remember?"

"I'll message her."

I pick up the computer to send a text and see that she's accepted my friend request and that she's also sent me a message. Shit you've joined FB. Is hell going to freeze over??? I roll my eyes and reply. Yeah, you asked me to find Linda. Right? This is bad but I can't remember her surname. There's no reply for a bit and then it comes through. Um, Smith, I think? Yeah, that was it.

There are millions of Linda Smiths. My life's become infinitely harder. But it comes back to me now in a flood, a pale face, dark hair, always where we didn't want her. No, I have to stop thinking in this way. I have to stop thinking of her as an enemy. I try to picture her in the dock instead, her face as the jury foreman said, "Guilty," to the charge of culpable homicide. She'd half slumped when he said, "Not guilty," to murder, but the desperation flowed from her in waves afterward as the judge sentenced her to a seven-year term of imprisonment. I walked out of the courtroom, never saw her again.

I raise my hand to type her name in the search box, but something stops me. "I need to gear myself up for this," I say. "I will do it. Maybe when you're out working later. But I have to work myself up to it."

Gareth puts his arm around me. "I understand," he says. "I know this is hard. I'm sorry I'm going to be out this evening."

"It's OK. It's my problem, after all. You've helped me loads already."

With that, I shut the laptop and turn to him, kissing him properly for the first time since I've arrived, and all thoughts of the past are soon pushed out of my mind.

Later, much later, I hear Gareth come back in from work. I hear the door close quietly, the creak of his footsteps on the wooden floor. The smell of him, sweat and onions and cigarette smoke, carries through the air and a tremor of longing passes through me before ebbing away again. I keep my breathing slow, steady, trying to calm the palpitations I've felt, the nerves, ever since I found Linda, her photo not far from how I remembered her from all those years back, and I pressed Send on the message I took so long to compose to her.

Gareth gets into bed, curling up behind me, his arm around me, but I keep up the breathing. I don't want to tell him I'm awake, don't want to talk. Don't want to do anything. If I do start to speak, it's going to start pouring out. I'm going to tell him what message Linda's sent back to me, and once I've said the words out loud, it's going to be real, and I don't know if I'm ready for that now. I don't know if I'm ever going to be ready. Gareth's breathing soon moves into sleep, but I lie on my side, eyes open, watching the moon shadows slide across the dark of the room, fear deep in my heart.

23

Gareth doesn't ask and I don't tell in the morning whether I've made any progress. We wake at dawn and fuck, gently at first, but increasing in intensity until we both come at the same time.

"Wow," I say. "That doesn't happen often."

He smiles from above me, withdraws. "We got some chemistry going on here, that's for sure."

We lie quietly for a little but then Gareth jumps out of bed. "Let's not waste the time we've got left this weekend," he says, clearly thinking about the train I'm due to catch later in the day.

"What did you have in mind?"

"I think we should go to Gullane. I want to get a sense of the place, after everything you've told me about that party."

My stomach flips, curls up. It's like I've been winded. "I don't know if I'm ready for that."

"You're going to have to face your demons sometime, if she gets back to you. Even if she doesn't."

"I suppose..." I sit up, still reluctant.

"Look, tell me to back off if you want, but I think this is something that you need to do. Just for yourself, if no one else. Something like this... It must have been eating you up all these years."

"I suppose," I say again, hesitant. "I mean, like I said last night, it was such a long time ago. I know I should have felt guilty. There must have been a time when I did, but I shut it all down. I honestly haven't thought about it for years."

Gareth's face is grave. I feel suddenly as if he's judging me, disappointed that I don't have a clearer sense of shame for what I did. "I felt it so much at the start. It was awful when it happened. I wasn't sure I'd be able to go on for a while. I'd wake up at night and be suffocated by the thought of it."

"What changed?"

"I went to university, far away. None of the same people. I didn't keep up with anyone at school. Not even Tess. By the time we met again, I was a different person. So was she. I packed it all up and buried it inside me. Tess too. We had to get on with our lives."

He's still for a moment.

"What would you have done?" I say.

"I can't answer that," he says. "But yes, I hear what you say."

I take in a deep breath. "Let's go to the beach. You're right. I do need to face this."

We drive out of Edinburgh toward Gullane in Gareth's car, a refrigerated van with the logo of his catering company emblazoned on the side.

"Very smart," I say. "Tess and I always thought a band had made it if they had their own van."

"Ha, I guess you could say the same for caterers," he says. "My own industrial unit, too."

"You'd make a good serial killer. Everything you need for body disposal." I laugh, but he doesn't laugh back. "Hey, I'm not saying you're a serial killer."

"Obviously not. Sorry, just concentrating on the road."

It's not that busy, too early on the Sunday morning still for the road to be full. We head for the city bypass, reaching the turn off the dual carriageway before too long. Aberlady, the long wall to one side of the road, the bay stretching out to the other, flocks of seagulls swooping overhead. Then the golf courses through which the road curves before hitting Gullane town itself, a sharp left at a ruined church before we're at the car park.

It's been twenty years. It could be yesterday. I know it all already, the playground, the path that leads behind the dunes. The gorse bushes. The rocks that lie just below the surface. I skate over it all in my mind.

"Where was the party?" Gareth says, holding my hand in his as we walk along from the car park.

"It's all the way along," I say. "There's a hollow at the other end."

We walk along the path I remember so well. My skin is itching, a prickling again under the collar of my jumper. At least it's cold, not the beating heat I remember from that midsummer so long ago. The trees are bare of leaves, the tall grass dying back a little. Instead of the yellow flowers on the gorse bushes, there are hedges full of bright-orange sea buckthorn berries.

"I should have brought a bag, picked some," Gareth says. "They're nice with fish."

"Foraging. Fancy," I say, trying to keep my voice light. My heart's jumping a bit, though, memories still thick. Here Tess and I stopped to light a cigarette before going to the party, here I twisted my ankle because I was wearing stupid shoes...

"Bringing back any memories?" he says, walking ahead of me by a few steps.

"Not really," I say, holding it all close to my chest.

We keep walking, one behind the other, all the way along. As we pass one part, a bend with a thicket to one side, a rock sticking up from the sandy earth, I start to shiver from deep inside. I know that if I held my hand out, it would shake. I tuck them both firmly into my pockets, averting my gaze. It takes all my self-control not to turn round and run away. Despite what I've told Gareth, I remember it all so clearly.

"Can you remember where his body was found?" Gareth says as we pass through a particularly overgrown part of the path. I stop in my tracks, astonished at the question. He sounds as if he's on a day out, a murder mystery tour. Easy when it's someone else's life, I guess. I don't answer, striding out ahead of him.

After a few hundred meters we come out at last by the sea, a narrow stretch of beach between sand dunes and the high-tide mark along which we walk before we come to the hollow, a space set back from the sea, enclosed on three sides by sand dunes. There's the site of an old bonfire in the middle where I remember it, blackened logs tumbled at its center. I look at it now; flames dance before my eyes from my memory, Linda a silhouette against the flames as she whirled round faster and faster, her long hair whipping out behind her as she spun.

I'm shriveling into myself now. She's turning, laughing. She's mouthing words at me. I can't make out what they are, not at first. But then I see. *You ruined my life.* I shake my head clear. It's a chimera. She's not real.

The words are, though. When I found her the night before, I sent a message.

Linda. It's Sylvie. I don't know if you remember me. I wondered if we could talk.

Her response was swift. Swifter than I'd expect after the gulf of twenty years stretching between us.

> Sylvie. How could I forget you?
> You ruined my life. You and that friend of yours.
> Why would I want to talk to you?

"You OK?" Gareth says, moving closer to me, though not quite touching me. "You're very pale."

"I'm OK. It's just…strange, to be back here again. I never thought I'd see the place again."

"It's so easy to imagine it," he says. "This is the perfect place for a party."

"It was," I say. "Until it all went wrong."

There's a timelessness to the place. Any minute now Tess could jump out from over the top of the dunes, Campbell and Stewart with her. I shiver again, this time unable to control my movement.

"You're shaking," Gareth says. "Maybe we should light a fire."

I look up at him in surprise. In reply he pulls firelighters and matches out of his pocket.

"I saw lots of dry driftwood over there," he says. "We can get a fire going in no time."

Unresisting, I sit on a flat stone and watch him build the bits of wood into a pyramid, a firelighter at the bottom to which he touches a lit match. Soon, flames start to crackle up the side. A small plume of smoke curls up over the top of the pyramid. It's caught by a gust of wind and blows straight into my face. I cough, my eyes watering. My sense of timelessness grows. It's now and it's then, the smell of bonfire always enough to bring me back to this hollow where I'm sitting now.

Gareth walks around the fire, kicking at the logs. The sound pulls me back into the present, but not entirely. I watch him as he moves, a shadow on top of older shadows, a palimpsest of memory. He's standing now where Linda was dancing, now where Stewart was when he lunged, now where Tess was watching, so drunk she barely knew what she was watching, what had been unleashed.

"You any warmer?" he asks, coming over to where I'm sitting.

I hold my hands up to him. He takes them in his.

"You're freezing," he says.

"I should have brought a thicker jacket."

I get up, stamping on the sand to bring some blood back into my feet, get the circulation moving. My head is spinning a little, dizzy from the onslaught of memory. I stumble slightly and reach out to Gareth to break my fall.

"I don't like it here. It feels as if something really bad happened here. I'm beginning to get the creeps."

"From what you said, something really bad *did* happen here," Gareth says, his voice somber.

I shiver. Someone's walked on my grave.

He puts his hands on my shoulders and draws me in. "I'm sorry. I didn't mean to upset you, bringing you here. I thought it might help. I know what it's like to lose someone to cancer. It's what killed my sister. This is going to be hard for you. Tess is only going to get more and more ill. If this is something you can do to help her, I can see why you want to do it."

I look at him, speechless. He keeps talking.

"Maybe it's something you need to do for yourself, too. You might think you've dealt with it, but the only way you'll find peace in yourself is to confront it all. I know myself how unfinished business can eat away at you. Drive you mad, even. It was hell after my sister died. I kept going over the things I never got to say to her. Maybe the only way to forgive yourself will be to see Linda face-to-face, tell her how you feel."

I look up at him. His face is full of concern, his eyes warm.

"It's so difficult," I say.

He puts his arms around me. I'm rigid at first in his embrace before dropping my head against his shoulder. If I shut my eyes, maybe it'll all go away.

24

We're silent on the drive home. Without discussion, Gareth's decided to take the coast road all the way back in, the length of Aberlady, Longniddry, the power station at Cockenzie, Prestonpans. I stare at it all as we pass, drinking it in. I've missed it all so much during these years of exile. I've lived south longer than I did in Edinburgh, but it's still the place of my birth, my childhood, my formative years. It's in my bones.

"Would you like an ice cream?" Gareth says as we approach Musselburgh. I blink in surprise.

"Isn't it too cold for ice cream?"

"It's never too cold for ice cream from Luca's."

The tension breaks. I nod in agreement and we stop and buy cones, eat them in the car. More memories flooding back, but these are kinder, more innocent; summer days on the beach at Yellowcraig followed up by a pink ice cream on the way home. We're still sitting in silence in the car as we drive but there's been a shift, a sweetening of the air as I lick the sugar from my lips.

I had chocolate, him mint choc chip. I taste it on him as we kiss goodbye when he drops me at Market Street a bit later for my train back to London.

"It was lovely," I say. I mean it, too. Mostly. The stresses weren't of his making. I'm about to get out of the car when he reaches out and takes hold of my arm.

"You can tell me anything, you know," he says. "I want to know everything about you."

Words hang in the air, the ones I've only ever said to one other person in my life. I brush them away. Too much, too soon.

"I know," I say. "But there really isn't that much to know." I lean over and kiss him again. "I'd better go."

The journey back to London is less scenic by far. It's dark outside now, and all I can see in the window are reflections from inside the carriage, orange lights and my face pale in the glass. I lean my head against it, trying to calm the thoughts that are spiraling round. I've been in denial for years, desperate to forget what happened that night, but now it's come roaring back, like a smoldering log at last given the oxygen it needs to burn.

I pull my phone out of my bag. I've had it switched off all day. Since last night, after reading Linda's message, realizing the animosity that still blazed. Not a question of leaving a sleeping dog to lie if the dog in question was simply chained, slavering and dripping with hunger at the jaw, waiting for the first opportunity to break free.

There's another message from her on Facebook, sent earlier today.

You say you want to talk to me. What do you want to talk about?

Civil enough. Images of gnashing teeth fade from my mind. I think for a moment, reply.

That night. You. How you are. How life has been. All of it.

A long pause. Then:

You know what, Sylvie. You're unbelievable. How do you think I am? Just fuck off and leave me alone.

I can't say I'm surprised. I would be the same in her position. But despite the gnawing feeling of shame in the pit of my stomach, I feel a small ray of hope. Perhaps Tess will take this as the answer she needs. We're not wanted here. There's no absolution to be found. Linda will not be forgiving or forgetting in a hurry, and perhaps we need to accept that and move on. *That would suit you just fine*, a jeering voice says in my head, but I ignore it.

I should call Tess, let her know that Linda has told me quite comprehensively to fuck off, but I scroll through my emails and messages first, checking nothing's come up since I last looked yesterday morning. Nothing. Not even from Tess. I take it as a sign that I don't need to get in touch with her tonight.

I'm tired. It's been a long weekend starting with the shambles of the trial, the animosity of Philip's QC. The way that Marcus was behaving in the pub. The desperation I'd felt. And that was only Friday. Add to it the rushed visit to Scotland, seeing Gareth, the messages from Linda, the trauma of revisiting that place.

I shut my eyes. It's too much to think about. Rocked by the rhythm of the train, I fall asleep, waking only when we arrive back at King's Cross. I take a cab home, too tired to want to think about the Tube, and collapse into bed, leaving my phone on the kitchen table. It's peace I want, not worry that I'm going to receive another message from Linda, more bad news from Tess.

Then I remember, I'd promised to tell Gareth I was home. I drag myself up and stumble into the kitchen. I find a photo of Gareth's cat that I took the day before and send it to Gareth with the caption Here's a photo of your pussy. Underneath it I send a second message thanking him for the weekend. It was great to see you. Sorry I was a bit distracted. The ice cream was lush.

Done. It's time for bed. I'm not going to wait for a reply. I turn my phone off, and within moments of getting back into bed, I'm carried away on long waves of sleep.

PART 2

12:03:53

Over now. It's all over. Life bleeding out in front of me.

No one's coming now. No one cares.

When I'm dead, they'll pull me off and burn me, dump my ashes in the sea.

I'm weeping now, the tears mixing with the blood and dripping through my hair into the ground. It's over now.

THE FIREFIGHTER

We did one of these before. Mind you, he wasn't dead. Poor bloke, he'd fallen headlong into a railing on Dundas Street. It went straight through his jaw. Lucky to be alive, he was.

You'd think this job would be easier. Given they're dead. It's not, though. The officer in charge keeps fussing round us, talking about preserving the evidence as if we've never carried out any kind of procedure.

I'm in charge of the band saw, a big hydraulic number. We have to work out how best to do it so that the bodies don't fall backward into the basement area. At least they're not on top of each other, like a kebab.

I shouldn't keep making cracks like that. One of the coppers asks if we'll be using an oxyacetylene torch to cut through the railings. I say we'll need to be careful or they'll start cooking. Everyone'll be after a bacon sandwich.

The younger copper looks like he's going to throw up.

We've got it planned out. First, we'll take the bloke off. Couple of people to support the corpse, couple of people to cut through the railings, done. She's going to be more complicated. The way she's fallen, the body is bent over the railings. We'll have to be careful how to cut, so we don't cause any further injury to it. If we photograph it properly beforehand, then the pathologist can discount any subsequent injuries.

You need to think about these things.

25

A ring at the doorbell. Another.

A third.

Banging. An insistent banging that doesn't stop even though I've put my head under the pillow. The ringing again, and now thumps on the ceiling. It must be my neighbor telling me to deal with the racket, whatever's causing it. I pull on my dressing gown and pick up my phone from the table in the kitchen before going to the front door. It's not even six yet, no light outside.

Another bang and I look through the spyhole, anxious to check it's not a burglar. Some old client who's decided to track me down, someone I've jailed coming back to get me now they're free. It's not a criminal, though.

It's police. At least four of them, two vans behind them on the road, all lights flashing. It looks serious. Even though I have no idea what they want with me, my throat tightens, a guilty conscience never far from the surface, however unwarranted it may be. Then I think again. Jesus, Linda. She's told the police I must have committed perjury, and even after all these years, they're going to arrest me. It can't be that, though. That would be unimaginable—

"Open the door immediately," one of the police officers shouts, and the thumping starts again. It's going to wake the street. It's already woken my neighbors, an aggrieved tapping still coming through my ceiling from the flat above. "Open up. We have a warrant."

A warrant. My heart drops out of my chest to the pit of my stomach. I reach out and open the door, my hand shaking. They shout words at me that I don't follow, a notice subject to PACE Section 8, a paper thrust in my hand. This is a moment when if I were defending a client, I'd be scrutinizing what the police did and said down to the shortest syllable. But it's me, and I have no idea why they're there, not the faintest clue why suddenly my small flat is full of men opening drawers, pulling out papers and picking up my laptop, my iPad, my phone and putting them all in evidence bags.

"What the hell are you doing?" I manage to say at last. They barely look up from their task. No one replies. I remember the paper in my hand, my copy of the warrant, and I skim through it. They're searching for computer equipment that may have been used in the commission of an offense contrary to Section 67 of the Serious Crime Act 2015. I cast around in my mind, but I can't think what offense this is, what the hell they might be doing here.

I need to look it up. I go to find my phone but too late, it's been taken. I try to argue with the officer holding it in its bag but he's stony-faced.

"You should take legal advice," he says, "but I have the right to take this. I'm afraid I don't have the authority to let you look at it."

I protest, incoherent, and it passes over him like a breeze on an ocean. He's unruffled. I'm aware suddenly of my unwashed hair, my pajamas, the manky fleece I've thrown over a loose vest. The fact that I'm not wearing a bra. I hug my arms around myself, self-conscious.

As he holds the phone in his hand, it beeps with a message. It's so early, it can only be Gareth, up to cater the conference today. As if automatically, the police officer turns the phone over in his hand and looks at the screen. His mouth twitches. Disgust? Disapproval? It's hard to read his expression.

"From a Gareth, miss," he says, his tone dry as he reads it aloud. "Nice pussy."

The blood rushes up into my face, my cheeks burning, before it seeps away, leaving me colder than before, pale in the bright lights of my flat. It's never looked like this before, like someone else's home, all my possessions so lovingly assembled looking cheap now, flimsy, worn out, and saggy at the seams.

"The warrant also permits us to search your chambers, miss," another of the police officers says. "We would be entitled just to go there, but we appreciate that might bring some embarrassment. Will you consent to traveling with us and letting us in so that we can carry out the search with the minimum of disruption?"

I look again around my living room, at the ruin that's been wrought in it. If they search chambers, my career is over. Not because of anything they might find, but because the shame of it will destroy me. My home is already wrecked, everywhere the police have touched covered with an invisible layer of slime, as if contaminated by a thousand snails.

"Is this acceptable to you?" he says, and slowly I turn to him.

"Do I have a choice?" I say.

"It would make the process rather more straightforward," he says. "Minimum of fuss. As you can see, our focus is on electronic devices. At this moment."

I laugh, a short, sharp bark that forces its way out of my mouth, deep from the back of my throat. Nothing is funny. "You've got all my devices. I don't have any in chambers. I work on that laptop."

"No desktop computer there, no other tablet that you might access?"

"None. Look, what the hell is this about? Why are you going through all of my phone stuff?"

"Ah, yes. A good point. Will you be prepared to give us the pass-codes to your phone and computer?"

I blink. This is serious. But I have no idea what they're after. I've been sifting through statutes in my mind, trying to remember what Section 67 of the Serious Crime Act is in practice, but I'm still blank.

"It's tricky," I say. "There's communication there from clients, in relation to cases. Privileged material."

"We won't be going through that, miss," he says. "We know what we're after." His mouth snaps shut, as if he's said too much.

"What the hell is it, then?" I say, but that elicits no response. Frustration is building in me, anger at this unwarranted invasion, warranted as it may be. They've come bursting in here at some god-forsaken hour in the morning, treating me as if I'm some common criminal. "What the fuck do you want?"

"So if you're prepared to let us into your chambers so we can check that it's correct that you don't have any devices there, shall we make a move? We can be in and out before anyone else is around," he says, impassive. I could smash a vase over his head, that big one there in the corner, and he'd still have the same impassive look, an automaton behind his eyes.

"This will have to be quick. I'm due in court. And I'll need to get dressed first," I say. There's no point fighting anymore. Not that it's a fight. Just me, raging against a brick wall. He nods, the first indication he's given that he can hear me, and I go through to the bedroom, shutting the door behind me.

"Hold on a second," a voice says from outside. "Please don't shut the door. We haven't finished in there yet."

Now I'm beginning to lose it, the anger I've felt from the start bubbling up. "What do you think I'm going to do? Stick a hidden phone up my cunt?" I fling the door open and rip off my fleece, my vest top too. "There, is that what you wanted to see?"

"Now, miss, there's no need for this," the robot officer says. "Get yourself covered up there and stop making a scene."

It takes all of my self-control not to spit in his eye as he stands, impassive still. The rage disappears as quickly as it came and now I'm drenched in shame, conscious of my seminudity, sweat prickling between my breasts. I dress quickly, jeans and a jumper. It's so early, I'll have time to get back and scrub it all off me before going to court, clean the house and restore it to its normal state.

As soon as I'm dressed, I march to the front door. "Can I drive myself? Or do you want me to come in the van?"

"I think it'll be best if you come in the van," I'm told. "Do you have your keys?"

Such solicitude, from someone who has been systematically violating my space. I go back to the kitchen and take the keys from the kitchen table where I left them last night. I look around for my phone, too, the movement as instinctive as breathing, before I remember. I march out to the van with my head down. While I wait for the door to be opened, I'm struck again by the feeling of rage that overwhelmed me before.

"Yes, I'm going in a police van," I shout out to the street, to anyone who might be watching from behind their lace curtains, their tasteful wooden blinds. "I'm being carried off like some criminal. You just keep watching."

"If you don't calm down, we might have to arrest you," the police officer says and lets me into the van. I slump down against the sticky plastic seat, the smell of sweat and an undertone of vomit thick in the interior. I'm silent as we drive up to chambers, Waterloo Bridge and the river stretching out unseen before me, before they park on a yellow line in Fleet Street.

It's still not seven o'clock and there's no one around, the alleyways and squares of Inner Temple empty of the usual traffic of men in dark suits and boys pushing trolleys of papers around. I unlock the door of chambers and enter the code into the keypad by the entrance. We walk past the clerks' room, and one of the officers sticks his head through the doors.

"Lots of computers here," he says.

"I don't have access to them," I say. "This isn't the room I work in."

"Right."

They follow me up two flights of stairs to my room at the end of the corridor. I turn on the light and stand back to let them in, thankful to my core that I don't share the space with anyone else. The men work their way through my desk efficiently, this time causing no disruption, putting everything back in the place where it had been found. As I said, there are no devices there, though they linger over a small pile of photographs on the desk.

"They're part of a brief," I say. "A GBH I'm defending. It's the site visit." I shut myself up. They don't care, but my nerves are strung so tight, jangling so loudly I'm amazed the police can't hear them.

They search for a few minutes more and then they're done.

"Are you going to tell me what this is about?" I say again.

"We'll be in touch," the officer in charge says. "Don't go away anywhere, just in case. We'd like to know where you are."

They walk out of the room, their footsteps fading away as they go back down the stairs. But the robot officer comes back, sticking his head round the door.

"Your passcodes, miss? We can make an application if you refuse, but it would make everyone's life easier if you were just to comply."

I sigh, all fight gone out of me. I pick up a Post-it note and scrawl the codes down for him, practically throwing the paper at him. He picks it up, examines it, folds it, and puts it in his pocket before leaving without saying any more. I don't follow, don't offer to show them out. I'm exhausted, wrung out by the strangeness of it all, the invasion. Unlike at home, they've left nothing to show they were here, the piles of papers on my desk still as tidy as they were before.

I'm still clutching the original warrant in my hand. Section 67 of the Serious Crime Act, 2015. It's time to look it up, see if it gives me any clearer idea of what the fuck this is all about. There's an old copy of *Archbold* on the shelf, a couple of years out of date, but I don't think that'll matter. Taking a deep breath, I turn to the index and look up the page number.

Once I have it, I pause for a moment. I'm filled again with dread, a foreboding that what I'm about to see, the offense of which I'm accused, at least sufficient to justify the granting of a search warrant, will be something that, once seen, I'll never be able to unsee. That once I've read it, it's going to set off a chain of events that will take me somewhere out beyond all control. This is the point at which if I were sleeping, I would force myself awake from the nightmare. But this is no sleep, and the nightmare is real.

I open the page, read. Close it again, gently, gently. Too much is broken already. It's what I had known from the start, the only reason they would be behaving like this. Sexual communication with a child. I'm suspected of sending sexual material of some sort to a child.

Horror takes hold and sinks me back into the chair, keeps me immobile. My mind is racing but it has nowhere to go. I don't know any children. I haven't sent any sexual material. Nothing of the sort.

But then a thought strikes me. In my mind's eye, I see Philip's face, flushed with fury, leering from the dock as Liam gave his damning evidence. Surely, though, it can't be. There's no way anything like that is even possible. Then I think about the way he turned, glaring at me, and deep dread strikes me down.

26

I don't know how long I sit in my room, head in hands. My life at the bar has flashed past me: the first days of learning about law, suppressed giggles at the case of *R v. Brown*, Operation Spanner, in which it was held that you couldn't give consent for someone else to nail your foreskin to a board. The pride of being called to the bar. The first time of wearing a wig, the scratchy feel of it a triumph, not a chore. First magistrates' court trial, first Crown Court mention. First time on my feet without a pupil supervisor close on my tail. First robbery, rape. First junior brief on a murder. First time to send someone to jail.

Now this. Facing jail myself, for all I know. For the first time, I start properly to understand how my clients might feel. My belief in the system being fundamentally fair has just taken a knock. With a growing sense of shame I begin to understand the privilege under which I've operated all my life, the benefits that have accrued to me simply as a matter of birth, class, race. I'm used to being in control, having an answer to every question, a solution to every problem. Now, it's out of my hands. I have no idea what I'm meant to have done, what's been alleged against me. Who's made the allegation.

It's crumbling to dust around me. A morning raid, my electronics seized, my house violated. I hug my arms close around me. The adrenaline is wearing off now and my hands are shaking, tremors running through my whole body. I know I should go home, tidy it up. But I sit as though fixed to the spot, my feet stuck to the floor, gravity too heavy for me.

People are beginning to arrive in chambers now. I can hear voices, footsteps, the sound of the front door opening and closing. There's a scent of coffee on the air, a crashing of scaffolding from the renovations on the building next door. The sun is fully up now, the sky a bright, beautiful blue, the kind of blue that normally allays all fear, calms me. I should be walking through Temple Gardens down to the Thames, to cross the river and stroll along the South Bank.

I inhale slowly, exhale, trying to bring myself under some sort of control, calm the tremors in my hands. I need to get home. After a few moments, I'm ready, and I push myself up to my feet as slowly as if I were eighty, my knees weak, my legs trembling beneath me. I'm about to leave my room when I hear a loud bellowing from the clerks' room.

"If she's here, I bloody well want to see her right now," a man is shouting, his accent cut-glass even if shaking with anger. "I've never heard of anything so disgraceful."

"We haven't seen her come in this morning, sir," one of the junior clerks says. I'm too shaken to work out which, or who is doing the shouting. I don't even know for sure that it has anything to do with me, but at the same time, it seems entirely clear that it must.

"I want to see that Munro woman right now," the man shouts again, and any tiny doubt that might have remained goes. Of course it's me. "You go check upstairs right now, my good man, and tell her to get the *fuck* down here *now* before I tell the whole building what she's been getting up to with my client."

I hear footsteps up the stairs, the gait hesitant, heavy. It's

Matthew the senior clerk—I'd recognize his step anywhere. His face appears around the side of my door, blank with astonishment at the situation. He opens his mouth to speak but I put my hand up to stop him.

"It's OK," I say. "I heard the shouting."

"It's Mr. Lamb," he says. "The QC. He seems quite anxious to see you."

I almost laugh at the euphemism. I don't, though. This situation isn't Matthew's fault. He hasn't asked for his chambers to be searched by the police, for one of his tenants to be treated as a prospective criminal.

"It's OK," I say again. "I'll come down." I stand up, and now gravity has stopped pulling at me. My feet are light, my body too, moving without me in it, as I float somewhere up to the ceiling, watching it all play out underneath me. This is all too much for me to cope with while fully present. I'm aware vaguely of the disassociation. I don't care. Whatever it takes to get me through this encounter. At least it might take me closer to the truth of what's happened.

I get to the bottom of the stairs to be greeted by David Lamb, his face puce. He'd looked pissed off enough times the week before when we were dealing with the youth court trial. Now he looks as if he might explode, his face is so suffused with blood.

"What the *fuck* do you think you're doing? Propositioning my client in a restaurant toilet? Sending him pornographic images? He's *fifteen years old*."

I can't believe what I'm hearing. I remember when I saw Philip on the stairs going down to the toilets in the restaurant. We didn't even brush arms with each other as we passed. He's lying. But the photographs… The police wouldn't have taken the steps they've taken if there weren't something. I'm being set up… I can't look at David. I focus instead on Matthew's face, before looking quickly away. His mouth is open, his eyes wide, his whole demeanor one of shock and outrage.

"You can't just barge in here accusing Miss Munro of something like this," he says, and I feel a momentary flicker of warmth against the chill I've felt since the early morning.

"I can and what's more, I bloody well will," David says, spittle flying out of his mouth and landing on Matthew's jacket collar. I want to reach out and wipe it off with my sleeve, but I'm frozen to the spot. "I've seen the photos. I tell you, I've never been more shocked in my life."

"I have no idea what you're talking about," I finally manage to say, the words grating, my mouth dry.

"Come off it," David says. He looks straight at me and I quail at the blaze of fury in his eyes, bulging blue irises, red-rimmed. "I don't know where the fuck you get off, sending that, that *filth* to my client. He's just a child."

"I didn't," I say. "I have no interest in your client. Why on earth would I send pornographic photographs to him?"

"You tell me," he says. "You tell me. I can't begin to fathom it. And not just pornographic photographs, pornographic photos of yourself." He looks me up and down, his face rigid with revulsion. "You should be ashamed of yourself."

"Um, Miss Munro, do you know what Mr. Lamb is referring to?" Matthew says. He won't look straight at me.

"I don't know," I say. "I don't understand what's happening at all. Maybe it's some kind of fake? Mocked-up photos with my face on them?"

Lamb shakes his head, a deliberate movement left to right, back to left. "Believe me, what I saw was no fake, Sylvie. How could you? The family is distraught. It's destroyed the whole trial. It's made a mockery of everything." He steps back, suddenly pale, and sits down abruptly on one of the chairs in the hallway. After taking a moment to compose himself, he looks straight through me.

"It was me who called the police, Sylvie. I'm making a formal complaint to the Bar Council this morning. I've informed the other representatives in the trial, too. The prosecution will have no option but to give it up and go for a retrial with a proper judge. Not a shit show like you. You should be suspended until this matter is concluded. Even if there's no suspension, you need to take yourself home and stay there. You have no right to represent any client right now, let alone sit in judgment upon anyone."

With that, he stands up and leaves. Matthew is silent. All I can hear is the hammering of my heart in my ears, my vision blurred. David is right. While this is hanging over me, I can't possibly continue to work. But without work, what do I have? I slump down in the same chair that he's vacated, putting my head down between my knees as a roaring sound threatens to engulf me.

"Miss Munro," Matthew says, hesitation in his tone. Deep concern, too. He does not stand close to me, though, nor extend a hand of comfort. "I'm going to have to let the head of chambers know about this." He's hiding behind formality. I know without looking that he's pulling himself up, straightening his shoulders and puffing up his chest in the way that he does when he has to face down truculent solicitors. I want to argue with him, try to reassure him that it's a load of bollocks, that a moment's investigation will clarify that I haven't done anything wrong. I know it's pointless, though. I get to my feet and, without looking at him, walk out of the building and away, trying to keep myself together at least until I'm out of Temple, away from any further audience to my humiliation.

Somehow, I manage to take myself down to the river. I don't run into anyone I know, and after some long minutes spent leaning against the wall by the side of the Thames, I'm calm enough to know that if I'm going to cry, it's not going to be yet. It's time to sort myself out, or at least to try to find out what the hell is happening. Without a phone, that won't be possible, so I need to get a new one fast. The thought stirs at the back of my mind that perhaps I shouldn't be accessing my online accounts, but I dismiss it. I haven't been arrested, I'm only under investigation, and they may not even charge me.

I'm calmer now. I know that I've done nothing wrong, so there will be nothing for them to find. This is a misunderstanding. A grim, damaging misunderstanding, but a misunderstanding nonetheless. It will all be OK. Thus comforted (even though I don't really believe my self-soothing words), I head for Fleet Street to buy a new phone and a replacement SIM card.

27

It's almost eleven by the time I've sorted out a new, basic iPhone and installed my email. I sit in a café near Ludgate Circus and go through it all. There's the usual spam and a message from the head of chambers, confirming that he's been made aware that very serious allegations have been made against me, and that while he's sure that I will clear my name entirely, in the meantime he is appealing to my good judgment to take myself out of practice "just for a few weeks until all this is resolved. We will be happy to take care of everything for you."

A few weeks. I think about the trials I have coming up in my diary. There's a particularly juicy attempted murder that I've been looking forward to. I'll bet they'll be happy to take care of everything. When I come back to work eventually, I'll find my practice stripped bare. But I can't even think about that now, not when the trial I've been presiding over lies in ruins. Liam's face flashes into my mind, the determined bravery of it as he told his truth, and I sink my head, weighed down with concern and fury. There's no way they'll get Ryan back to give evidence for a second time. Liam will lose his nerve… He'll think the system has betrayed him completely. Philip is going to get away with it scot-free. I just hope they let Daniel out in the meantime. It's such a fucking mess.

Fuck's sake. What about Gareth? It's the first time I've dared to think about him since they ripped me from sleep this morning. I don't know what to say to him, how even to raise it. *Hey, they're investigating me for sending nudes to a minor, but it's a pack of lies.* I select his number, poise my finger ready to call him, but I know I can't. Not yet.

Nude photographs. My thoughts stumble. There is someone who has taken nude photographs of me, who's seen me naked on their screen. Gareth. I sit, motionless, horror trickling cold through my veins. Then the espresso machine in the corner bangs and emits a huge head of steam. The noise brings me back down to earth. I'm being ridiculous.

The Facebook app has downloaded while I've been neuroticizing over Gareth, so instead I open it and enter my log-in details. It opens, showing that I've had some more friend requests: Gareth, a few more colleagues. Someone from primary school.

I can't deal with it now. I'll decide later whether to accept his request. This is why I've eschewed social media all my life. I've no desire whatsoever to have all the pieces of my past fit together into some sort of accusatory jigsaw puzzle, accessible at the touch of a button.

Right on cue, a message notification pops up. I go to the Messenger app and once it's verified it's me, I see who has sent the message. Linda. I open it and it's a paragraph of text. Before I read it, I look around me in the café, nerves back on edge again. There's no one behind me—I deliberately chose a seat with my back to the wall—and no one to my left or right. Resisting the urge to swipe on it, delete it, as if that would make it all disappear, Linda cease to exist, instead I focus on it properly, moving the text up the screen slowly as I read.

You still haven't answered my question. What do you want? I can still see you standing there, you and Tess, thick as thieves as you screwed my life up. Tess was lying through her teeth. Or you were. One of you, both of you. You could have been brave, Sylvie. You could have told the truth. But you never had the balls. Why are you hassling me now?

I sit, chewing the inside of my lip. The urge to delete is still overwhelming. But I've promised Tess. She wants to resolve this.

It's because of Tess. She has cancer. She wanted me to find you, see if there was some way of moving forward from everything that happened. It's been on her mind. We're still best friends, and I promised to help her.

I hit Send. The time that it takes for the message to be read seems to stretch out for eternity, the gray dots hovering on the screen. Finally, a reply.

We all have shit to deal with. Leave me the fuck alone. If you don't…well, I've looked you up. I've seen you're a lawyer now. Would they be pleased to know that you committed perjury?

I drop the phone onto the table, my fingers cold. Another potential complaint, when I'm already in this situation? I don't know anyone whose reputation could withstand that. The false confidence with which I'd boosted myself earlier ebbs away. It's over. Between this and the allegations of the morning, I feel crushed in a vice.

My coffee's cold now and the waiter is glaring at me as a queue for seats forms. It's nearly lunchtime. I drain what's left in one gulp and walk out, head held high, but the moment that I'm out of sight, I slump down against a wall. I don't know what to do. I don't know where to go. I mean, I should go home, but the idea of facing the mess defeats me.

Tess. I'll go and see Tess. She'll help me make sense of all this. She's always been good at calming situations down. She'll tell me I have nothing to worry about, and she'll agree to drop all this Linda business now that she can see that no good is going to come from it. I start walking toward the bus stop in the direction of her house in Islington, my steps breaking into a run. Tess will make everything better, just like she always has.

She makes me a cup of tea while I sit at the table in her pristine kitchen, words flowing from me without pause. All the horror of the morning, the shame of it, the feeling of helplessness. She puts the tea in front of me, sits opposite me, her fingers laced tightly together, her face blank, unreadable. After a while I realize she's made no sound, no noise of sympathy or encouragement.

"Are you all right?" I say. "I'm sorry, I haven't even asked how you are."

"Not really," she says. "I saw the specialist last week."

"You didn't tell me."

"I'm telling you now. It's not good, Sylvie. It's inoperable."

All my petty troubles fall away, washed away by shame that I could burden her with such meaningless bullshit when she's facing something so huge.

"What do you mean, inoperable?"

"Exactly that," she says. "It's in too deep. It's not very big, but they don't like the look of it at all. They're worried that the effects of surgery would be so dangerous that it's not worth the risk. They're going to watch and wait, that's what they call it. I'll have to have a scan every two months so they can see how it's progressing."

"I can't believe there's nothing they can do," I say.

Her head is bowed. She's plucking at the sleeve of her jumper, pleating it over and over again. At this she looks up, her eyes like pebbles. "They're not saying it, not in as many words. They aren't saying I don't have long left. But the oncologist. He looked so sad. Before I left, he said really gently that if there was anything I'd ever wanted to do, anything at all, now was the time to do it."

"What did he mean?" I say, stupid in shock.

She shakes her head, a ghost of a smile touching her lips. "Oh, Sylvie. You know what he meant." She reaches over the table and grabs my wrist, her fingers tight. "That's why it's so important to me that we sort out the Linda situation."

Linda. Yes. Of course. I'd hoped we could leave the subject behind. I should never have underestimated Tess's tenacity, though.

"She's made contact," I say. "But I don't think she's very happy to hear from me."

Silence from Tess. I look over at her before jumping up in shock. It's like what happened the time before, the seizure that she suffered. But this time she's fallen awkwardly on the floor, bashing her head on the corner of the table as she's gone down. There's a trickle of blood seeping across her forehead. As before, I clear the space around her, pushing the table away from her and the chair, too.

Again like last time, it's over in less than a minute, but again, not before she's lost control of her bladder. Once the seizure subsides, I lean down beside her, pulling her into my arms.

"I'm sorry, Tess. I'm so sorry," I say. "Are you OK?"

She blinks up at me, groggy. "What's happened? Have I had another seizure?"

I nod. "Yes, you did. Can you sit up? Your head is bleeding."

Slowly, she maneuvers herself up, leaning against me. I can feel her pee seeping into my tracksuit bottoms, her back warm against me. She puts her hand up to her head and dabs at the blood, holding her fingers up in front of her afterward, staring at the viscous stain.

"I should get you to bed," I say. "You shouldn't keep sitting on the floor. Do you need to speak to your doctor?"

After a moment Tess turns to me, blinking. "I don't need to," she says. "They warned me that this might keep happening until the new medication kicks in. They've given me something that helps to control them, though it'll take a while to kick in. Lev…levetisomething. I can't remember the name now."

"Glad they've got you on something that might help, anyway," I say. "Now come on. Let's get you upstairs and changed. Would you like to have a shower?"

The pee is starting to smell. I can feel it cooling now, the sodden material clinging clammy to my leg as I stand up. Tess leans on me heavily, and I walk with her upstairs to the bathroom. She slumps down on the side of the bath and I turn on the shower, holding my hand underneath the stream of water to check that it's warmed up.

Once it's hot, I turn to Tess. She's stripped off, standing naked in the middle of the pile of her clothes. I don't mean to, but I start in surprise. She's very upright, her chin raised, as if she's defying something. I haven't seen her naked since we were in our teens, but now I can't look away. Her stomach is flat, unmarked, her limbs lithe. I've got more stretch marks than she has. Our gazes meet and for a moment we lock eyes before I realize that I've sucked in my tummy and I'm holding my breath. I move away from the shower, breathing out as slowly as I can so that it's not obvious that I've been holding in my gut.

She moves past me into the shower. "Can you stay in here with me, Sylvie? I'm just worried in case it happens again and I hit my head."

"Sure, yes," I say. I really don't want to be in here anymore, too conscious now of my appearance in comparison to hers, the hours I haven't spent working out, but I catch myself. I might be feeling defensive, but it's not some competition. Tess is desperately ill, not flaunting her physical perfection in front of me.

I sit down on the bath while she showers, looking anywhere but at the shower cubicle, pulling the damp material of my joggers away from my leg.

"Can I have a towel, please?" Tess says, and I go to the towel rail and give her the towel, handing it over still without looking at her. She makes her way out slowly, and I follow her into her bedroom where she dresses in clean clothes, slowly, her movements almost languorous.

"What were you saying? Before, I mean? Did you say something about Linda?" Tess finally says once she's fully dressed and rubbing at her wet hair with her towel.

"I did, yes. I found her on Facebook, sent her a message. She got back to me."

"How does she sound?"

"Angry. Really, really angry."

"In what way?"

"In an angry way," I say, irritated with Tess's questioning despite my concern for her. "She said you were lying, asked why I had backed you up. She says we knew what we saw."

Tess puts down the towel and picks up a comb, running it through her hair in a slow, deliberate way before she answers. "It was all so confusing."

"That's what I was going to tell her," I say, my words rushing out of me.

Tess looks over at me, her eyes piercing through me. "I was so sure for years that I didn't see Stewart lunge at her. The more I think about it, though, the more unsure I am. I can't even remember where you were when she hit him. I'm so scared we got it all wrong. We were both hammered. How could we be so certain that she attacked him unprovoked?"

I'm frozen to the floor. "You were sure at the time. That's why I backed you up."

She ignores what I've said. "It's been bothering me so much. Even worse, what we said to Stewart beforehand. That preys on my mind."

I don't know what to say for a moment. I'm completely winded. Finally, I get my breath back under control. "Why are you doing this, Tess? I don't understand. I thought we'd left it all behind forever."

"Sylvie, Sylvie." Her voice is a caress. "The chances are, I'm going to die pretty soon. It's just, the more I think about it, the worse it seems that we lied all those years ago. We protected ourselves instead of backing her up, and I can't forgive myself for that. If you're honest with yourself, I bet you can't forgive yourself, either."

My jaw is clenched shut. I don't dare reply. She continues talking.

"I know you've done your best to do the right thing over these last years, but I also know how important it is that people are honest. I'm not meaning to sound preachy, but I'm bothered about your application to become a judge. I think we committed perjury and it's really worrying me."

Something's stirring inside me, breaking through the shock. It's white-hot, searing. It's rage. Tess has always been jealous of my career, the way I succeeded where she failed. Her support has always been lukewarm, her resentment of my work conversations with Marcus palpable in the way she always tries to change the subject. Now I understand. Underneath all the talk of making amends and finding closure, I can see the truth. She's setting me up somehow, trying to fuck with my head in the way that only Tess can do.

But then I look at the cut on her head, I smell the whiff of her urine from my clothes and the rage subsides. She's facing something bigger than I can possibly comprehend. Sure, it might make no sense that she's decided to fixate on all this now, but who's to say how someone reacts, given a serious diagnosis of illness. I might have put Linda out of my mind, packed it all away from the moment that I left Edinburgh. But I can see it's important to Tess.

"What do you want to do?" I say in the end.

"Confess to Linda. Tell her we were protecting ourselves. Protecting Stewart, too."

I take a deep breath. "I understand how strongly you feel," I say, "but I'm really worried about this. Not just for my own sake, but for yours. It's not just that we didn't back her up in court, didn't confirm that Stewart had lunged at her and wasn't letting go. It's why he did it. What he thought. Is that really something we want to go into? Could you handle that coming out?"

She nods her head. "However bad, it would make me feel so much better, knowing that it was all out in the open," Tess says. "This is going to be so hard to deal with as it is, without having that hanging over me."

I want to say that I don't understand why it should be hanging over her. It's not like it's her future that's at stake. She'll feel better about herself, that's all. My career will be in ruins. But I know what Tess's conscience is like, a slumbering beast, slow to rouse, but unstoppable in its fury once it's fully stirred. It is inarguable that without our testimony, Linda might have been cleared, the verdict at worst not proven. By saying we didn't think we'd seen Stewart touch her, it ruined her claims of self-defense, made it look like an unprovoked attack. I do understand it.

Tess is beginning to look more and more distressed. I can't bear the idea that I might drive her to another seizure. I know how much she already has to deal with, and I'm overcome now with guilt that I've added to that.

"I'll speak to her," I say. "I'll tell her what we did. Why we did it."

"You do that," Tess says. "Do it fast. We don't have much time."

"I promise." With that, I leave.

But as I walk away from her house, Marcus's words come back to me.

Maybe this whole brain tumor story is a lie...

I shake my head, keep walking. The thought doesn't leave me, though, a little smear of mud across an unmarked screen. Along with the doubt still lurking in the back of my mind. I thought Gareth was safe. But maybe he's not what he seems, either.

28

Time's done something strange. It's stretched, curled round itself. I can't get a handle on it, days merging. Without work, I'm a paragraph without punctuation, the words running over into each other without an end in sight. I give no one my new number; no one calls my landline. Not that anyone has for years. I sent one message to Linda, right after leaving Tess's that afternoon, the one that seems now so far away. Only a few words.

I need to tell you something. You're right—we lied. I'm sorry.

I sent it, then deleted the app from the phone. I can't bear to look again to see what reply she might have sent. Just as I can't bear to log into my email, or check in at chambers, see if anyone has left any messages for me. They've taken my diary, my cases; they can deal with any issues that might arise. I've got nothing to add.

I sit in my flat, night blurring into day and back to night again. I scavenge from the fridge, the back of the freezer. Even the old packs of noodles that have been sitting there for years. I can't bear the idea of walking into a shop for fresh food, dealing with people. Or daylight. I don't want anyone to see me. I can't face running into someone I know, trying to make idle chitchat, *Fine, yes, you? Not so good, under investigation for sending indecent images to a child.* Not the way the conversation should go.

The mess is still where the police left it, the piles of clothes from the drawers that they emptied, the papers strewn across the floor. I can't bring myself to tidy up. I can't bring myself to wash, to change my clothes. I'm slowly putrefying in the dark of my flat, the blinds shut at all hours. The doorbell rings occasionally but I ignore it, pushing the missed delivery cards to one side when I go out occasionally for walks at the dead of night.

The only way that I mark time is watching box sets, all the series I've meant to watch for years, never had time. *The Wire, The Sopranos, The Deuce*, segue to the Godfather films. I even manage *The Seventh Seal,* Death playing chess almost a welcome diversion from my bounded reality. The nightmare isn't a dream. I'm not going to wake up from it because it's here already, pressing down on me. Even if all this bullshit about Philip is resolved, there's still the truth of the matter with Linda.

*If it's the truth...*I'm not listening to the doubts Marcus has seeded in my ear. Of course it's what he'd want to think.

And the matter of what lies behind that, too. I'm not going to think about that, though it stalks my dreams.

Good as I am at ignoring the doorbell, this time I can't. Someone's leaning on it. It's been going for at least ten minutes, and while I thought it would get easier to tune it out as it kept going, it hasn't. It's gotten louder and louder in my head, building up to a crescendo of noise that's threatening to burst my head open. The bell is going continuously and the person is thumping now on the door, an angry noise, and I can't deal with it any more, I want it to stop because it hurts, everything hurts. I get up from the sofa where I've been sitting for the hours and stagger to the door, flinching from the sunlight that streams through once I open it.

It's so bright and I'm so dazzled by the glare after all those hours spent sitting in the dark that I can't tell who it is that's making all the noise. A figure stands against the sunlight before a voice says "Sylvie," and now I know. It's Gareth. I shrink back inside.

He pushes past me into the flat, stopping and looking around him as if in disgust or confusion.

"It's after twelve, Sylvie. Why are you still in the dark? It stinks in here."

He opens the blinds, and even though it's cold, the beginnings of winter, he pushes the windows up, too, as far as they'll go before they hit the locks. A gust of crisp air blows through the room, cutting through the fug of stale sweat and old food.

"Jesus, what the fuck is going on? I've been trying to get hold of you for days," he says.

Days. I guess it has been. Blinking still in the light, I shuffle back to the corner of the sofa in which I've been nestled and curl my feet back under me, wrapping myself in the blanket that's stiffened into place around me, it's been left unshaken and festering for so long. Gareth sits down next to me, but not too close. I can see his nose twitching. I know I smell, but I've become inured to it. I'm still in the same tracksuit bottoms I wore to Tess's house, her urine still ingrained in them.

"Sylvie, seriously. What the hell is happening? Your phone goes straight to voicemail, and you're not replying to emails. You haven't looked at Facebook for days. I don't have a landline number for you."

"No one uses their landline," I interrupt.

He pays no attention. "Your chambers said you were on an

extended leave of absence. I ran out of options to find you. So I came down. I was coming anyway to meet your friend Tess, finalize the arrangements for her party at New Year. I've been really worried about you."

"I'm fine," I say, though I know it's pathetic to try to pretend. Obviously, I'm not fine. I'm very far from fine.

"Are you going to tell me what's going on?"

"It's…it's really difficult. I don't even know. But the police…the police think that I…" I'm trying to speak, but putting it into words is hard, so hard. I haven't spoken to anyone for the best part of a week and my tongue feels swollen now, stuck to the roof of my mouth, my throat like sandpaper.

"What do the police think?"

"They think I sent indecent photos to a child. And that I made a pass at him," I say, rushing the words out so that I don't have to hear them, and without any warning, tears spring out of my eyes and I start to sob, great raucous noises bursting from me, snot streaming out of my nose. Gareth makes no move to comfort me but sits, watching me, though it takes me some time to realize that he's at such a remove from me.

Eventually my tears subside. "I'm sorry, it's been a really bad week," I say.

"Why do the police think that?" he says.

I can't ignore his distance anymore. It's almost palpable. "I don't know. They haven't given me any information. They've taken all my devices and searched the flat. That's why it's such a mess."

"Have they charged you?"

"No, they haven't. As I said, I don't know what's going on." I'm curling up tighter and tighter in my corner, bewildered at the tone of his voice, the edge that's emerging. "Do you think it's something I'd do, Gareth? Do you seriously think I'd send dirty photos to a fifteen-year-old defendant in one of the trials I'm presiding over? Don't you know me any better than that?"

"I'm beginning to think I don't know you at all."

His contempt stirs something up in me, a smolder of anger. "You're the only person who has any nude photos of me, Gareth. How do I know it wasn't you?"

His face goes completely still. I don't dare meet his eyes in case I turn to stone.

"I'm sorry…" I can't finish the sentence. This is all wrong, very, very wrong. "Of course I didn't do it. Or you. Someone is setting me up. Most likely the defendant himself, or one of his friends."

Gareth's face relaxes, only by a tiny amount, a shift at one corner of his mouth perhaps a tiny sign that he's hearing what I'm saying. He uncrosses his legs and crosses them again, but this time his foot is pointing in my direction, his torso too, even if his head is still averted somewhat. He might be listening.

I press on. "Believe me, I've done nothing but think about this. I've sat here for hours and hours, trying to work it out. Between this and Linda—"

"What about Linda?"

"I told her I lied," I say. "It was the last message I sent before I turned my phone off."

"What did she say?"

"I don't know," I say. "I'm too scared to find out. I'm too scared to do anything. I don't know what's going to happen to me, Gareth, I really don't. I don't understand how any of this happened."

I start to cry again, quieter this time but no less impassioned, and this time I feel Gareth's hand on my shoulder, his arm round me, and I sob into his chest until I've exhausted all the tears I have left to cry.

After a while, Gareth gets up and starts to tidy. Now that I've calmed down, I'm conscious of how rancid my clothes are, how greasy my hair is. I need to have a shower. It's too shaming to be like this with Gareth here, all clean and smelling of shampoo and aftershave.

"I must wash," I say.

"You're not kidding," he says. "How long has it been anyway?"

"I'm not sure. What day is it today?"

"You really don't know? It's Saturday. Saturday lunchtime. I'm going to meet your friend late afternoon. We don't have much time left to decide what she wants for this party. I don't even know how many people are coming."

I shrug. "She hasn't told me that detail yet. I just know what I have to wear."

"What is it?"

"The fucking awful bridesmaid dress that she put me in twenty years ago. I look like shit in it."

"Can't wait to see that," he says.

The surge of energy I'd felt subsides. "That's if she still wants me," I say. "She seemed pretty pissed off with me when I saw her at the beginning of the week."

Gareth comes over and puts his arm around me again. The fact that he's not completely repelled by my stench is warming.

"Look, babe, she's worried about you. That's what she said to me when we talked earlier this week about the catering. She said she couldn't get hold of you."

"She's got my landline," I say, going over to the red phone in the corner that's encrusted with dust, it's been so long since I've used it. But when I pick it up, there's no ring tone.

"See? No way of getting hold of you, short of breaking your door down," Gareth says. "She's probably not well enough for that, either."

Shame eats into me, gnawing into my stomach. I remember how she looked when I left her house.

"Why don't you come with me?" Gareth says. "Once you've decontaminated yourself."

I nod, go to the shower and wash off the last days. For a flicker of a moment, I hope that Gareth will join me, but I quash it immediately. I'm lucky he's still speaking to me, let alone trying to shag me. Would I be as tolerant if he were accused of molesting a minor?

Soon I'm out of the shower and dressed in clean clothes, the jeans uncomfortable after days of wearing my jogging bottoms. I brush through my hair and pick up the dirty clothes, ramming them into the washing machine along with the solidified blanket, putting it all onto a hot wash.

"You look more human now," Gareth says.

"I feel more human. Thank you for sorting out the flat, too," I say, gesturing around at the space that he's tidied, almost transformed back to how it ought to be.

"That's OK. I couldn't leave it like this. Look, can you at least give me your new number? I want to be able to get hold of you. I won't call if you don't want me to, I promise. I want you to be able to get hold of me, too. If there's a problem."

I nearly laugh. There's nothing but problems. I nod, switching on the new phone that I've barely used. I take down the number he dictates to me, the one entry in my Contacts, and text him a blank message so that at least he has it. He nods, pleased, as he saves it to his own device.

"Why don't you come here and give me a proper welcome?" Gareth says after he's finished with his phone, holding his arms out to me. I go over and we start to kiss, tentative at first, but increasingly passionate. His hand is on my breast, mine at his throat, when the doorbell rings.

"Ignore it," he groans, and I want to, but as when he rang, it goes on and on, not letting up at all, followed by a heavy thumping.

"I don't think I can," I say, and I walk to the door, slowly, deliberately, because I know who's there, and I know what's going to happen. The urgency of that summons can mean only one thing.

29

Sylvie Munro, I am arresting you on suspicion of indecent assault of a boy aged fifteen contrary to Section 3 of the Sexual Offenses Act 2003 and on suspicion of sexual communications with a child, contrary to Section 67 of the Serious Crimes Act 2015.

I don't turn to look at Gareth. I can't bear to see the look in his eye, the disappointment, the horror, before he withdraws from me entirely. I nod, letting the police lead me out of my flat, take me to the car. I dip my head automatically as I get in, leaning my head against the glass as they drive me to the police station at Kennington, process me at the custody suite before putting me in a cell to wait for interview.

You do not have to say anything, but it may harm your defense if you do not mention anything you later rely on in court.

It wasn't me. I didn't do it. Someone's setting me up. All the defenses I've ever put forward on behalf of my clients, my skepticism growing with each denial. Now I'm one of them.

Anything you do say may be given in evidence.

I told Gareth to call Lola Adebayo, one of my best instructing solicitors, but when I arrive at the station, I decide I'd better do it myself to ensure she gets the message. He wasn't looking as if he was registering fully what I was saying, that's for sure. I put my one call in to her and she agrees immediately to come, though she doesn't know how long it'll take for her to get there.

I sit and wait in the cell, strangely calm. I know it can't last. I know I'm facing the destruction of everything I've worked so hard for, that even if I don't end up in court, it will be permanently on my record that I've been charged with something as vile as this. It's almost laughable that anyone could believe that I would demean myself to this extent. But not laughable enough.

She doesn't arrive for nearly two hours, by which time I'm fully acquainted with every crack and chip of paint in the cell. They've taken my new phone off me as well, and I didn't have the sense to bring anything to read with me. I'm bored, bored and tense, my spiking adrenaline calmed a little by the wait but only superficially. I know the moment there's any action it'll go through the roof again.

I've been in police stations on and off over the years. This very one, about fifteen years ago. Ironically enough, to view some indecent images of children in a magazine that had been found in my then-client's house. The photographs were so appalling they had to be kept under lock and key. *I'm a mother*, the police officer had said repeatedly, as if only by having children of one's own could one understand fully the horror of the images. I didn't need to be a mother to see how awful they were. It's sickening that I should be accused of anything remotely similar now.

They were kinder to me when I was a child. Seventeen, sweet and innocent, my eyes wide as the police officers asked me gently what had happened. What I'd seen. They watched me like a hawk, but I kept my voice low, my head bent lower. I wish I were back there now. The problems then seemed insurmountable. I thought this was the worst life could throw at me.

I know better now.

The minute Lola is let into my cell, I nearly jump on her but I restrain myself, just as she restrains her reaction, too, almost hiding the shock in her eyes at my appearance. Normally I'm slick, hair tied back, suit sharp. Now I look like I've been dragged through a hedge backward. I didn't even have a chance to dry my hair before they took me away, though I'm grateful that Gareth had made me wash. My armpits are prickling with sweat, though, and smelling the aromatic perfume that Lola is wearing, I'm reminded now that I didn't put deodorant on. I might be clean, but it won't be long before I'm stinking like a polecat again.

"We don't have long," she says. "We need to come up with a plan."

After some discussion we decide that the best approach is for Lola to read out a statement on my behalf in advance of the interview, and I will then answer no comment to all questions.

"We need to put them to proof," she says. "If you don't have any explanation for what's happening."

"None whatsoever," I say. "I walked past the boy on the stairs in a restaurant. We didn't touch as we passed. We didn't even make eye contact. As far as the photos are concerned, I have no idea what they're talking about."

Lola nods. "There's no way that anyone could have accessed nude photographs of you?"

For a split second Gareth's face flashes before me. I blink, hard, willing it away. "Lola!" I say, sitting on my hands. "What do you take me for?"

"Look, it's blatantly ridiculous. Of course you've not been sending nudes of yourself to some schoolboy. I have to ask the questions, though. You know this."

"Of course. I understand."

I thought it was almost laughable, before. No one is laughing now, no one at all, after Lola has finished reading out the statement we've prepared together in which I deny any allegation whatsoever that I have ever touched a fifteen-year-old or sent him any indecent images or words, and that the only explanation can be that the story has been manufactured because he resents the decisions that I've taken in the course of his trial.

Then the interviewing officers show me a series of photographs printed off from the messages folder on Philip's Instagram account. Inappropriate as it might be, my first reaction is one of relief. They're not any of the photos that Gareth has taken. It's nothing to do with him. For a moment I'm almost faint with relief. But then I look again, blanching. They're fakes, but they're horrifically realistic. If I didn't know my own body, I'd think it was me, not just a superimposition of my head onto these images ripped from the internet. It's more like me almost than I am myself—stretch marks, saggy, my unexpurgated self. I look over at Lola, an involuntary movement I immediately want to take back, and she raises an eyebrow. I'm desperate to scream at her that they're not me but I keep myself under control. I stare at her closely, hoping she can see them for the fakes they are.

Terrified she might not.

"You're making a face there, Sylvie," the interviewing officer says. "Do you want to tell us what that expression means?"

Fuck you. "No comment." I grit my teeth.

"Because while I'm no expert, it looked like you recognized yourself in these photos. Am I right?"

"No comment."

Lola holds up her hand. "I'd ask the officer to stick to the questions rather than speculating about the meaning of my client's facial expressions."

"But of course," he says, spreading the photographs out in a fan shape in front of him, the images facing in my direction. "These photographs bear a great resemblance to you, Sylvie, don't they?"

No no no no no. "No comment."

"So much so, that to suggest they're fakes seems deeply improbable, don't you agree?"

Of course they're fucking fake. "No comment."

"Sylvie Munro is shaking her head," the officer says to the recording. "Now, to move on. These images were all contained in messages sent to one Philip Presley on his Instagram account with the username @presleyPhilip. They were found in the message requests folder as the sender was not following Philip who has a private account. In other words, he has to grant permission to a user to follow him. With me so far?"

I nearly forget, say yes. Remember. "No comment."

"So these messages were unsolicited, Philip states. He had no relationship with the sender and had not requested any images of this sort. Yes?"

Of course he fucking hadn't. "No comment."

"On checking his messages folder two weeks ago, while the trial was still ongoing, he saw the first of these messages. He did not recognize the name, but on opening the images, recognized that the naked woman in question was the judge presiding over the trial. He checked the name again, and found it to be @MissSylvieMunro. That's your name, isn't it?"

I'm about to explode. *I've never had a fucking Instagram account in my life.* "No comment." I bite down on my inside lip so hard I taste blood.

"Is this your Instagram account?"

No. "No comment."

"Would anyone else be able to log onto your Instagram account?"

Jaw clenched. "No comment."

"If we go into the settings of this Instagram account, we can see that it's been set up to a Gmail account: sylvie_ munro@gmail.co.uk. Is this your email address?"

No. My nails are dug deep into my palms. Out of the corner of my eye I see Lola twitch, a tiny movement. "No comment."

"I'm looking at your mobile phone now, Sylvie. At the email address that comes up on the Mail screen. Let me read it out to you: sylvie_munro@gmail.co.uk. Do you agree that this is the same email address as that registered to the Instagram account?"

I've never seen it before in my life. "No comment."

"Right. Well. If we can turn again to these photographs, they look as if they've been taken by you by way of a selfie, is that right?"

Lola interrupts again. "No admission has been made as to these photographs being of my client."

"Noted," the officer says.

I try not to look at the pictures. The one nearest the top is a body that isn't mine with breasts that aren't mine squashed together with one arm, the camera held out in the other hand. Not my body, but my face is laughing at the camera.

The image of my face has been taken from one of the three photos I've uploaded to Facebook. Gareth took it, snapping it on his phone as I came out of the bathroom, a towel wrapped round me, my shoulders bare. I'm biting my lip so hard I can taste blood.

"No comment."

"So the implication is clear that the person who has taken these photos is also the one who has sent them to Philip?"

"No comment."

"Or are you able to offer any other explanation as to how they might have made their way onto Philip's phone?"

They're fucking fake. "No comment," I say, but my brain's exploding. The coppers are actually taking this seriously, and it's freaking the hell out of me. I open my mouth, about to protest my innocence, but Lola flicks a glance at me hard as if she'd kicked me on the ankle.

"Something to say, Sylvie?"

I clench my jaw. "No comment."

After a few more passes the officers give up trying to make me cough to it. There's no real air of disappointment or resignation. They must have known before we even came in that I would go no comment.

The interviewing officer piles the photographs up in a heap. As he does so, one of them comes loose, falling out into the middle of the table. It's headless, a woman sitting with her legs open, the camera pointed straight up between them. Pubic hair. Labia. Not mine. He raises an eyebrow.

"No comment."

More questions. They'd searched my phone, my computer. OK, these photos weren't saved in the photo library. But it didn't mean they weren't photos of me. That's their line.

"I'm going to ask you again, Sylvie. Can you offer any reasonable explanation as to how these photographs made their way to Philip's Instagram messages via your Instagram account if it wasn't you who sent them?"

I'm being set up. "No comment."

"Let's move on now," the officer says. "Have you been to Trullo Restaurant in the last month?"

You know perfectly well I have. "No comment."

"You were there at the same time as the complainant, Philip, and his family?"

"No comment."

"His legal representative too?"

You mean his godfather. "No comment."

"And while you were in the restaurant, you went downstairs to the toilet. When you were in the basement, you bumped into Philip as he came out of the gents'?"

"No comment."

"You suggested to him that you could be persuaded to let the trial go a certain way in return for certain favors, and you cupped your hand round his crotch, backing him up against the wall and attempting to kiss him."

My mouth is hanging open. I can't even mouth the words I want to say. I'm stuck in a nightmare.

"It was only when the boy's father came downstairs and shouted that you let go of the victim."

The nightmare's closing in, the walls too. My breaths are becoming shallower, my heart rate elevated.

"I'll read out the statement that's been provided by the victim's father."

What the fuck?

A buzzing in my ears now. I can't hear anymore.

I won't.

"For fuck's sake, there's got to be an explanation," I say to Lola after we leave the police station a couple of hours later. "They're lying. They're all lying."

"You can't prove it, though."

I swing round at her, stopping so suddenly that a woman behind me bashes into me and stumbles onto the pavement before moving past me, telling me to fuck off as she goes.

"It's not up to me to prove anything," I say. "Remember the burden of proof? It's on the prosecution. Yes?" I'm so cross I'm shouting.

Lola pinches the bridge of her nose between finger and thumb. She looks tired. "There's no need to shout at me," she says. "It's not my fault that there's a witness to this. We'll get an expert onto the photographs, at least. If they are fake, we'll be able to ascertain that pretty easily."

If... I want to shout again, but now the words won't come out, drowned in a wave of fear, of shame that washes a red flush from my cheeks down to my chest. Charged. I've been charged. The next time I face that officer, it'll be in court when I make my first appearance to face this.

"Why would I grope some fifteen-year-old? Why the fuck would I want to send naked photos to a child? I told you, they're not of me."

Lola just looks at me. She doesn't reply. She has a look in her eyes that I recognize from defending only too well, the one that says *It's not my job to believe you; it's my job to defend you no matter what.* When I see that, it hits me now properly, smashing through the sense of unreality that has shrouded me from the moment that I was taken to the police station and my fingerprints taken, my mug shot too, as if I were one of my clients.

She doesn't offer to drop me home and I walk back, head down, ramming my way through any groups I encounter on the pavement. It's early December, the shops full of gifts and Christmas lights, but I'm dark inside, oblivious to festivity. One man I run into starts to swear at me but when I turn to him in challenge, he backs off, sensing how little I care. How little I have to lose.

It's gone.

As is Gareth when I get home. His bag is gone, too, and the house is unnaturally tidy, everything put away but in fractionally the wrong place as if it's been tilted, just a little, then returned to its axis. I'm off-kilter too, discombobulated. I've spent over twenty years running from justice. It's karma time. This must have been how Linda felt, being trapped in a net of dishonesty, lies told by schoolkids trying to save their own skins. If I hadn't had Cambridge lined up, maybe I'd have been a better person. Philip and his family are obviously fighting for his future, despise them for it as I might.

I guess I've had it coming, but this is not how I expected it to catch me, a smutty pic in the inbox of a snot-nosed kid. Someone is setting me up and I've no idea how, or who. I need to fight but I'm tired now, so fucking tired. I lie down on my sofa, the stale smell comforting. Cursing myself for the fact that I put my blanket in the wash earlier, I get my coat and roll myself up in it, willing myself to sleep, desperate for oblivion.

I can't sleep, though. There's too much buzzing in my head and besides, it's too early. I'm being stupid. I sit up, pace round the living room, repositioning the ornaments, the books. Then I go to make a coffee. Perhaps the caffeine will cut through the fug in my head. I go through to the kitchen to see a piece of paper on the side.

Gareth. At last. He hasn't just cleared out and left me. *Gone to your friend Tess's house for the party food tasting. Call me.*

At least I saved his number on my new phone. There's nothing else for it. Much as I'd like to lock myself in my flat and never leave, I know I can't do that. I put my coat on. This is one time that I know I need the support of friends. The thought of Gareth, Tess, and Marcus together gives me hope, a glow of warmth that they'll help me, they'll stand with me as I face this trial. Suddenly my steps lighten and I'm practically running as I go onto the street, hailing the first cab I see.

SPRING TERM
March 1990

A different night, back at Stewart's brother's flat. We went through into the living room, still as grotty as it had been at New Year, the Stone Roses still playing in the background. The coffee table in the middle of the room was stained with wine and beer, concentric circles of grime all overlapping like a Venn diagram of the night, here the juxtaposition of tequila and red wine that made me so sick. Stewart slammed down a six-pack of Tennent's and Tess pulled a half of vodka out of her pocket.

Campbell knelt down at the table and pushed the cans aside before taking a small paper wrap out of his pocket. He shook out the contents onto the table, a small pile of white powder.

"Give us a card," he said, and without saying anything, Stewart pulled his wallet out of his back pocket and gave one to him.

"Blockbusters," Campbell said, turning the card over in his hand. "Classy."

Stewart shrugged.

"And a note."

Again, Stewart rummaged in his wallet and came up with a grubby fiver. He rolled it into a tight cylinder and held it while Campbell divided the powder into fat lines, four of them. One for each of us. As the preparations took shape, I felt more and more twitchy, nerves even more exposed.

Tess leaned forward. "You'd best give Sylvie a smaller one," she said. "She's not done it before."

"And you have?" I said, outraged at this insult to my dignity.

"I know what I can handle, Sylvie," she said. "Unlike you."

I snarled under my breath. Secretly I felt a little relieved as I watched Campbell take some off one of the lines and divvy it up between the others, but I wasn't going to show it. I just hoped to fuck I wasn't going to be asked to go first. I might have seen *Goodfellas* recently, but I wasn't totally confident about what I was meant to do, how I was meant to inhale the drug. Ian Brown wanted to be adored, crooning from the speakers. I just didn't want to make a complete twat of myself.

"Is this coke, then?" Stewart said. "Thought you said you hadn't been able to get hold of any."

"Nah, it's speed," Campbell said. "But let's not spoil the illusion." He bent his head and snorted a line so quickly that I didn't have time to see how he did it.

"Dirty drug," Stewart said, and they laughed.

Tess tucked her hair back behind her ears before leaning forward, careful not to dislodge the lines that remained on the table. I gazed intently as she pressed one nostril in, held the note to the other, snorted up the drug, wiping white residue away from her nose with the back of her hand before handing the note on to Stewart. He had his, and now everyone was finished, looking at me. I shivered, unable to control the movement, feeling suddenly like a slab of meat in the middle of a skulk of jackals, slaver dripping from their jaws, red glinting from their eyes.

Stewart gave me the rolled-up money and I nearly flinched as the soggy end of it touched my hand. I didn't want to think about all the noses it had been up, or the gunk it had hoovered up from the table along with the drugs. My skin started to crawl at the thought, the millions of bacteria, the spores of mold that would be growing microscopically on the stains on the table. Horror at the thought of it held me rigid, even as Tess started to jeer at me for my cowardice. She took the lid off the bottle of vodka and drank a draft straight from it, unable to control a sharp intake of breath at the end, a puckering of her mouth.

The spell holding me in place broke. I could wash away any germs with the vodka, I thought, and bent down to take the speed, surprising myself with the efficiency with which I cleaned it off the table and up my nose. The chemical hit the back of my throat with bitter force. I sat back and took the vodka from Tess, taking a gulp and washing it round my mouth before swallowing it. I don't know what I'd expected, an immediate transformation, like Popeye after eating a tin of spinach, but there was nothing, no great revelation, no moment of epiphany.

Images were moving on the television, shifting forms, no soundtrack. I wasn't looking closely at it, but Tess cried out in surprise. "It's porn," she said, and started to laugh, more nerves than mirth judging by the high-pitched sound. I looked more closely and yes, it was porn, a naked girl on all fours in between two men who seemed much older than her, one taking her from behind, the other with his cock in her mouth. I shivered again, but the boys laughed, an avidity to their gaze, like the way that they'd looked at me earlier, slaver back dripping down their maws.

Stewart was gurning, his jaw moving rhythmically in time to the music, and suddenly he leaped to his feet and pulled me up, too, grinding himself against me, hard against my thigh. I was getting off on the music, too, the rushing feeling that was building in my head, sweat starting to prickle at my temples. I let go of him to scratch at my face, my arm, the rushing happening all over my skin now.

Campbell was grinding up against me from behind now, and Stewart laughed as if he were welcoming him in, but I saw Tess's face over his shoulder and I pulled myself away. Stewart took me back firmly into his arms and started kissing me. Even though normally I preferred it if we were alone, wanting to avoid any PDAs, I didn't mind right now. If anything, I was into it, kissing him back with more enthusiasm than normal. My eyes were tight shut but I opened them after a moment to see that Campbell was sitting on the sofa next to Tess, his hand down her top, her tongue in his ear, but it was me he was looking at, and it was for him that I started to perform, bringing myself round to face Campbell while grinding my arse into Stewart.

He bit at my neck for a while, but then muttered in my ear, "I want to fuck your brains out," and I laughed *yes yes yes*. He led me by the hand out of the room, all the time my eyes on Campbell as he watched me leave, and then we were back in the bedroom, the room I knew so well. We were kissing still and he was pushing me back on the bed and I was in it completely, until an image of Linda came into my mind, her kissing him, her lying back on this very bed with him. Her falling unconscious and him continuing to have his way with her. I pushed him off and sat up.

"What?" Stewart said and pulled at me, so I stood up and walked over to the door.

"Why did you do it, Stewart? Why did you get off with Linda at Hogmanay? She told me that you brought her back here."

He groaned in response. "It was her suggestion," he said. "She was the one who wanted to come back here. I was so out of it I didn't really have any idea what was going on."

"That's what she said, too. That she was out of it."

"There you go. Maybe we were both out of it. Maybe it got out of control. It shouldn't have happened. If you'd just stuck with me instead of getting off with all those blokes, none of it would have happened."

It was your idea nearly burst from my lips, but now I wasn't sure what had happened. Whether it even mattered. I looked at him and his words from earlier reverberated in my head, *I want to fuck your brains out*, and actually, that was what I wanted, too. The effect of the speed was rushing through my blood, and I definitely wanted it right here, right now. He held his hand out to me and I took it, sitting back down beside him before he pulled my top off over my head and undid my bra.

After a while he rolled over and fumbled through his jeans, which were on the floor.

"Just getting a condom," he said. I didn't bother to reply, listening to the music thumping from outside the room, wondering what Campbell and Tess were doing, whether they were fucking on the sofa.

"Get on top," Stewart said, and I pulled off the rest of my tights. Normally I would have shied away from it, too self-conscious about how to move, how fast, but now I didn't give a shit. I was guns blazing ready to ride. He took hold of my waist and thrust up once, twice. I tried to get a rhythm going but he wouldn't let go, driving up into me at his own pace. I started to get into it, welcoming the length of him as he withdrew fully, then thrust up again. He shifted me slightly, then once more drove up, but this time it wasn't pleasure, it was a sharp, intense pain of a kind I'd never felt before. I jumped up, breaking away from his grip, and realized then what had happened.

"You just fucked me up the arse," I said. "You just fucked me up the arse." The pain was still intense and I curled my knees up against my chest and held them close as I pushed myself up into the far corner of the bed.

"Sorry," he said, but he didn't sound sorry. He didn't look sorry, either, a smirk lifting the corners of his mouth as his jaw continued to contract.

"We should have talked about it first," I said.

"I thought you were more fun," he said. "Up for anything. Didn't take you for the frigid type."

"Not up for that. Do you want to ram something up your arse?"

He squirmed. "That's different."

"It's not different at all." I looked over at him, but he was smirking while I was still in pain. "Why didn't you ask me first?"

He shrugged. "It was an accident."

I climbed out of bed and dressed, my fingers clumsy as I rushed to cover myself. All I wanted was to get out of there, away from Stewart's mocking face and the grunting I could now hear from the living room as the music stopped. I slammed out of the bedroom without buttoning my shirt, my bra exposed, and stopped short as I saw Campbell fucking Tess from behind on the sofa, just like in the video. I stifled a sob.

I couldn't stay here anymore. Not like this. I turned and looked at Tess, one last look, checking whether she was OK, if she had registered my distress. She showed no sign of it, her eyes looking straight in front of her, no immediate flicker of awareness that I was there, though after a few seconds she seemed to register my presence. I wanted to ask her for help, tell her what had happened, but Campbell was still going at her from behind, and as I watched, Stewart emerged naked from the bedroom, erect cock in hand, and walked to where her head was, taking hold of her jaw as if in question, and she opened her mouth to let him in.

Shame washed over me. I'd passed myself off as a party girl, but I'd fallen short. Stewart would be telling everyone on Monday what a prude I was. I watched Tess some more, acquiescing to their treatment of her, desperate as ever to please. To show how much more fun she was than me. Sure, they'd say she was a goer, but Tess didn't care. All she wanted was to be wanted. It didn't matter what the consequences might be.

As I stood, transfixed, Campbell pulled away from her. She pushed at Stewart as if to say she was done, rolling over onto her side in a fetal position on the sofa, her back to me. I stood for a moment more, waiting for her to get up, come over to me, but she lay motionless.

I couldn't stifle the sobs anymore. I'd watched my best friend sucking off the bloke who'd just hurt me, who'd done something horrifically intimate without permission, without even warning, and I turned and ran, through the dark streets, past the pubs that were still open, still thumping with music, until I got to my front door and, realizing I didn't have my key, rang on the doorbell for one long ring after another, no longer caring now what my parents saw or thought might have happened to me, so desperate was I to have a long, hot bath and hide in my bed until the end of time.

THE WAITRESS

Shittiest party I've ever worked at, that's what I tell the police. No atmosphere to speak of, not many people. For the size of the house, I'd have expected at least a hundred guests. There were less than thirty people there.

Also, a renewal of vows? I mean, obviously I'm not the demographic, but I've only ever known one other person do that, my auntie's sister-in-law, and that was because she'd had an affair. Just looked weird, this woman in a tunic with long hair muttering over them in that big room upstairs.

Still, not my business what people do. A job's a job. I was getting the food ready downstairs, all the last bits of prep as the boss—Gareth—told me. Putting canapés together, garnishing salad, polishing glasses. That kind of thing. Once they'd finished the ceremony, I had to go round with drinks, then canapés, then get them downstairs for the buffet proper before taking them back up for the dancing later.

Dancing, I call it. I mean someone put an eighties selection on through Spotify, and some of them danced like they'd never done it before. Even more embarrassing than my dad. Which is saying something.

Did I notice any atmosphere between any of the guests? Not really. I mean, the woman who was in the bridesmaid's dress didn't seem very happy, but she cheered up later. She was drinking, but she wasn't the drunkest by a long shot.

Gareth told me beforehand that the bride was ill. He said that was why they were doing this. All I can say is that she didn't look ill to me. She looked lovely, beautiful dress and great skin. I guess you can't tell, can you? Her husband was being so sweet to her, always making sure that she had what she wanted.

I was one of the last to leave. Everyone went pretty early—there were a few old people who got out of there around eleven, and the rest went up town for the Hogmanay festival. They were mostly staying in hotels further along Princes Street. I didn't see Gareth or his girlfriend—or the bride and groom (well, you know what I mean)—before I left. I thought they might have gone upstairs. Gareth had told me I could leave at 11:45 p.m. and that's when I got out.

It was a shit party, but it's sad it ended this way. They were far too drunk to be going up on the roof. It's horrible, but it doesn't surprise me that there was an accident. Just what I would have predicted.

30

I stand at the front door ringing and ringing on the bell. It normally takes them a minute to answer but this wait stretches out for what feels like hours. I can imagine them there, checking the CCTV at the front door, discussing whether they should let me in. Gareth will have told them everything by now. Not that they wouldn't know anyway—the news will have spread around every barrister in London already. Marcus will be abreast of every single detail.

"Sylvie, I'm coming," I hear Marcus calling from behind the door, and he opens it. He doesn't reach to embrace me nor I him. We face each other for a moment before he bows his head, standing back to let me in. I go through to the kitchen without waiting for him to show me in. I see Gareth standing by the stove, Tess sitting on a stool on the other side of the island. My mouth tightens.

"This is cozy," I say, before stopping myself. I know what I want to say, a rant that says *I've been fighting for my life in that police station while you're stuffing yourself with food don't let ME disturb you* before turning on my heel and striding out. I restrain myself.

"Sylvie, come on," Gareth says. "You knew I was doing the tastings today. These are your friends. You asked me to help."

I glare, but I don't reply to him. I look over at Tess instead. "I might have known you'd go ahead with it, hell or high water. This vow renewal is the only thing that matters to you."

She blinks. "Well, not quite the only thing," she says quietly. I hear her, though. Her words fight their way into my head, followed by the emotions they provoke. Chagrin. Concern. Guilt. It's the guilt that wins out. I swoop down beside her, take her hand.

"I'm sorry, Tess. I'm really sorry. I know how much you have to deal with. I'm just scared, that's all."

"You don't think I'm scared?"

I watch it play out across Tess's face, the comparative losses that we fear. Me, my career. My name. Tess? Well, let's just say it's existential. I know that's the case. Rationally, at least. Though the loss of everything I've worked for feels close to death for me. I catch sight of myself reflected in the mirror on the wall. I've never looked so old, so tired. Gray skin, graying hair, clothes flapping loose against me. Despite everything, Tess looks glowing with health. I look like the one with cancer.

"Are you doing OK?" I say, going over to sit beside Tess. "That was scary to watch before, when you had that..." The word won't come out.

"Seizure?" she says briskly. "Fine. I told you what the oncologist said."

"I'm scared about all that, too," I say. "You're my best friend."

"Look, Sylvie," she says. "I think you should go home and have a nice bath and an early night. You're in shock from everything that's happened today. I think you just need to get some rest."

"What about the party? I was going to help you plan..."

Marcus butts in. "I know how much you've got on your plate," he says. "The situation's very serious. The Bar Council are concerned. There's never been anything like it."

I look over at him, trying to stop my eyebrows from shooting up. "That's not strictly true, is it? There have been lots of cases like it, lots of male barristers harassing their pupils. Sending unsolicited photos of their cocks to the girls, too, I'll bet. They don't get suspended, though. They get *sympathy* and *understanding* and *he's been under a lot of pressure lately.* God forbid they actually lose anything. Don't you know that it's different for girls?" The words are exploding out of me like bullets.

Marcus looks taken aback. Tess too. I don't dare look at Gareth. He hasn't made eye contact with me since the moment I walked in. I look at my friends, my boyfriend, and the disappointment I feel almost crushes me. I'd been so happy thinking of their support. But I got it completely wrong. There's nothing here for me.

"I should go," I say. I stand up, ready to walk out, ready never to return. But I can't. It's been too long. So long. The friendship is deep in my bones. I shake my head, trying to dislodge the thoughts.

Tess sighs. "I think you need an early night, but I don't want you leaving in this mood," she says. "I can't bear it to see you so unhappy. Stay, have some food. Then we'll get you home. Try Gareth's food. He's gone to all this trouble."

Gareth nods. He shuffles through some notes. "I was thinking this," he starts, and lists canapés, bowl food. A buffet as an alternative. "Twenty people, didn't you say?"

"I think it'll be about that. Perhaps even fewer. We're really just doing this for us. As long as we're there, my brother, Sylvie, that'll be enough," Marcus says.

"That's right," Tess says, smiling. "Just a few family members. My mother—she's maybe going to be able to come. A couple of cousins. Marcus's right, though. This is something we're doing for us. In my situation, it feels like an important thing to do."

Gareth nods his head, his expression thoughtful. I can feel the concern radiating off him. He's a nice man. Very nice. He deserves better than me.

"I'm all set to whip up the food that we discussed," he says, "if you've got in all the ingredients. Would you like me to get on with that?"

"Definitely," Marcus says. "We're starving."

I stay at the table, looking at the lists and photographs of floral arrangements in front of Tess, while Marcus shows Gareth where everything is. There's a clattering from the stove behind me, pots and pans, the scrape of a wooden spoon on a frying pan. The oven's humming, the smells of onion, chicken, beef permeating around me.

"Here you go," Gareth says, putting the plates down on the table. I gasp in pleasure. I've seen his food before, but nothing as nice as this: little jewels of food laid out in concentric circles, garnished to perfection, piles of salmon ceviche tumbling from curved silver spoons that he must have brought with him to demonstrate. It all tastes as good as it looks, too. I pick one up to try it, a small square of brioche topped with pâté and madeira jelly, but the intensity of its flavor, sweet, savory, little flecks of salt tangy on my tongue, sets me off and I eat another and another, practically batting Marcus's hand out of the way to get to the next.

Tess turns to Gareth and smiles, the sauce dripping from the side of her mouth.

"This is amazing, Gareth. All of it. Thanks so much… It's going to be great."

"It is," I say in agreement, but he doesn't look up at me. He's still arranging food, pushing miniature Yorkshire puddings around a serving platter delicately as if it's brain surgery. He looks up briefly, looks away again.

I know that look. He's backing away.

"Are you coming home with me later?" I say. I can't help myself.

"I can't, Sylvie," he says. "I need to finish up here and then I'm getting the train back tonight."

It's like a kick to the stomach. The pain billows off me in cold waves.

"OK," I say. "I'll go home, then. Will you be down before New Year?"

He won't look at me. "I don't think I can, no. I'm sorry."

"That's fine. I understand."

"I'll see you then, though," he says, reaching for a jaunty tone. Failing.

"It's fine," I say, and with that, I get up and walk out of the door. No one calls me back.

31

The weeks pass. I'm suspended from practice the week after I'm charged. Chambers suspends me too—removed overnight from the website. Erased. From the register of deputy district judges, too.

It's as if I never existed. I can imagine what they're saying about me. How sad. How much potential. How I could have been a judge. The thought of it exhausts me. I was so full of energy, so full of plans. Marcus was going to write a reference, David Lamb, too, if the trial had gone well.

All these years. Wasted.

I have my first appearance in the magistrates' court. I keep my head down, whisper, "Not guilty," into my hair so quietly the judge asks me to repeat myself. One more humiliation.

No one calls. I imagine Gareth talking to Tess about table settings, menus. I bet they don't mention my name. Strangely, the only person who'll talk to me is Linda. Not that they are conversations I want to have. If I could turn back time, I would. I bitterly regret doing what Tess asked. We should have left it all alone.

I want to know why you covered up for her. Why did you let Tess lie?

I do my best to calm her down.

It was all such a long time ago, Linda. So much has hap-
pened in all our lives. I tried to put it all out of my mind as
much as possible. I think we all needed to get on with our
lives.

Maybe not the best response.

Easy for you to say. You're not the one with a criminal record.
Not easy to leave that behind, now, is it?

This floors me. Do I tell her about the situation I'm facing or not?
Will it make things better? Or will she argue that I'm getting my just
deserts? I leave it alone.

That's true, Linda. It must have been very difficult. I'm
sorry for any part I might have played in that. I did what I
thought was right, though. We were all such children.

After this Linda doesn't respond for a few more days. I hope I've
choked her off. But no.

I wouldn't have chased you up, either of you. You and Tess
are the last people I ever wanted to see again, or speak to.
But once you got in touch with me…well, let's just say I'm
curious. What do you both want from me?

I take a day to reply.

Tess has been under a lot of pressure. I told you she's ill. I'm
sorry that you've been reminded about all this again.

Linda doesn't respond to that message. She still hasn't. It's two weeks and counting to New Year, and I'm hoping she's gone away now. Tess is finally in touch, to confirm that I'm still invited, still her bridesmaid. She lists her arrangements: the food, the venue. The guests. Her parents, Marcus's parents. Around twenty friends from recent years. It's funny—she tells me she's gone over the guest list from her actual wedding. She hasn't kept up with anyone from those days, no one at all.

Only me.

I know why. It's not about me, really. It matters to her, this link to her past. Sometimes it feels as if Tess is the last piece of mooring to my past, too. Without her, I'd be rootless, rudderless, floating off into the ether with no sense of time or place. However angry we are, we both need the other to keep us grounded.

She needs Marcus, too. We prop her up, her left and right hands. She can't operate without us. And much as I try to keep my distance, I can't operate without them, either.

"You need your friends," Tess says, handing me the mashed potatoes. "You know that we're here to support you, come what may."

I shoot a look at her across the table. My eyes are sore, bloodshot. I'm not really fit for company, but Tess insisted. "I guess," I say. "There's not much that you can do, though."

"Well, Marcus can write you a letter of support. Can't you, darling? That might help."

"If I get convicted," I say. "I suppose. He could be a character reference. But it might look as if we were trying to influence the jury, calling another judge to give evidence on my behalf."

Marcus shakes his head. "You know I'll do it if you need me to. I'm sure it's going to get kicked out before it gets to that point, though. It sounds completely ludicrous."

I shrug. I feel completely helpless. "It's an email address and an Instagram account in my name. Photographs of me. They're fake and I didn't set the accounts up, but the damage is done. You know how mud sticks. My reputation's fucked now. I mean, Philip's father is adamant about what he saw. The only thing is, I didn't do it."

Tess leans forward. "I didn't know you had Instagram, Sylvie. You said it was all bullshit."

"Yes, it is. I don't have time for any of that crap. You know why I joined Facebook—that was my limit. But somehow someone has managed to clone me and set one up in my name." I drain my glass of wine and pour myself another one. Tess glances at my glass—I can tell she wants to lean over and take the glass away from me. I bet she thinks I'm getting too worked up. She's not wrong. Emotion is leaking off me, anger building up inside.

I'm trying to keep it under control but it's too strong for me. Words burst out before I can stop them. "It's your fault," I say. "This has all happened since you made me set up that Facebook account."

"I didn't make you set up any Facebook account," Tess says. "I had nothing to do with that."

"If you hadn't wanted me to speak to Linda, none of this would have happened. Ever since then, it's all gone wrong."

Tess shakes her head. "You can't force a connection where there is none," she says. "The two things have nothing to do with each other."

I push out my lip, mutinous as a child. "It feels like they're connected."

"Well, they're not. It's a ghastly set of circumstances, that's all. A perfect storm. But like all storms, it'll pass. I promise."

I pour myself another glass of wine. I'm on a mission now. The way I always drink when I'm stressed. "I hope to fuck you're right," I say. "Right now it feels like I'm about to lose everything. This prosecution. The way Linda is talking to me. She's really angry. It's as if it all only happened yesterday. She's saying she wants to meet up so that we can talk about it."

"What did you say to that?"

"I said no. She was really insistent. She says she'll tell the police that I lied, otherwise."

Marcus leans over the table. "There's a statute of limitation on perjury, you know."

I practically spit I'm so cross. "Of course I know that," I say. "But even if they establish that this all happened twenty-five years ago, it'll still leave another black mark on my record. It won't help with anything."

"What are you going to tell her?" Tess asks.

"I don't know. I don't know what to say," I say. "I mean, we were all so sure that it was an unprovoked attack. You. Me. Campbell, even. No one saw anything."

"No one wanted to see anything," Tess says, her voice calm. "It doesn't mean we didn't, though."

"I'm beginning to wonder if I've got any idea at all what happened that night," I say, shaking my head. "I thought I was sure but the more that Linda questions me, the more I don't know."

There's pressure building in my head. I know this is important to Tess. It was important to me, too, but not anymore. It's been superseded by everything else that has happened.

"I don't want to deal with this, Tess," I say. "I don't think I can. Not right now. I'm starting to feel a bit... I think I'd best go home."

"We can't run away forever," Tess says.

I don't want to look at her. I don't want to look at Marcus, either. I want to crawl under the table and never get out again.

Tess picks up her phone and checks something before she says, "Right, we're getting the train up to Edinburgh on the thirtieth. I've booked seats on the 10:30 from King's Cross. And we're going for drinks that night, like a mini hen do. Just you and me. Not a big one, obviously, but time to visit the old haunts. Marcus can go out with his parents, maybe. Then on Hogmanay itself, the celebrant is coming to the house in Regent Terrace at five. We'll have the ceremony in the drawing room. Gareth and I have talked it all through, and he can source some chairs and flower displays for us. That'll only take half an hour, max, and then we'll crack into the champagne and have a proper shindig."

Marcus looks at Tess, his face full of admiration. "I can't believe you've managed to sort all of this out," he says. "Between all those appointments, too. It's brilliant."

"It wasn't that big a deal. It's only a couple of days up north. Gareth helped me with a lot of it, like tracking down a celebrant."

Marcus nods. "He seems like a nice guy. Better than Sylvie's usual."

It's as if I'm not in the room.

"I get it right occasionally," I say, and he colors, a dull pink moving up from his neck to his cheeks. I freeze. I don't want to watch Marcus's awkwardness, the suspicious expression I sometimes see on Tess's face when the three of us are together. It's misplaced, of course—I'd never betray my best friend—but sometimes the memory of Marcus's hands on me on the night of their wedding reaches out of the past and clutches at me.

I know she's often thought he was going to leave. She's always thought he wanted me, even though I've reassured her so many times that there's nothing in it. I can't bear to look at her now, to see that same worry on her face. I have to, though. I'm braced to face his shame, her accusatory expression.

They're not even looking at me. They're staring at each other, emotion so raw between them that it leaves me flayed, skinless and twitching. Something's changed between them, something at their core. For a moment I'm lost, before it comes to me.

Death. Of course. It's Tess's diagnosis. It's changed everything. It's a paradox; the worst news of her life has brought her everything she ever wanted. Center stage at last, Marcus's eyes only on her. It'll be an added bonus that my life's collapsed into the gutter. She's won.

It's almost as if she's been working to a plan.

PART 3

32

Though I'm still exhausted, demoralized, the idea of going up north, seeing Gareth, has brought me back to life and I travel up to King's Cross with a lighter heart than I've had in weeks, even if my suspicions of Tess haven't died. We get on the train and I try to insist that we sit on the right-hand side of the train on the way up to Edinburgh. Tess asks why and I remind her of the view, but she shrugs. When I go to sit down in the direction of travel, her face falls.

"That's the seat with the best view," I say. "Do you mind if I...?"

"I'm so sorry," she says, "but I get really sick if I don't face in the right direction. It didn't used to be the case, but over the last few months..."

She doesn't need to finish. I move immediately. Even though we're in a first-class carriage, the catering trolley is out of order, so Marcus and I run up and down to the buffet all the way, fetching coffees, teas, shortbread biscuits for Tess. Nothing is too much trouble. Every now and again I see her checking our luggage, the small cases in the rack by the door, the suit carrier containing her dress and mine. I wish someone would steal it. I'm tempted to throw it out of the window myself, letting it fly over the bridge into Newcastle. Despite having the best view, Tess spends most of the journey looking at her phone, her face pinched over the glow of the screen. I follow suit, reading through the file of papers I've been served by the prosecution in my case. I pore over and over Philip's father's statement, hoping I'll find something there to show his lies. At least Linda hasn't been in touch. I'd prefer not to be confronted with mine.

Tess drops the odd comment, telling me she's finalizing the menu for Gareth, reading the news. There's some footage of a person apparently dropping down dead in a street in China from a virus. She holds her phone out to show me.

"People will believe anything," she says. "What are you so engrossed by?"

Her comment makes my antennae twitch. Am I being too trusting? The seeds sown by Marcus's revelation about the false pregnancy all those weeks ago have started to sprout, a tangle of bindweed twisting through my thoughts. "Just looking through the witness statements for my case again, seeing if there's something I've missed," I say.

I put my phone back in my bag and watch Tess. She's finally looking out of the window, gesturing at me to have a look, too. It's the sea. The joy's gone, though, poisoned by my suspicion of her. How can she look so happy?

All the years of our friendship run through my mind, the agony of being a teenager, the ways we were learning how to be women, playing at being adults while we were still so firmly children. We always took everything so seriously, even then, reading so much into our relationships, so much more than was warranted.

We were a four back then, me going out with Stewart, her going out with his best friend, Campbell. It was all so tidy, the way that we met up, went out. There was a symmetry in it. If only Linda hadn't come along and spoiled it. If only we'd just been able to brush her off, ignore what was happening between her and Stewart. It's not like it meant anything. If I could have laughed it off, it wouldn't all have gone so terribly wrong.

I never thought we'd be friends again after I left that summer, after Stewart died. I saw Tess at the trial, but we didn't speak. After I gave evidence, I sat in court and watched her tell the jury what I'd told them. So blurry, so confused. Didn't know Linda, didn't really know Stewart. Didn't see anything happen between them until Linda hit him on the head with the driftwood. It was an unprovoked attack by her on him, out of the blue.

It could so nearly be true. Tess seemed sure by the time of the trial that it was true. I didn't want to argue with her certainty. We didn't need to bring up my relationship with Stewart, my dislike of Linda. I mean, I didn't see what happened. Not really. Not that I could swear to. It was better for Tess that way. But maybe for some reason Stewart did think Linda was up for it. Maybe he did try it on with her and she lashed out. I swore to it that I didn't see. I've always tried to protect Tess. But now we've found Linda, now we've played with that fire, it's time to see it through.

"So strange to be going up to Edinburgh on the train with you, after all these years," Tess says, finally turning away from the window, her cheeks pink. "After you left, I never thought we'd be so close again, or that we'd be returning in this way."

I smile. Our minds still work on the same lines, even now. A synchronicity.

Fast-forward through the years, running into her in London after university. Our friendship rekindling. I wanted her to meet my new friend. To show that I'd moved on from that terrible time, from my obsession with Stewart. I still remember it, the moment he walked over to the table where we were both sitting. I knew from the look in her eye what would happen, even as I introduced her for the first time. She leaned over, smiling fit to burst. "Tess, this is Marcus."

I didn't stand a chance after that. She was thin, funny, gorgeous. All the things I loved her for at school. All the things I hated her for after that. I was so close to getting a new relationship, Marcus and I were so nearly there. But Tess came along. The frisson between us didn't die, though. It smoldered on. All these years I've felt his eyes on me, wondering what might have been.

The train's pulling into Edinburgh Waverley. We pick up our bags. Well, I pick up mine, but Marcus won't let Tess carry anything. He's treating her like she's made of glass, like she'll shatter if she falls. It's taken a cancer diagnosis to make him realize how much he cares.

We go up to Market Street to wait for a taxi. We could walk, but again Marcus won't let Tess, too worried that she'll exhaust herself. She tries to reassure him, smiling brightly and cracking jokes in the cab on the way to Regent Terrace. He doesn't look convinced, though, worry lurking all the time behind his eyes. It's as if everything he said to me about his suspicions has gone out of his head. I'm trying hard not to think about it all, but I can't. If she could lie about a pregnancy, she could lie about this. I'm not sure anything is beyond her.

I have to stop thinking like this. I'm being a terrible friend. The worst imaginable. Tess is facing a potential death sentence, and I'm sour with suspicion. By the time we get to Regent Terrace, I've calmed myself down. The sight of where we're staying knocks all residual unpleasantness from my mind. From the ornate, spiked railings outside to the facade of the Georgian house, three windows wide, it's a dream.

"This is amazing," I say. "Where did you find it again?"

"A specialist company," Tess says. "One of their deluxe bookings. That's how we've been able to arrange the party. Though it was so helpful for you to recommend Gareth. He's been amazing."

A shadow passes over me. "That's great."

"I'm sorry," she says. "I know it must be awkward. Has he not been in touch?"

Tears start in the corners of my eyes. I dash them away with my fingers and laugh, a little shaky. "No, he hasn't. But at least I'll see him tomorrow. Maybe we can work it out."

We walk up the stairs to the front door. It's opened by a man from the lettings agency who shows us round. He keeps telling us about the features of each of the rooms, but I want him to leave. We want to explore for ourselves. We listen as politely as we can but get him out as soon as possible. When he's left, Tess stands in the middle of the drawing room, a huge room the width of the house, and pirouettes.

"We made it," she says. "We're here. It's going to be glorious."

Marcus goes over to Tess and puts his arms around her and for a moment they embrace. I step back. I'm excluded again. Seeing their happiness brings home my own misery.

But Tess reaches her hand out to me and pulls me into the circle.

"Here we all are," she says. "Back where we began." She squeezes my hand in hers. "It's amazing to be here with you. I'll do a proper speech tomorrow, but for now, I want to tell you how much we appreciate your friendship, Marcus and me. You really are our best friend."

Marcus nods, patting me on the shoulder. There's nothing sexual in it. I feel like his child. So much has changed since Tess told us about the death sentence hanging over her head.

"I just want tomorrow to be perfect," she says.

"It will be," Marcus says. "And then we've got the holiday to look forward to."

"Holiday?" I say.

"Yes, a honeymoon. As it were. Tess booked it," Marcus says.

"Where are you going?"

"Mauritius," Tess says.

"How lovely," I say. I even manage a smile. They'll be jetting off while I return to London to deal with the wreckage of my career. I try not to dwell on the contrast.

33

My room is on the third floor, above the master suite on the second floor. I can hear Tess and Marcus's voices through the floor, though not the actual words. Are they arguing again? I wouldn't put it past them, even on the day of their vow renewal. So many rows. So many misunderstandings.

It's going to be strange, being out with her in Edinburgh again. I'd never have anticipated it all those years ago, when I thought we were saying goodbye forever. The fact that our lives have been so entwined is one of the foundations of my life. It's a scary thought that it might change. Sometimes the ivy is the only thing holding the crumbling stones together.

That won't be the case here. They need to move forward. I need to get on with my life, too, get this travesty of a trial behind me and get my career back on track. My relationship with Gareth, as well. Maybe it's time for me to see this renewal of vows not as a self-indulgence but more as an ending and a beginning, burning clean all the infection and suppuration from the past.

The cab driver doesn't look impressed when we say that we want to go to St. Stephen Street—it's hardly worth the fare for him—but he takes us, going round corners slightly too fast so that we're thrown into each other, teeth jangling as we drive over the stone setts in the road. Soon enough we're there, down the stairs into the Antiquary.

Tess orders a soft drink but I hit it harder, ordering doubles to every glass of her sparkling water and throwing the drinks back so fast she soon has a queue of glasses waiting for her attention.

"Take it easy," she says, but I don't pay any attention. I've tried to cheer up but I'm feeling morose, the drink not lifting me but rather pulling me down.

"Easy for you to say," I tell her. "You're sorted. Lovely vow renewal with your lovely husband, lovely trip off to Mauritius. Lovebirds on sea."

Tess raises an eyebrow. "Well, sorted for now. I think you might be forgetting something, though. Why do you think I'm not drinking? It doesn't agree with my medication."

I glare at her before I lower my head. "I'm sorry. I know I should remember. It's just hard, sometimes. You look like normal, you talk like normal. It's hard sometimes to keep in mind what's happening."

"I know," she says. "It's about as far from normal as it can be, though. It's like sitting on a bomb. Or a firework. Someone's lit the fuse, but I don't know how long it is, how soon it might go off. I'm constantly on edge."

"I'm sorry," I say. "This is hard for me, too. I feel as if everything is changing."

"It *is* changing," she says. "That's why. It would be bound to with a diagnosis like this."

"You can't change the past, though. You do know that, don't you?"

I put my chin up as I say this, a defiance to the question, and Tess puts her chin up, too.

"It's not about changing it. It's about making it right. Accepting we were wrong. Saying we're sorry."

I try to stare her out, but her gaze is unwavering. I lower my eyes first.

So many ghosts lie between us. The dead are not always quiet.

Tess's glass is empty at last. Mine too. Not half-full. Or half-empty. Drained to the dregs.

"Shall we go somewhere else?" she says.

"Where?"

"Well, we could go along to the Bailie for one. Or down to Shambles—I think it's called something else now, something like Maison Hector. More revisiting of our youth."

I pull a face. "I dunno. I like it here. It's always been my favorite. Can't believe I haven't been here for so long."

I look around as I say this. Not much has changed, the bar still in the middle, curving out into the two rooms of which it's the center. There's still a blackboard on the wall, listing the bands that will be playing over the next month. At least it's not a fucking folk night.

"I want to move on," Tess says. "This may be the last time..." She doesn't finish the sentence. She doesn't need to. I bite my lip, but fury builds up in me.

"Is this what it's going to be like for the rest of it?" I say after a moment, unable to contain myself.

"What?"

"You, pulling out the cancer card every time you want to get your own way?"

Time stops. We're at the heart of it, time before, time after, a moment of still. I look at Tess as the vibrations from the words I've said travel through her ear canals to her eardrums. I can feel the movement of the ossicles as if they were mine, translating the vibrations into sounds, the words forcing their way through her cochleas and down her auditory nerve until they make their way into her brain, like a shit posted through a letter box, stinking and unwanted. As what I've said sinks in, I see revulsion growing on her face. Not as fast as my self-loathing. But it's too late to unsay it now.

"Did you just accuse me of playing the cancer card?" she says. I want to die in my chair right here, right now, my mouth stuck half-open.

"I… Of course not. I mean, I…"

I've lost the power of speech.

"I want to go back to the house, Sylvie," Tess says. "I've had enough now."

I nod, eager in my movements, though it's too late now to show how keen I am to do what Tess wants.

We stride back through the dark streets. I guess this isn't how it was meant to be. Not the triumphant return Tess hoped for, a time for us to luxuriate together in our shared past. Perhaps this is how it was always going to be, though. At some point I was going to lose it, goaded past endurance by Tess's insinuations, her rewriting of history. It was always a competition between us.

From the moment she said she had cancer, it was always a competition I was going to lose.

It's cold now, but bright moonlight cuts through the night sky and lights our path, merging with the orange glow of the streetlamps that reflects up from the damp pavements. There's still Christmas in the air, trees lit up in windows, and the occasional firework, a warm-up for the extravaganza that'll happen for the Hogmanay celebrations tomorrow. We get to the end of St. Stephen Street, St.

Vincent Street, cross the bottom of Howe Street, past the clock tower that measured out my childhood. Along the gray facades of Great King Street, through Drummond Place, London Street, and up to Broughton Street. So many memories we pass, so many corners when I stopped and snogged someone or had an illicit fag before my return home, always later than I said. I'm crying now, tears running down my face that I'm too angry to wipe away. This is not how it was meant to be. We were meant to walk back arm in arm, *do you remember, wasn't it here…*

I stop again, but now I'm laughing. Of course it was always going to end this way, me furious, her in a strop because as ever I've said the wrong thing, been a stupid cow. I knew it from the start, and so did she.

"Tess," I say, "Tess."

I think for a moment she's going to ignore me, keep stomping on like a juggernaut, but she slows, turns, icebreaker slow.

"What."

It's not a question. Not really.

"Let's not do this now. Let's forget about it. All of it. We're here now. Let's enjoy it and stop fighting."

Slowly she walks toward me, feet still heavy, her shoulders drooping as if she's under a great weight.

"I'm sorry, Tess. I shouldn't have said that."

"I know," she says, but she holds out her hand.

34

Even though it's Edinburgh, where the weather can switch to wind and rain in the blink of an eye, it stays sunny throughout the morning. Marcus and Tess eventually emerge down to the huge open-plan kitchen for breakfast, where I'm drinking black coffee. I don't meet their eyes as they walk in, despite the brightness of Tess's greeting.

Tess says that both her parents and Marcus's are on their way up on the train and plan to check in at the Balmoral Hotel above Waverley Station. They'll be able to share a cab over to the house in time for the ceremony in the afternoon. Some of their friends have messaged to say they're here, the couples who have made the trek excited at the idea of a Scottish Hogmanay.

"Jeff and Serena are on the way," Marcus says, looking up from his own phone.

I freeze. "As in the people from your chambers? Jeff the judge?"

"Didn't Tess mention it?" Marcus says.

"I'm sorry, Sylvie. I totally forgot. It'll be fine, though. Don't worry about it. This is a party. It's not work."

I shake my head. "Jesus, this is going to be humiliating."

Tess shakes hers back at me. "No, it's not. Not if you don't let it. This isn't about you, Sylvie. It's about Marcus and me. Everyone is here to celebrate that. Call it an armistice day, if you must, but literally no one will be talking about you or anything you're supposed to have done."

"Promise?" I feel utterly exposed. Vulnerable.

"I promise," she says.

Maybe because we've gotten up so late, the day flies by. Marcus goes out at lunchtime to meet up with his friends and family at a pub they've booked down in Stockbridge. I'm about to go out, too, until Tess reminds me that we're getting our hair and makeup done. I want to tell her to fuck off, my lips practically forming the word, but I restrain myself.

"Lovely," I force myself to say, and I put my coat back down on the chair in the hall.

While we wait for the hairdresser to turn up, Tess walks me around the house again, talking incessantly about how pleased she is at how well it's turned out. The drawing room is the perfect size for the intimate ceremony that she has in mind. Gareth will be arriving soon to start doing the food for the reception and to set up the room. I dig my fingernails into my palms when I hear his name.

Tess has thought of every detail. The house is no smoking—of course—so there's a tall ashtray to put out on the front step. Only a couple of people still smoke—the barristers, of course—but she wants to be accommodating to everyone. It's going to be great. She says it so much she almost sounds as if she believes it.

A flurry of arrivals, the hairdresser first, swiftly followed by the makeup artist. Tess sends me upstairs, saying she's waiting to let in Gareth. I don't argue. It might help to be all done up before I see him.

They make me sit on a chair in the middle of the master bedroom in a mist of Elnett. They don't ask me what I want. Even if they did, I wouldn't be able to say. I put myself completely in their hands. After a while, Tess comes into the room.

"What do you think?" she says.

"I haven't looked yet. They said it should be a surprise," I say, waving my hand at the stylist.

"You look lovely," the hairdresser says.

I know I should react, smile, but I feel like a soft toy with a hole in it, the stuffing falling out of me. I can't even sit up straight.

"Why don't you put your dress on?" Tess says. "It's hanging up in the wardrobe over there."

I shrug. "If you want." I get myself up to my feet, the movements slow, almost painful. Again, I'm struck by the thought that it's me who looks ill, not Tess. I'm wearing gray jogging bottoms and a gray sweatshirt and as I walk across the room, I feel as if I'm already dressed for prison, all washed out and dreich.

Tess opens the wardrobe and pulls out the long purple dress, hands it to me. I undress, careless as to audience. I know how much weight I've lost, but there's nothing I can do about it now. My ribs are visible under my skin, like a xylophone. I've never seen myself so thin before. After all these years I've achieved the holy grail, massive weight loss. It does not suit me.

At least it means I don't have to worry about the dress fitting me. It glides up over my hips without a hitch. I reach behind me and pull the zip up as far as I can before standing, helpless. No one in the room moves until I say, "Tess, can you help me?"

Tess comes over to me and zips the dress up to the top. I turn round and she smiles.

"How do I look?" I say.

"Amazing. You haven't aged at all. It could be our wedding day."

I almost crack a smile. "I don't believe you."

"No, honestly. It's great. Go and have a look." She points at the upright mirror that's standing in the far corner. I walk over to it, the purple satin rustling with each step, before standing in front of it.

I want to cry. They can all tell me I look lovely till they're blue in the face. They're wrong, and I'm right. I look appalling, all updo and fancy frock, my face peering out of it all like a corpse daubed in undertakers' paint. I'm a whited sepulchre, the outer finery masking the rot within.

"Thanks," I say. "You've worked wonders." I smile, my lips tight, and take my place at Tess's side.

SUMMER TERM 1990

"I can't fucking believe you're wearing those," Tess said, glaring at the high-heeled sandals I'd packed to wear for the party.

"What's wrong with them?"

"We're going to have to walk for miles on the beach. Don't you know where it is?"

I looked at her blankly. "Gullane? It's close to the car park, isn't it?"

"No. It's a hollow way along at the other end. Fucking miles. Fucking stupid, too. I don't know how we're going to get all the drink there."

Typical Tess. She always thought she knew best. She hadn't been up for organizing the party, though. The grunt work was always left up to other people. Lesser people. Not people like Tess.

I shouldn't have still been speaking to her. I wanted to ignore her, but she bounced into school the Monday after as if nothing had happened. I didn't want to be the one to make a fuss, show myself up as being prudish, or boring. No one else was as much fun as Tess, after all. When she was nice, she was lovely—funny, self-deprecating, full of compliments and support. I had to wipe out what had happened, the image of her between Campbell and Stewart. It was just one of those nights. Stewart and I continued seamlessly, too. It was as if the events of the Friday had never even occurred. I took my place on his arm and the crowd in the playground parted for us, like the waves of the Red Sea.

When she asked if I wanted to come to the party with her, I jumped at the chance. The exams were tough, long days spent in on my own revising. My parents weren't keen on my going out, but they said it was OK if I drove. They trusted me not to drink. I was happy to stay sober, too fraught about my exam results, the conditional place I had at Cambridge, everything riding on these marks.

It was time to go. I kept my trainers on—there was no point wearing the heels. Besides, I was hardly dressed up, a long beige skirt and a strappy top, denim jacket over the top. Tess bounded in front of me, legs toned in a pair of short denim shorts. She'd freeze later, I thought.

Music loud, windows open to let out the fag smoke, we hit the coast road by Aberlady. Tess pulled out a vodka bottle and took a long pull before waving it at me. I shook my head. I was going too fast to be able to risk losing concentration, swerving to avoid a branch lying on the road. I thought about the accident that had happened there the year before, three teenagers killed when their car flipped on the corner, and kept my eyes pinned to the road.

We made it, though, staggering out of the car after squeezing into a parking place in the car park above the beach at Gullane. Tess hung onto my arm while I straightened myself up, head still swaying from the drive. It was a beautiful evening, the sea stretched out blue in front of us, and for a moment, I thought I could let go, forget about everything that had happened.

The light was falling golden. Stewart and Campbell had arrived in someone else's car and they were clowning around on the grass. They were bathed in light, their faces laughing. I could feel the warmth of the evening sun on my face, too, music blaring out of someone's car, and actually, I was happy. As happy as I'd been for months.

Even the walk along to the hollow for the party didn't piss me off. I carried as much beer as I could hold, a couple of bottles of vodka in my bag which the boys asked me to take. We were laughing the whole way, stopping every ten minutes to light another fag.

"You'll want to watch putting those out," an old man said as we passed him, glaring at us. "Else you'll set the place up like wildfire."

I rolled my eyes. The others, too. Though I was more careful, the closer we got to the marram grass of the dune. As we neared the site of the party, I could hear music thumping from a stereo, laughter.

"Some of the rugby team came along earlier," Stewart said, turning back to me. "We wanted to make sure that we got the spot saved."

"Good job too," Campbell said. "Don't want to share the space with anyone else."

We kept walking. Despite no booze, I felt drunk, buoyed by the golden light, the blue sky, the fact that exams were over and this night, tonight, was nearing the end of everything. I joined arms with Stewart, Campbell bumping into me in a friendly way as we went along.

Round the corner and now here we were in the hollow. There were already about twenty, thirty people, all from the upper sixth, all shouting to each other over the strains of the Pixies blasting from someone's boom box. Campbell pulled me by the hand into the heart of the group and then we were dancing, Stewart and Tess beside us, the night stretched out before us, no limits on what it had to offer.

The mood changed the minute that Linda arrived. No one was expecting her until she exploded into the area beside the bonfire with a great whooping noise.

"What the fuck's she doing here?" I said to Tess.

"I guess she's come to see everyone off," she said.

Stewart ran over to her, hugged her, spun her in the air. My blood ran cold.

Not again…

THE PATHOLOGIST

Well, this isn't much of a puzzle. The officer in charge looks at me, one eyebrow raised. He wants a cause of death.

I look at the bodies, twisted up under the cloths we've had to cover them with. They're too big for normal refrigeration—they're still on the sodding railings, for God's sake. Getting these bodies ready for the funeral won't be fun. At least it's not my job to make them presentable.

I've got to stop being facetious. I'm just tired. The bloody fireworks kept me awake half the night, and I've got a nagging hangover behind my right eye.

Anyway, time to begin.

First: male, around forty, well nourished, no signs of illness. Brain and all other organs in good order. No signs of defensive injury, only those consistent from a fall. Some bruising to the arms and hands. Cause of death: a penetrating trauma to the back of the neck protruding through to the front, severing the jugular. The blood loss alone enough to kill him. Further penetrating trauma to the left thigh, again where the railing spike has gone all the way through. Death would have been within minutes, if not shorter.

Second: female, early forties, also well nourished, no signs of illness. Brain and all other organs (other than those affected by the blunt trauma penetration) in good order. No sign of defensive injuries. Cause of death:

a penetrating trauma to the stomach and to the liver, where the victim fell face forward onto spiked railings. The victim would have died quickly from immense blood loss from the injuries; like the other it would only have taken minutes, five at the most.

35

I need to get it under control, any rage I feel, any frustration. This is not the time. I might think I look like shit but I'm not going to say anything.

Tess looks stunning. Marcus will only have eyes for her. As he always did.

I don't like my dress, but grudgingly, I must admit, I look fine. Nowhere near as good as Tess, but not as bad as I initially thought. We stand together, faces peering out from the mirror in the hall, the sublime and the not-so-ridiculous. I catch her eye in the reflection and she looks so lovely, so pure, I can't help it. I start laughing, something of the happiness of the day finally infecting me.

Tess starts laughing, too, holding her arms out to me, and mad as I am with her, I can't, I simply can't. It's her day. She's ill. At least, I'm choosing to believe she's ill. She's the only friend I've got left. I lean in to her and we give each other a hug. A proper hug. It's the most connected I've felt to someone since my world came crashing down.

"Maybe I don't look that absurd," I say, when I finally pull away.

"You look like the years have stayed still," she says. "It's wonderful."

At that moment, Tess's father appears, extending his elbow to her. It's time. They walk into the drawing room to the strains of a string quartet. I'm going to try to enjoy the ceremony, not think about what's going to happen later.

The celebrant is better than I thought she'd be, less mawkish, despite her rather eccentric appearance, all long beads and floaty sleeves. She speaks in a businesslike tone and even the vows aren't too sentimental. Despite his initial skepticism, Marcus looks as if he's thrown himself into it wholeheartedly, wiping away a tear at the requisite moment when he and Tess join hands and turn to face the congregation.

It's heartwarming, but I can't be distracted from my fears about Philip, Linda, the complete mess I'm in. I see some barristers in the audience, Marcus's colleagues, carefully ignoring me from a distance. My gut starts to crawl, sending spasms through my nerves. I'm doing my best to pretend that the space they're occupying is in fact empty, a void, but when I turn round to scan the room, they're still there, awkward smiles and nods all round.

It'll be easier once I've had a drink. I hold off until the end of the ceremony, determined not to fall over in front of everyone. My stock is so low, I can't bear to make it lower still. I stand in the corner of the dining room. The moment anyone comes anywhere near me, I turn away, slipping from room to room to avoid any awkward conversation. Any conversation at all.

I have a brief conversation with Tess's parents, who have never really forgiven me for the situations Tess and I got into all those years ago. They greet me quickly, eyes turned down, and move on. Marcus's parents are even more evasive, unwilling to acknowledge that we've ever met before.

Seeing Marcus and Tess together, standing in front of the celebrant like that, it's brought it back. Could it have been me? Should it have been me? It's too late for that now. I take another glass of champagne, neck it. Trays of canapés are circulating along with the champagne, beautiful miniatures of food. I know they'll be delicious, a testament to Gareth's handiwork, but the thought of food chokes me. Even imagining swallowing one of the mini Yorkshire puddings triggers my gag reflex. I turn away.

Tess is circulating, the hostess with the most. Everything, she's got. Including a glass in her hand. I squint and she raises it to toast me. I shake my head. It's not for me to judge, though. Maybe she's decided that one drink or two won't kill her today, regardless of the medication.

I'm about to go over and talk to her when I feel my phone vibrate in my bag. It's been quiet all day—these days it's always quiet. I pull it out and see there's a message from Linda.

I'm coming to Regent Terrace soon. I want to see you both.

How the hell does she know we're here? I'd hoped she'd gone away. I approach Tess, my face grave. She stiffens, looks at her glass as if she thinks I'm going to bollock her for drinking, then takes my arm and steers me out of the dining room.

"Linda's on the way. Here. She knows we're here."

Tess nods. It doesn't seem to come as a surprise.

"Did you know that?"

"Yes," Tess says. "She's been in touch with me, too. We've been talking. A lot."

I can feel the color leaching out of my cheeks. "What have you been talking about?" I say, barely keeping my voice under control.

"This and that," Tess says. "Exchanging stories about old times. That kind of thing."

I look down. Tess is still smiling.

"You invited her?" I say.

"I thought it might be nice. A good way to bury the hatchet. It's been over twenty years, after all."

I twitch. "I thought today was meant to be your special day."

"It is. It will be. This isn't going to spoil it," Tess says. "A quick chat, a couple of apologies, then she'll be on her way."

"So you're definitely going to let her in?"

"I am, yes. You don't seem very happy about this, you know," Tess says.

"It's fine," I say. "There's just a lot happening."

I pause after I say this, wondering if Tess might say something kind. She doesn't. I can practically hear her thoughts. *She's brought it all on herself. I don't want to listen to her moaning continuously about everything that's gone wrong in her life. Not now. I'll be sympathetic tomorrow, but for now, I want to drink with my friends.*

After the silence has stretched out for a few seconds longer, my face crumples, tears about to come.

"I'll ask Gareth to let her in and show her to a different room so that we can have a proper chat when she gets here," Tess says, oblivious. "Then we can get on with the party."

"I wish this had never happened. None of this," I say.

"Me too, Sylvie. Me too. But it is what it is."

She pushes past me into the dining room, and a few seconds later, I hear her greeting Serena and Jeff, her voice tinkling lightly as if we haven't had our exchange. She's always been good at this, switching on and performing for the crowd. I laugh, a sound bereft of any humor, and make my own way back to the dining room.

That's when I see Gareth. He's watching me. I don't know how long he's been there, but his gaze is steady and true, the only person in the room with any kindness for me. I hold up one hand in greeting, a tiny wave, so slight that he can pretend not to see it, and it hangs in the air, a moment of possibility... Will he, won't he acknowledge I'm there.

He does. He smiles, jerks his head upward as if to say, *Come over here.* I slide across the room to face him, eyeball to eyeball, and for the first time since the arrest, the police, we're actually seeing each other. I can tell it by the lift of the corners of his mouth.

"It's good to see you," he says. "I'm sorry."

I hold my hand up to silence him.

"I understand," I say. "I'd have done the same. But it's good to see you, too."

"Are you OK? You look beautiful."

He's just being nice. I'm about to tell him to fuck off but looking up I can see sincerity glowing from him. Not what I was expecting.

"Are you having a nice time?" he says.

"Honestly? Not really. It's a bit much. I'm desperate to get pissed but I can't. Not yet."

"Why not?"

"For some godforsaken reason Tess has set up a meeting with Linda, sometime this evening."

"Yes, she's asked me to let her in and take her upstairs," Gareth says. "I'll come and get you."

"I don't understand it." I pause for a moment, then continue. "Well, I do really. Tess has gotten in her head she wants to see her. I don't know what Tess thinks is going to be achieved by it, but I guess we should apologize to Linda for not supporting her."

I'm trying to make light of it as I talk to Gareth, but the gnawing in my guts is back. This can't end well. I'm being set up. I look over at Tess, her head tilted back as she roars with laughter at something that Marcus is whispering into her ear.

As I watch her, I cease to hear the sounds of the party. They're replaced by a dull roar, as if of a wave approaching. I can see all her teeth, and now it's not humor I see in her expression, it's something more primal. It's as if I'm looking straight through to the skull beneath the skin. I turn my gaze away from her, horrified, but now all the people around her have become skeletons, angled grotesquely in a danse macabre.

I've had too much to drink. I'm tired. I'm stressed. I shake my head, dumping my glass down on the side, and push my way through the guests to find a chair at the side of the room, where I sit, head down, breathing in, out, until my vision is clear again.

36

It takes me a while to get my breathing back under control, my vision clear. No one comes to ask if I'm all right. It's as if there's a force field around me, keeping everyone away. Scratch that. I'm the leper at the feast, the suppurating flesh no one wants to touch in case it's catching. My social disgrace is absolute. I don't understand why Tess kept me on as bridesmaid, unless it was to punish me.

I look over at her again, and this time she catches my eye and smiles. My heart rate slows down a little. It can't be that. We've been through so much together, we can weather anything. I'm getting paranoid, that's all. I go over and join her, welcomed immediately into the group, and it's normal again. Or I can pretend it is. All the bones are hidden. The teeth too.

"Sylvie, here you are," she says, and draws me into the circle.

Later, much later, when all the champagne has been drunk and we're onto red wine, music starts to pound through the speakers in the drawing room upstairs, the occasional banging of fireworks outside as Edinburgh begins warming up for the Hogmanay party. Despite my good intentions of staying sober until I've dealt with Linda, I'm half-cut now, the room hazy. It's a good feeling, though; I'm almost a happy drunk. My paranoia's still there but it's happening over in the other corner, to someone else. There's no sign of Linda, and I'm beginning to wonder if she's going to show at all.

Gareth is fussing around the buffet, directing the waitresses to clear up the leftover food, and after he's done that, he comes over to our group. It's just the three of us, Tess, Marcus, and me, a small bubble in the middle of the guests. Like my paranoia, the tension between us is still there, but I'm ignoring it. Gareth stands to the side of me, too polite to intrude, but I take his arm and pull him in, kissing him on the cheek.

"He's a genius chef, isn't he?" I say. "That was fantastic."

"It was great," Tess says. "Thank you for organizing everything. We really appreciate all your help." She leans into Marcus and he kisses her hair, more intimate than if he'd started ramming his tongue down her throat. I move closer to Gareth, who puts his arm around me.

"I think we should get the dancing started," Gareth says. "People have begun to move upstairs. We'll finish clearing up in here and then we'll be done."

"You're not going to go, though?" I say. "You'll stay?"

He looks over at Tess and Marcus, one eyebrow raised as if to ask if it's OK, and Tess rushes to reassure him. My paranoia subsides even further.

We go upstairs to the drawing room, where the chairs have been cleared to the sides of the room. It's not a big crowd dancing, perhaps only ten people, but they're totally into it, pogoing away to Nirvana like we never left university. We don't get many chances these days.

I dump my bag and glass down at the side and barge into the middle of the floor, Gareth in tow, and we get down and dirty to it, thrusting away to Prince and Madonna, any dignity ground to dust beneath my heels. I've forgotten nothing, all the strains, the stresses, the way that anyone who knows me even vaguely has avoided me all night, the fact that I'm on bail for something as sordid as groping a fifteen-year-old, sending naked photographs to a teenage boy, but I'm dancing like it's the end of the world. Technotronic starts to "Pump Up the Jam" and I am there for it, hips swaying, arms extended above my head.

The people around me are drifting away. They're talking about going out into the street to watch the fireworks, join in the Hogmanay celebrations. I'm ignoring them though, giving it large on the dance floor, not caring if Gareth and I are the only ones left.

Gareth pulls away suddenly. I catch hold of him.

"Don't go!" I say.

"I heard the doorbell. I need to get that."

"I didn't hear anything."

He looks at me, smiling. "You're pissed off your head," he says. "I'll be back."

I keep dancing, but I'm off beat now, my movements heavier, less fluid. I look down at the purple dress and see it's torn on the bodice, near the shoulder strap. The top of my bra is showing. I pull at the material to hide my underwear, but it tears worse.

I can't do it anymore. It's suddenly too much, the way I've been treated all night by Tess and Marcus's guests, their expressions full of scorn as they look me up and down like some piece of shit they've found on their shoe. I stop for breath, ready to go and find another drink, when Gareth appears again. His face is somber.

"It's Linda," he says. "She's arrived. I showed her upstairs so that you can speak uninterrupted—go and join her."

I look at him, frozen to the spot. I don't want to move. I don't want to see her. I don't want to have to tell her anything, let alone what really happened that night. I don't want to have anything to do with it.

"Come on," he says. "They'll be waiting."

"They?"

"She and Tess. I told Tess she'd arrived. She's gone up already."

This galvanizes me. I don't want to see Linda, but I don't want Tess to spend any more time than necessary speaking to her on her own. God knows what Tess'll have said about me by now. I find a glass and a half-full bottle of wine and pour myself a slug to strengthen my nerves, knocking it back in one go.

"Right," I say. "Let's go."

He shakes his head. "I think you and Tess should deal with this. The woman seemed pretty upset. I think if she has to deal with anyone other than the two of you, she might lose the plot."

Upset. She's not the only one. Doesn't look like I can get out of it anymore, though. I put the glass down, raise my chin.

"OK," I say. "I'm ready."

"They'll be upstairs," he says. He reaches out and puts his hand on my shoulder. The weight is comforting. All I want to do is sink my head into his shoulder, shut the world out with his warmth until it's all gone away. Not an option, though.

Bracing myself, I leave the drawing room, pausing on the landing at the bottom of the stairs. Despite all the wine I've drunk, the champagne too, I feel completely sober now, my vision razor sharp. For the first time I can see the chips on the paintwork, the nicks on the wooden banister. I thought the house was flawless before. I look over my shoulder to see Gareth smiling at me from just inside the drawing room. Again, details jump out: the yellowness of his teeth, the way his canine teeth are pointed like fangs.

Like Tess before, his smile ceases to be a smile and starts to be a grimace, a threat.

I turn away, put one foot on the stairs. Time to cross the Rubicon. Though the acoustics can't rationally be behaving this way, it's as if the music fades to nothing the higher I get, the only sound I hear in my ears the thumping of the blood round my head, the build of pressure behind my eyes. My breaths are fast, shallow, a pain jagging through the left-hand side of my chest.

The top of the stairs now. My heart's racing like I've just scaled Everest. The door to my bedroom is to my left and it calls to me. I could go in there, barricade the door with the big mahogany dresser, curl up in a ball under my duvet until it all stopped. I know I can't, though. I look along to my left, trying to work out where they might be.

A door at the other end of the corridor is open. I walk along, my steps quiet, hoping I might catch Tess and Linda talking, get some sense of which direction Tess is taking it. I'm not kidding myself anymore. The sudden sobriety has also rammed home the message that Tess is going to do all she can to pin the blame for everything that happened on me. The thought's weighing heavy across my shoulders. *Are you just going to let her?* a small voice sneers in my head, and it gives me the kick I need to walk the final steps along the landing and open the door.

To my surprise, it isn't another bedroom, but rather a small storage room, with shelves built in all the way round. In the middle of the floor, facing the door, is a wooden stepladder leading up to an open trapdoor in the ceiling. I'm hesitant, mindful of my long dress, high heels, but then I see Tess's shoes kicked off to one side, round the back of the ladder, and that decides me. I remove my own shoes and pull my dress up above my knees before putting my hands to the ladder and taking the first step up.

I can't imagine why they've decided to hold the showdown in the loft, but to be fair, it's the place where privacy is most guaranteed. Maybe there'll be a decent view of the fireworks, too. The triviality of that thought almost makes me laugh. The only fireworks that we'll be noticing will be the ones exploding between us. I can quite see Tess lobbing in a hand grenade or two to get herself off the hook. I bet she wishes she'd never started all this...

One step up, two, and I'm slowing down. I don't want to face it, this final confrontation. The flash of courage I'd felt has deserted me, the wood cold under my hands, the steps creaking. Stairs to a scaffold, the long drop before me, a sense of doom so strong upon me again that it's all I can do to keep standing, let alone climbing. There's nothing left of me now but fear, a small, crumpled ball in the face of a storm.

Deep breath. Another. I brace myself and continue to climb. I'm up the ladder now, and I pull myself into the loft space, the sloping ceiling low above my head. I'm not tall, but I need to stoop a little. Again, there's no one here, only an open hatch at the point where the ceiling comes down almost to meet the floor. I walk over to it, still hesitant, before sticking my head out and looking around. It leads out onto the lowest point of the valley between the two pitched roofs to the front and back of the house.

Gingerly, I pull myself through, standing on the slates, the cold striking against the thin tights I'm wearing. I'm not bothered by the cold, though, fueled by booze and adrenaline. I look around me, searching for any sign of Tess or Linda. I'd laugh at the absurdity of the situation if I weren't so scared at my core.

There's a screech straight above my head, and I jump, nearly losing my footing on the slate. I look up and see it's a rocket, a huge purple flower cascading its petals out over me. I smile, despite myself, the sky so clear beyond it, even stars are visible. I haven't seen stars in London for years.

"Sylvie," a voice calls out, disturbing my reverie, and I look over to see Tess silhouetted against the sky, up on the peak of the roof to the front of the house. I raise my hand and clamber up to where she's crouching. It's a good thing the roof's a double one, I think. This could be risky if there were a straight drop down.

I'm surprised to see her on her own, though I don't say anything until I've reached the top, sitting down next to her, my hands holding firmly onto the leads on the roof at the top. Instead of greeting her, I look at the view. It's breathtaking, Arthur's Seat and Salisbury Crags laid out in front of me. I look over to my left, and I can just make out the castle. The firework display will be spectacular from here.

"Sylvie," Tess says again, "where's Linda? I thought she'd be coming up with you."

"Not with me, no," I say. "I thought she was up here already."

"I haven't seen her. I found the hatch open. That's why I came out."

"Me too."

We hold each other's gaze in the dark. I can't see what expression she's wearing, but she sounds calm.

"Did Gareth tell you she was here?" I say.

"She messaged me. Told me to come up. She thought it would be good to watch the fireworks while we're up here."

There's a thump behind me and I jump again, nearly losing my balance. I grip hold of the roof tight with my hands. I'm overreacting to everything now. It must be my nerves. They're already stretched almost as far as I can bear.

There's another thump. It's definitely the sound of someone coming.

"This must be her," Tess says, and I nod, forgetting that she's unlikely to be able to see me. Another noise, someone crawling through the hatch, and I rotate as I sit, moving round a hundred and eighty degrees so that I'm facing down in the valley of the roofs.

There is a figure appearing at the bottom, leaning back over the hatch, doing something. I take a sharp intake of breath.

37

"Where are you?" Gareth calls up.

As soon as I hear his voice, I calm down. My fear's irrational. This is going to be unpleasant. It's not going to be dangerous, though. I'll get through it, especially if Gareth is here to support me.

"Where are you both?" Gareth says again, this time with more urgency in his voice, and he starts to make his way up to the top of the roof.

"I thought you were Linda," Tess says, and I add my voice in agreement. "Do you know where she is?"

"For fuck's sake," Gareth says, and there's a note there I haven't heard before. He starts to move faster, looming over us when he reaches the top. "You still think she's coming?"

"I don't understand what you're talking about," Tess says. "What's it to you?"

"She's not here," he says. "Just me. And you two."

"Gareth," I start. "What's going on?"

"Exposing you for the liars you are," he says. He gets closer to Tess, who backs further down toward me. I'm crouching, confused by the anger I'm witnessing.

"What are you talking about, Gareth?"

He starts to laugh, though it's not funny, nothing is funny, the sound more threat than merriment. "Oh, I know everything," he says. "Everything. She told me the lot."

"Who? Sylvie?" Tess says.

"No," he says. They're practically nose to nose now, balancing on the narrow roof pitch.

"Who then? Linda?" Tess says, the malice gone, replaced with disbelief. Also, a slight note of fear, lurking deep beneath.

"Yes, Linda," he says, and everything stops around me, another fearful moment of clarity.

"How do you know Linda?" Tess says. I clutch even more tightly at the roof. I want the answer, too, though I'm scared that if I speak, all that will come out is an incoherent wail. I bite my lip, hard.

"My sister," he says. "She's my sister."

My head's spinning. Sister. Sister. Why the fuck hasn't he told me? The air in front of me shimmers, a break in time. But then a memory stirs in me. Smith. Quarry.

"You don't have the same name," I say, my tongue thick in my mouth.

He laughs. My nerves prickle. "You remember her name well enough now," he says. "Though you forgot for all those years. It's our mum's maiden name. I changed it when she died, so I'd be ready when I found you. But I should have known I didn't need to bother disguising myself. You're so fucking self-obsessed."

"Disguising yourself?"

"I've been waiting for this moment for a long time, Sylvie. I made a promise when Linda was dying that I'd find you both, make you accountable for what you'd done to her."

"It wasn't all on us, though," I say. "She was just unlucky. Maybe she was telling the truth that Stewart assaulted her, that she was acting in self-defense. But I didn't see! Not enough to be sure. None of us did. It wasn't my fault." I'm trying to be controlled but it's not working. I'm talking too fast, my words tumbling over each other. Panic's searing through me. This is the man I've shared a bed with so often over the last few months. How could I not have known?

"That's not true," Tess says. "We did see it happen. We did see Stewart assault Linda. She was acting in self-defense."

Silence between us. Fireworks banging in the distance but my heart's pounding louder, a thumping in my ears.

"Do you know what you're saying, Tess? Because if you tell him this, you're going to have to tell him why Stewart thought it was all right to try it on with Linda. What we've covered up for all these years."

Tess carries on as if I haven't spoken. "You told me it was all my fault," she says. "That's why I went along with it. I had so many blanks about the evening that you could have made me believe practically anything had happened. But I don't think it's true anymore."

"You're lying," I say. "You're trying to get out of this. Now I understand what this has all been about. You want me to take the blame for what happened so you have a clear conscience, polish up the halo on your martyrdom."

"Sylvie, that's not what this is about at all," Tess says. "You need to face up to what you did. It's the one thing I can do before I die."

Darkness is taking hold of me, a rage building up inside me so great that I don't give a shit any more. I'm out of fucks to give. Careless now of my precarious position on the roof, I pound my way up to where she's standing and shout in her face. "Are you dying, Tess? Are you really fucking dying? I don't believe you!"

A massive bang to my left, a burst like gunshot to my right. The tension running between Tess and me, Gareth, it's stronger than any explosion.

"I might be," Tess says. "And this ends now."

Gareth interrupts. "Linda told me everything," he says. "Both of you lied. Both of you stood there and watched Stewart molest her. She couldn't work out for ages why you protected him in this way, why you said that it had been an unprovoked attack. Then she put two and two together. *She told me you were up for it.* That's what he said to her. He screamed it in her ear as he groped her." He looks from me to Tess and back again before he continues, his voice relentless.

"One of you told Stewart that Linda fancied him, knowing it was a lie. He was guilty of assaulting her, but one of you was just as guilty for telling him to do it. Obviously you couldn't admit what you'd done. But that changes now. That's what I want to find out. I want to know who."

An explosion, the golden stars lighting up Tess's face. She's staring at me, her face frozen in an expression of horror.

"It was Tess. It wasn't me," I say, desperation building. "I didn't say that to Stewart. I didn't tell him to get off with Linda. I didn't see him doing anything to her. I told you. She hit him out of nowhere."

"You told me I said it," Tess says. "You told me you remembered me saying it. For years I thought it must be true."

"Are you saying it wasn't you?" Gareth says, turning his head toward her. Tess ignores him, keeps talking at me.

"I'm not sure I ever believed you," she says. "But I went along with you. You were the one with the brilliant future. I didn't want you to be ruined before you began, having to admit you'd encouraged someone to carry out a sexual assault. But I know the truth now." Her voice is implacable, not loud, but clear as the toll of a bell.

"You've got to believe me," I say, pleading now with Gareth. "Linda will tell you. I was always friendly to her. I'd never have set her up. Tess was always the manipulative one. That's why she's trying to ruin my life."

He's silhouetted against the sky, his head shaking as he looks from one to the other of us.

"Linda can't tell me anything more now," he says. "She's dead. She died from cancer nearly ten years ago."

Tess's face is pale, her eyes black sockets in the darkness.

"Who have I been talking to, then?" I say.

Another massive bang, another purple chrysanthemum lighting up the sky, golden showers all around it. Gareth might be speaking but I can't hear him. I don't need to hear him. I know what he's going to say. It's clear, now. From the moment that he spotted my name badge at the conference in Edinburgh all those months ago. It's a setup.

"Who the fuck do you *think* you've been speaking to, Sylvie?" Gareth says, spitting the words out with force.

"You bastard," I say, another kick to my guts.

Tess laughs, a sharp, angry bark. Gareth turns on her. She takes a step backward, another. She's getting near to the edge and I know I should call out, tell her to be careful, but I'm frozen to the spot, images of the last months speeding through my brain as I piece it all together.

Tess is clearly piecing things together, too. She starts shouting again.

"It's your fault, Sylvie. If you hadn't told Stewart to try it on with Linda in the first place, none of it might have happened."

I push myself up to my feet, shock outweighing my fear of falling. "That's bullshit, Tess, and you know it. I never told him to do that. It was you."

"I remember now, Sylvie. For all these years I took your word for it that you were sure about what happened, that this was for the best because I'd get in trouble, too. You made me believe it was me, but it wasn't."

"Why would I have told Stewart to go for Linda? He was my boyfriend. I hated her. I hated the fact he'd gotten off with her before," I say. Old jealousies, long forgotten, bursting up inside me now.

"You could hardly blame Linda for that. Are you still refusing to admit what Stewart was like?" Tess says. "Fuck's sake. At some point you need to accept the truth. He was a complete shit." She's agitated, a note in her voice close to panic. But she's on the attack, no longer wounded prey. "That's what I told Linda... I mean Gareth. You could never see Stewart for what he was."

Another bang. I jump, nerves shredded now. The impact of what Tess has said is sinking in. I'm standing now, careless as to my balance, where I'm standing on the pitched roof. Tess is sneering and fury is beginning to rise up in me, bubbling up from the bottom of my stomach.

"What do you mean, that's what you told Linda? Have you been trying to blame me for everything?"

Gareth turns his wrath on me. "Stop fucking lying, Sylvie. You owe me the truth. We're going to settle this, once and for all."

I'm panting now, anger, dread, adrenaline all coursing through me. I can hear Tess breathing heavily, too, Gareth breathing easy, light on the balls of his feet like a boxer ready to land his next punch.

"I can explain. It all happened so fast," I say. "None of us could be sure what happened. But Stewart didn't deserve to die."

Tess is laughing again, a high-pitched hysteria. If stress is a trigger, any minute now she's going to have another seizure. If it's true she's ill, that is.

"I can't think of anyone who deserved to die more than Stewart," Tess says. "He was a complete shit. We should have stopped him."

"Then why didn't you?" Gareth says.

There are more fireworks now, more banging. Midnight must be approaching. I'm hanging on Gareth's every word, Tess's too, trying to catch every nuance of what they're saying. Tess hasn't replied and I look over to her to see her clutching her head, bent over against the sky. She's so close to the edge…

"Please stop it. I'm not feeling well," she says. "I think I'm going to…"

"Oh, please," I say. "You don't think we believe you, do you? The whole thing's a lie. Brain cancer doesn't look like this."

"It's exactly what it looks like. Linda had a secondary brain tumor. It's what killed her in the end," Gareth says. I've been dumped in ice, my body freezing now, my head submerged too.

Tess looks up, her face contorted. "I told you I was ill. You have to believe me. And you have to start telling the truth. Linda didn't seduce Stewart. He assaulted her. Stewart raped me, did you know that? The night you thought I had a threesome with them. It wasn't what I wanted. You kept covering for him and covering for him, but all the time…"

Words that change it all. Everything I've ever thought, turned on its head. Stewart the aggressor, Linda the victim. Tess the victim, too. Me? All I've ever done is see myself as the victim, closed myself off from any truth that might threaten my future.

"Tess," I say, "Tess, what the fuck?"

She's crouched over now, a seizure taking hold. I'm frozen in place.

"What's going on?" It's Marcus. He's on the roof now, looking around him wildly. He catches sight of Tess on the edge, pushes past me, Gareth too. By now he's going too fast. Both men lose their footing, slipping down the slope of the roof.

Tess is on her side, convulsions taking hold of her. She's caught by a low parapet, but Gareth goes straight over it, falling over the edge. Marcus is only a few seconds behind, but his legs have caught on the parapet.

Time's stopped. The bullet in the matrix but it's slipped through my fingers. Too late to catch Gareth's fall. The words Tess has spoken crash through my mind. Rape. Stewart. Her cancer.

It's real.

The shield I've built around me all these years is cracking. I can't deny it anymore. It was all my fault.

"I'm sorry," I say. "I'm sorry." Then I move.

Gareth's gone. I can't even think. Tess is in front of me, her body juddering. The ice that's bound me in place shatters, fire now in my veins. I move over her as fast as I can, throwing myself at Marcus's legs, pulling at him to bring him back up. But Tess's body arches, and she kicks me in the back so hard I stumble, fall. I'm over the edge now, still holding on to Marcus. She kicks me again.

She's right. I've always known the truth. I just couldn't handle it.

Marcus has nearly managed to pull himself up. He's almost safe. He gives one last wrench, throwing himself sideways to catch at the edge, bring himself over, and as he does, I lose my grip. The past is crashing down on me. Too tired to break my fall. I'm at the edge now, hands grabbing onto nothing, my leg catching onto part of the structure. All that holds me there.

Bangs in the sky, great thumps. Headlong over the edge now, nothing between me and the ground but air...

It's a blur of pain now, shooting agony from my leg. The drop's looming below me. My leg caught on the parapet, my dress too. I'm being held by a thread. I try to drag myself up but I can't, gravity's pull too strong on me. I'm screaming, my mouth wide open, but nothing's coming out.

More noises on the roof above. More bangs. Fucking fireworks. The pain's unbearable in my leg. There's no one to help me. I shout again, twisting madly, trying over and over again to pull myself up, flailing like a broken puppet in the void.

The pain's excruciating now, bolts of electricity searing up my leg from my ankle. A crack of metal and the pain stops. But now I'm falling.

Flashes of red, gold, green, purple.

Sparks. Smoke. An artillery of explosions.

Midnight.

12:04:59

It's nearly over now. A minute more, maybe two. It's going to end. This agony will be over. Though the pain has lessened, adrenaline spiking through.

I can see so clearly now. Everything I buried has come to the surface. I was always chasing my dream. Too caught in ambition to deal with the truth. It's almost funny. A tragedy, right there.

I did make Tess take the blame for it. It was safer. She didn't have plans; I had everything to lose. So I told her what she'd done and she believed me. What she thought she knew, what I knew I knew, all these years…

I hope the boy gets off lightly, that boy who told the truth in court. I looked at him and wished I'd had the strength. I was too selfish, though.

My mind's wandering. I'm jumping from place to place, year to year. The pain's nearly gone. Seconds left, at most.

Back at the beach now. I remember. Everything I've hidden. I did tell him to go for Linda. Pride—I didn't want him to see how hurt I was, that I'd meant so little to him. Spite too. I'd persuaded myself it was all Linda's fault. If he'd never gotten off with her that New Year, none of the rest of it would have happened. I didn't care what she wanted. I didn't care what he did to her now. I wanted her to suffer like I was. Or at least a part of me did.

I couldn't watch it, though. I ran away. But then I came back. Stewart bumped into me. He was staggering. Confused. I thought he was drunk. He saw me, almost fell upon me, and the smell of him, the weight…it took me straight back to that night, the pain I'd felt. The shame.

I pushed him off me, watched him fall, a sick thud as his head hit a jagged rock on the ground under the sea buckthorn. I ran away without stopping to check. I didn't know he'd already suffered one head injury.

I didn't know he was going to die.

I wonder if it felt like this. Did he know? Did it hurt?

I wish I could say I'm sorry.

Not to him. To Linda. To Tess, for making her feel so guilty all these years. It was my fault. I was covering up so many lies, I made myself forget what was true.

No more hiding now. Too late.

All too late.

It's the end…

TESS

It's February before I can face returning to the place where it happened. Marcus and I take the train, the short taxi drive to Regent Terrace. I look at the iron railings, the gap cut in the front from where they removed the bodies. I lay a bunch of white roses, Sylvie's favorite.

The days after that night are still a blur. I spent most of them in bed, shaking. I don't remember much from being brought down from the roof other than being wrapped in a blanket and held tight in a warm room. The police tried to talk to me, but I couldn't stop crying.

Whenever a firework went off, I started to scream. I'm not sure I'll ever be able to hear them without screaming. They asked so many questions. It was endless. We went up to watch the fireworks; it ended in disaster. Drunk people and roofs don't mix. We should have known better.

The toxicology report for Sylvie shows a considerable level of alcohol. A few times over the legal limit to drive. Of course she wouldn't have been able to stand up.

I should hate Gareth for what he did, how much he lied to us. Somehow that's all gone. He must have been hoping for years that he'd find me or Sylvie, furious at how we'd let his sister go to prison, convinced that the stress of this was what caused her to develop cancer. Die. After that he took his mother's name, his camouflage in place for the day he tracked us down. It would have been hard for him to find us at first because of Sylvie's avoidance of social media, my marriage and change of name. When he saw Sylvie's name badge at the conference, he must have known it was his only chance to get close. When I asked her to start looking for Linda, it was a gift from heaven to him, the opportunity at last to work out what happened. Who set his sister up.

Sylvie didn't know how much I hated Stewart. How scared I was of him. But she'd been terrified of losing him. He'd been her ticket out of obscurity, the wallflower lingering too long at the sides of the room. When he started going out with her, she was made, no door at school left unopened. She turned a blind eye to everything.

I was too drunk to be sure what happened that night. I thought I saw Stewart put his hands on Linda. I saw her back away. I thought I heard him shout something, maybe even *She told me you were up for it*. I saw Linda lean down, pick up the piece of driftwood from by the fire. I saw her hit Stewart on the head, how he staggered back, away from the fire. I voiced my suspicions as to what I'd seen to Sylvie, but she said no. She said I was drunk, I'd gotten myself confused. The more she said it, the less sure I was of what I'd seen, the images dissipating in my mind like smoke in wind.

When the police asked their questions, I told them nothing of what I thought I'd seen.

Sylvie was adamant nothing happened. She was standing right there and she saw nothing. I agreed because I didn't know what else to say. What else to do. She was my best friend. I didn't want to see her get into trouble.

I knew how much she liked him, how possessive she was of him. It made no sense that she'd have encouraged him to go after someone else. It was all Linda's fault. That's what I thought for years... The dead boy was Sylvie's ex-boyfriend. Linda was nothing to us.

Not back then.

The thought of her never left me, though. It built and built, her face in the fire, her face in court, the betrayal we wrought on her day on day, year on year. I knew what Stewart was like. I did nothing to stop him. Linda told me what he did to her, and I didn't pay attention.

So much for the sisterhood.

"Linda was acting in self-defense. We should never have protected him. I was so drunk and Sylvie was so adamant that Linda had assaulted Stewart out of the blue..."

"She was adamant about a lot of things. She was convinced your cancer wasn't real, you know," Marcus says. "And that I was secretly in love with her, too."

"She always had such a thing for you," I say. "Even though you were only ever just friends. She thought I stole you off her. It was really sad. I guess I didn't realize how much pressure she was under. If I'd left it alone..."

"You can't blame yourself," Marcus says. "She was tricky before, but after she was charged. It's as if she'd lost all grip on reality. I was going to tell you, her head of chambers has been in touch. She's completely exonerated. It was all a setup by the boy. His dad backed him up because he didn't want to get him into trouble, but when they established that the photographs were fakes, he came clean, told them it was all lies. The QC is being investigated, too. He's a close family friend of the defendant's dad and was turning a blind eye to it all. Forget robbery—they're being done for attempting to pervert the course of justice. They've dropped the charges against the other two boys. Sylvie's name would have been clear. She'd have been a judge. It's so sad…"

"It is sad," I say. "But that's what she did to Linda. OK, in a different way, but Sylvie was happy to let her be convicted for something she didn't do. She was always desperate to protect her own reputation, make sure nothing got in the way of her career. Even back at school. I knew I had to get her to stop and take a proper look at herself."

"You were doing the right thing," Marcus says. "She needed to confront her part in the past. Someone went to prison because of her."

"Because of me, too," I say.

"I think you're being punished enough," Marcus says.

"Maybe."

"Are you sure you're doing OK on your own?" he says. "I could move back in. Treatment can be really hard."

I shake my head. "You know it's not what either of us want," I say. "We knew it from the start, really. I'll be OK. They say the treatment's working. I'll have to wait and see."

"I'll keep in touch," he says. "If you'd like me to."

I hug my arms round myself. "I know it was all too late, but I did try," I say. "I did try to get her to tell the truth."

Marcus pauses for a while before he replies. "At least she came right at the end."

"She did."

She saved him. Her hands on him, pulling him back. If only I hadn't lost control at that moment, unable to restrain myself from kicking out at Sylvie. She was hanging on to Marcus for dear life. He so nearly went over the edge, too. I gaze at him for a moment, wondering if he knows how near to death he came.

Turning away, I look at the iron spikes on what's left of the railing, tracing one of them with the tips of my finger. All those years of friendship, of rivalry. It ended here.

A shiver runs across my scalp, a breath of cold wind. I wrap my coat round me. It's time to go.

Reading Group Guide

1.   Question

2.   Question

3.   Question

A Conversation with the Author

Question

Answer

Question

Answer

Acknowledgments

My time during sixth form was in some ways similar (all the good bits), and in some ways very different (all the bad bits). I was lucky not to be surrounded by boys like those in this book, but by boys (and girls) who remain close friends of mine to this day. But, as I looked back on what were to me almost halcyon days, I was at the same time reading with horror the stories as they emerged from the Everyone's Invited website, and this horror worked its way through into my writing. I think those of us who grew up before the age of internet porn were really very lucky indeed.

My deepest thanks go to my editors, Jack Butler, Kate Stephenson, and Shana Drehs; my agent, Veronique Baxter; Rosie Margesson; Joe Yule; the Rights Team; and the superb teams at Wildfire, Headline, and Sourcebooks. None of this would be possible without you.

Russell, Neil, Fergus, Og, Gav, Norms, Sandra, Susan, George, Steven, Justin, Alan, Jim—I love you all and the others, too. 1990 was a very good year.

Sarah, I miss you. Thank you for marrying someone as great as Kris.

Emmie, Louise, Kate, Katie, Trevor—thanks so much for reading the early drafts.

Sarah P—thanks for talking me down and keeping me sane. You belong in the above group but you deserve a special mention, too.

Nat, Freddy, Eloise—you know how much I love you all. Thank you for letting me get on with it.

A special thanks to Jill Whitehouse and Gareth Quarry for donating their names to me by taking part in the Books for Vaccines auction.

About the Author

© Rory Lewis Photography

Harriet Tyce grew up in Edinburgh and studied English at Oxford University before gaining legal qualifications. She practiced as a criminal barrister in London for nearly a decade and subsequently completed an MA in creative writing–crime fiction at the University of East Anglia.

Blood Orange, her debut novel, was a Richard and Judy Book Club pick and a *Sunday Times* bestseller. *The Lies You Told*, her second novel, was also a *Sunday Times* bestseller. *It Ends at Midnight* is her third novel.

CPSIA information can be obtained
at www.ICGtesting.com
Printed in the USA
LVHW040559160722
723244LV00002B/2